SAC

D0098658

OUTFOXED

ALSO BY DAVID ROSENFELT

ANDY CARPENTER NOVELS
Who Let the Dog Out?
Hounded
Unleashed
Leader of the Pack
One Dog Night
Dog Tags
New Tricks
Play Dead
Dead Center
Sudden Death
Bury the Lead
First Degree
Open and Shut

THRILLERS
Blackout
Without Warning
Airtight
Heart of a Killer
On Borrowed Time
Down to the Wire
Don't Tell a Soul

NONFICTION
Lessons from Tara: Life Advice from the World's Most Brilliant Dog
Dogtripping: 25 Rescues, 11 Volunteers, and 3 RVs on Our Canine
        Cross-Country Adventure

OUTFOXED

David Rosenfelt

MINOTAUR BOOKS
NEW YORK

OUTFOXED. Copyright © 2016 by Tara Productions, Inc. All rights reserved. Printed in the United States of America. For information, address St. Martin's Press, 175 Fifth Avenue, New York, N.Y. 10010.

www.minotaurbooks.com

Library of Congress Cataloging-in-Publication Data

Names: Rosenfelt, David, author.
Title: Outfoxed / David Rosenfelt.
Description: First edition. | New York : Minotaur Books, 2016. | Series: An Andy
    Carpenter novel ; 14
Identifiers: LCCN 2016008508| ISBN 9781250055347 (hardcover) | ISBN 9781466859920
    (ebook)
Subjects: LCSH: Carpenter, Andy (Fictitious character)—Fiction. | Agency (Law)—
    New Jersey—Fiction. | Murder—Investigation—Fiction. | Escaped prisoners—Fiction. |
    Animal shelters—Fiction. | Dog rescue—Fiction. | BISAC: FICTION / Mystery &
    Detective / General. | FICTION / Suspense. | GSAFD: Suspense fiction. | Mystery fiction.
Classification: LCC PS3618.O838 O88 2016 | DDC 813/.6—dc23
LC record available at http://lccn.loc.gov/2016008508

Our books may be purchased in bulk for promotional, educational, or business use. Please contact your local bookseller or the Macmillan Corporate and Premium Sales Department at 1-800-221-7945, extension 5442, or by e-mail at MacmillanSpecialMarkets@macmillan.com.

First Edition: July 2016

10 9 8 7 6 5 4 3 2 1

OUTFOXED

I've been enjoying work lately. I'd have to check my diary, but I think the last time I said that was never. Of course, the last time I wrote in a diary was also never, but that's another story.

My change in job satisfaction is probably because I'm doing very different work these days. I'm a defense attorney, have been my whole life, but lately I've been successful in not taking on new clients, leaving me no one to defend. I like it that way; trials can be very trying.

I wouldn't say that I've retired, it's more like taking a year off, much in the way a baseball pitcher does when he blows out his elbow. I like to say that I haven't had "Tommy John surgery," it's more like "F. Lee Bailey surgery."

My current work involves dogs, which are pretty much my favorite things, living or otherwise, on the planet. My partner, Willie Miller, and I run the Tara Foundation, a dog rescue group in Haledon, New Jersey, that covers Paterson and surrounding communities.

I've been spending a great deal of time helping Willie and his wife, Sondra, handle the day-to-day activities of the foundation, work that I couldn't do as a practicing lawyer, especially during trials. The days are enjoyable and rewarding, no more than when I watch a dog go to his or her new home with a terrific family.

And, best of all, I don't have to cringe and wait for a jury to decide whether I did well or not. All I need to see is a wagging tail.

I'm also heading up a program called Prison Pals. Passaic County has followed the lead of a number of other communities around the country in bringing rescue dogs in need of training and socialization into prisons to be trained by the inmates.

It's a win-win: the dogs get needed training and loving care, and the prisoners get the chance to interact and bond with some really great dogs.

Because I have a familiarity with the prison and criminal justice systems, and because I corun a dog rescue foundation, I was the county's choice to run this program, and I was glad to accept. I am Andy Carpenter, spreader of human and canine happiness everywhere. And the truth is that I've enjoyed every second of it.

One of the inmates working in the program is Brian Atkins, who is also a client. His lawyer had been Nathan Cantwell, a legend in New Jersey legal circles for sixty years. I had dinner with Nathan a couple of years ago and he told me that he would never retire, that even though at that point he didn't have many clients, the only way he would quit working would be by dying.

And dying is exactly what he did, three days later, at the age of eighty-seven. He had neglected to mention at the dinner that his will included a request for me to watch over his clients. Had he mentioned it, I would have pleaded for him to reconsider.

But Brian, at least, has been an easy client. He has served three years of a five-year term after being convicted of embezzlement and fraud, the victim being the software company that he cofounded. He's in the minimum-security area of East Jersey State Prison, and he will be up for parole in four months. I have it on good authority that he'll be granted that parole.

Today I'm bringing dogs and trainers to the prison, including the dog that Brian has been working with, an adorable fox terrier named Boomer. He clearly loves Boomer, and in a way it's a shame that Boomer is almost done with the program and will be finding a permanent home. If the timing had been just a little different, he could have been Brian's dog when he gets out. I really like Brian, so I'm looking forward to this conversation.

"Fred will be coming in, but I wanted to talk to you first," I say, referring to Fred Cummings, the trainer who has been working with Brian and Boomer.

"So you're not staying while Fred is here?" he asks, petting Boomer the whole time.

It seems like an odd question, but I say, "No, I'm meeting Laurie for lunch, and then we've got a parent-teacher meeting at the school. I just wanted to tell you that I've been pretty much assured you'll be getting your parole. You'll be out in no more than four months."

He nods. "Good. Thanks."

It seems like a strangely muted, unenthusiastic response, but my guess is he is just in "I'll believe it when I see it" mode.

"You okay?" I ask.

"I'm fine, Andy. Thanks."

"The parole hearing itself will be in three months, but it's basically a formality. We'll have time to prepare."

"Okay . . . I understand."

I'm not sensing any excitement here. "Any questions?" I ask.

"No. Thanks again."

S he has no idea what she's talking about."

"Mrs. Dembeck?" Laurie asks. "How would you know that? All she said so far is 'Hello' and 'I'll be right back.'"

"She's had Ricky in her class for less than two months. How can she know anything about him?"

Ricky is the child that Laurie and I adopted six months ago, and Mrs. Dembeck is his third-grade teacher at School Number Twenty. We're sitting in her classroom, squashed into two of the kids' desks. These desks were a lot bigger when I went to school here.

The session has already started in an ominous fashion. As we were coming in, we saw our friends Sally and Brian Rubenstein, who had just finished their meeting about their son, Will.

Will, Ricky's best friend, is a great athlete, excellent student, and all-around terrific kid. Brian and Sally were all smiles with Mrs. Dembeck; no doubt their perfect child got a perfect report, and she's saving the bad stuff for Ricky.

I hate perfect kids.

"Just give her a chance, Andy."

"These teachers don't know how to handle kids; they never have and they never will. When I was in third grade, the teacher would put me out in the hall for talking."

5

She thinks for a moment. "That's a good idea . . . maybe I'll try it when we get home."

"If she says anything bad about Ricky, she will live to regret it."

"Hold that thought," Laurie whispers, as the door opens and Mrs. Dembeck walks into the room, an evil smile on her face.

"Sorry to keep you waiting," she says, as she sits at her desk. It's right in front of us, and even though she's maybe five foot four, with us hunched in these little desks, she towers over us. Her goal is obviously to gain the psychological advantage.

"So let's talk about Ricky," she says, looking through some papers in a folder in front of her. "I'm sure you know this, but he is a very special, very wonderful child."

I nod and smile. It is a pleasure to hear a trained, dedicated professional like this talk about her work.

She goes on to talk about how friendly Ricky is, how popular he is among his classmates, and how he clearly is a leader among his peers. This is a woman who knows what she is talking about.

"Let's talk about individual subjects," she then says. "He's particularly proficient in mathematics."

Laurie smiles. "I know; sometimes the calculations he makes in his head amaze me."

Mrs. Dembeck returns the smile. "I overheard him the other day lecturing his friends about point spreads."

Uh-oh. I'm about to be busted. "Kids," I say.

"You mean point spreads like in betting on sports?" Laurie asks her.

"Yes. He's quite knowledgeable on the subject."

"Kids," I repeat. "The things they pick up from their friends."

Laurie is staring at me in a way that indicates she is not buying the bullshit I am selling. This comes as no great surprise to me. "How's he doing in history?" I ask.

Laurie rolls her eyes as Mrs. Dembeck opens her mouth, almost as if the movements are synchronized. "History isn't part of the curriculum," she says, "but Ricky—"

She stops when the door behind us opens. It's the principal of the school, Ms. Jansing. "I'm sorry to interrupt," she says, "but there is an urgent phone call for Mr. Carpenter."

I stand and immediately head for the door. I'm worried, because in my experience the word *urgent* isn't used when the news is terrific. The other thing in my mind is how few people, if any, knew I was here.

I follow Ms. Jansing down the hall to her office, and I pick up the phone that is lying on her desk. "Hello?"

"Andy, it's Pete."

Pete Stanton is a close friend of mine and a captain in the Paterson Police Department. The fact that it's him is further evidence that this is not going to be good, and I experience a moment of panicked worry about Ricky, even though I know he is down the hall at gym class.

"Is this bad news?" I ask.

"Bad and worse," he says. "The bad news is that Brian Atkins escaped from prison."

This makes no sense to me, but I've got a feeling that it's going to be downhill from here. "And the worse news?" I ask.

"He killed two people."

I was right; that is way downhill, and doesn't compute with my understanding of him. "That can't be," I say.

"Oh, it be," Pete says. "Are you his lawyer?"

I'm not really sure how to answer that, so I say, "I was working with him on the parole hearing."

"I think you can safely put the parole preparation on hold. So, are you his lawyer, or not?"

"I guess I am, at least for now."

"Then you might want to come talk to me."

"Where are you?"

"I'm at the murder scene."

"Where is he?" I ask.

"That is the question of the day."

7

Your dog helped him escape." Those are Pete's first words to me when I meet him at the address he gave me in Englewood Cliffs. It's the home of Brian's ex-partner, Gerald Wright, who used to live here, when he was alive. And according to the coroner, he ceased to be alive about two hours ago, when he was stabbed seven times.

We're standing outside near Pete's car. The scene is as busy as every murder scene I've ever been at, and I've been at more than my share. It is a very fashionable neighborhood in a very expensive area; this house would definitely sell for seven figures, and the first number would be a crooked one.

Pete is in charge, but most of the work is being done by the forensics people. Pete has no doubt given them their marching orders, but they are pros and know what to do. The coroner's van has come and gone.

"What the hell does that mean? And which dog are we talking about?" I ask.

"I don't know; the dog is a fugitive as well. When we catch it I'll ask for a photo ID."

"How could a dog help him escape?" I ask.

"Atkins locked your trainer, one Fred Cummings, in a supply room and took his clothes and ID. Then he left with the dog, pretending to be the trainer."

"And that worked?"

Pete shrugs. "It's a big place, and it's minimum security. Plus the guard at the gate was new to the job, which your client probably was aware of."

"Aren't there cameras in the prison that would have recorded everything? Wouldn't someone have seen him do that to Fred? Is Fred okay?"

"He's fine," Pete says. "The camera in that particular hallway was awaiting repair. Your client did his homework."

"The dog must be Boomer," I say.

"Thanks for sharing that; it's a terrific clue."

"Who is the other victim?"

"A woman named Denise Atkins. That last name might ring a bell for you."

"Brian's wife?" He had told me a few visits ago that Denise had filed for divorce, but that it wasn't official yet. That filing is apparently now as moot as the parole hearing.

"One and the same. Apparently he found out his soon-to-be ex-wife was involved with his ex-partner, and that didn't sit well with him. If he contacts you, you might want to suggest that he turn himself in."

"Okay, good. Any other instructions for how I should deal with my client? I'm hanging on your every word."

"You think we're not going to find him anyway?"

"I'm surprised you found me." Then, "So you've made him for this murder already? Rushing to judgment, are we?"

"A neighbor walking by saw him running from the house. She knows him, so had no trouble recognizing him. And she saw the dog in the back of his car."

"Who found the bodies?"

"She did. Your client left the door open when he ran out. It seemed strange to her, so she went to the door and looked inside. The fact that there was blood everywhere tipped her off that something was amiss."

"You going to do any detecting, or just let it go at that?"

"I'll do my best, but it's a real whodunit."

The crowd in and around the house seems to be thinning somewhat, so I ask, "Okay if I go in and take a look around?"

"Gee, that's a tough call. We ordinarily love to invite defense attorneys into our active crime scenes, but maybe not this time."

There's not much more to be learned from staying here, and Pete is getting on my nerves, so I leave. I call Laurie and find out that the conferences are over and she is home from the school.

She's reading with Ricky, a ritual that they both really enjoy, so I don't ask her how the rest of the meeting went. I'm also afraid that the teacher revealed that Ricky is running a bookmaking operation at the school, utilizing the information he learned from me about point spreads.

The ride home gives me time to consider the situation with Brian. It doesn't seem likely that Brian is a person who could have committed the murder, though my knowledge of him is fairly limited. It's not like he was in jail for murder; he's a white-collar criminal, and one who has always professed his innocence of even that crime.

But while I can't quite picture him committing the brutal killings, his escape from jail doesn't really require visualization; it's a fact. And it is completely bizarre.

Here's a guy who has served three years already, and was to be released in a matter of months. Being in any jail is no fun, but Brian was not exactly pounding rocks and eating small helpings of porridge. This was a fairly comfortable, minimum-security prison, and his life was not terribly difficult.

Even after paying back the embezzled money and a fine, Brian is still a wealthy man. A comfortable life awaited him on the outside. The idea that he would run from staying in jail for a short time longer, and in the process expose himself to a life on the run and a longer jail term in a tougher prison when caught, defies logic. And there was nothing about Brian that said he was lacking in logic or smarts.

At least I now know why he reacted to my parole news with obvious indifference. Something was driving him to escape from the prison, acting irrationally and against his own self-interest. Whatever that force was also could have caused him to commit murder; that will not be known until he is caught. Pete is making the early assumption that jealousy and revenge were the driving factors, and a jury might certainly accept them as credible motives.

One thing is certain: he will be caught. Brian is not El Chapo; he does not rule a vast criminal empire filled with soldiers who will go to any lengths to protect him. Brian will be out there alone, with few allies, and no understanding of what it takes to elude a manhunt.

If he is lucky and smart, he will be taken into custody. If he's unlucky and stupid, he could get killed in the process.

Laurie is tucking Ricky into bed when I get home, so I get a chance to go in and kiss him good night. They had dinner together earlier, so while I eat she tells me that Mrs. Dembeck was basically glowing in her praise of his progress in school.

I then go on to tell her about Brian's escape and the subsequent murders. She never met him, but she's heard me talk positively about him these last few months. Regardless of Brian's true character, or lack of it, escaping prison a few months before parole is not an easy thing to understand.

After we talk about it for a few minutes, Laurie asks, "Have you checked the animal shelter? Is there any sign of the dog?"

"No. Maybe he still has Boomer with him. I hope he's okay."

"You would think he wouldn't want a dog with him. It just makes him easier to find."

It's not until I'm in bed, still thinking about this at three o'clock in the morning, that it hits me. I don't know where Brian is, but I sure as hell know where Boomer is. Or at least I know how to find out.

I wait until 6:30 A.M. to call Willie Miller. He's an early riser, so he's probably up by now. But either way, I don't want to wait any longer.

He answers on the first ring with the words, "I was about to call you. I saw the news; why didn't you call me yesterday?"

"Sorry," I say. "I should have." Willie loves every dog we take in, so I know he's worried about Boomer. I doubt he gives a damn either way about Brian.

"I'm going to get him," Willie says. "You want to come?"

Once again, Willie is way ahead of me. We put small GPS devices in the collars of all our rescue dogs, in case they get out or run away from owners that have adopted them. We've used it to great advantage a number of times. Willie has instantly realized this, while it took me until last night to do so.

"Have you checked the GPS?" I ask. The base unit is at the shelter, so Willie would have had to have gone down there early this morning.

"Just got back," he says. "Boomer is in Freehold, the address I've got is a motel."

Freehold is about an hour south of Paterson, and the fact that Boomer is there tells me one of two things. One could be that Brian wanted to get out of the immediate area, where the publicity

would be greater and there would be more chance that he would be noticed by someone.

The other, more likely possibility is that he is simply stopping there on a trip to take him much farther away . . . he could even be hoping to escape to Mexico.

I don't know if I care much about him either way; I certainly don't if he stabbed two people to death. But I do care about Boomer.

When we rescue dogs, we enter into a covenant of sorts with them, in that we promise to be responsible for their welfare on a permanent basis, even after they go to a new home. The adopting owners know that if they ever cannot care for their new dog, we are there for them.

"I'll pick you up," Willie says.

"I need to think this through."

"You can think it through while I'm driving over there," he says, and hangs up. It's fair to say that Willie doesn't hang on my every word.

But I really do need to analyze this situation carefully, especially the legalities of it. While we are going to get Boomer, at the very least we probably also will learn the whereabouts of a fugitive wanted for murder.

If it were just me, that wouldn't be a problem. I remain Brian's lawyer, so I have no obligation whatsoever to report his location to the authorities. In fact, I am prohibited by my oath from doing so.

Willie's position is somewhat different. My view is that even as a private citizen he does not have to turn Brian in, but there is one distinction: if he is asked specifically by a member of law enforcement if he knows where Brian is, then he has to surrender the information. Lying to the police is a crime.

I'm not too worried about this; there would seem to be no reason for law enforcement to think that Willie might have the information. And I'm not breaking privilege by bringing Willie with me; since he has the GPS device, he is actually showing me where Brian is, rather than Brian having revealed it.

So legally I think we're fine, but that is not the only consideration. There is also the fact that Brian might have brutally murdered two people with a knife, is on the run, and might be less than welcoming to someone who shows up unannounced.

Confronting a dangerous killer is something I have done involuntarily a number of times, and it wasn't on my bucket list in the first place. My instincts about Brian still tell me that he would not do anything to hurt me, but he may be desperate and not completely familiar with the attorney-client-privilege concept.

I could bring Marcus Clark, a private investigator that I often employ to protect me. I would feel comfortable confronting a Russian tank division with Marcus alongside me, but I'm not sure it's necessary in this case.

First of all, it might take a while to reach Marcus, and I don't want to take a chance by giving Brian and Boomer more time to get farther away. But more important, I'll have Willie with me.

Willie is a martial arts expert, and the toughest and most fearless guy I've ever met, with the exception of the aforementioned Marcus. Willie spent seven years in prison for a murder he didn't commit, and I represented him in the successful retrial. He had a number of violent skirmishes in prison, and if there is a prison version of *The Ring Magazine,* it would list him as undefeated.

The third and final consideration is what we hope to accomplish, if anything, beyond getting Boomer back. I think I need to play it by ear; we will just have to react in the moment depending on Brian's actions and attitude.

I talk it out with Laurie, which is pretty much what I do about every topic more important than what to have for breakfast. She offers to go along, and as a former police officer licensed to carry a gun, she would make us a much more formidable group.

But Ricky is home, and there's no one to leave him with. We tend to shy away from having him meet vicious murderers on the run, even the alleged kind, so she's going to stay here with him.

Laurie agrees that Willie should be able to handle Brian, but she strangely makes no mention of my potential contribution in a confrontation. Her only suggestion is, "Stay behind Willie."

By the time Willie pulls up, I've decided that it makes sense for us to go, and I've established a few ground rules that Willie needs to be made aware of before we leave. We'll take ten minutes to talk it out before heading out.

I go outside and wait for Willie at the curb. He pulls up, reaches over, and opens the passenger door, and says, "Get in."

So I do.

We can talk on the way.

We switch roles after a few minutes; I drive and Willie gets in the passenger seat. It has nothing to do with our driving abilities; it's because I don't have a clue about how to work the GPS device. We need to be watching it, in case Brian and Boomer leave the motel before we get to Freehold.

So Willie keeps it in his lap, alert for any sign that Boomer is moving. I use the time to tell him his legal obligations, and I extract a promise from him that he will not lie to law enforcement, in the unlikely event that he is ever asked if he knows where Brian is.

Willie has an intense air about him that I have seen before, and that can be intimidating. He does not take kindly to being wronged, in any fashion. I suspect it's a natural reaction for someone who had seven years of his life taken away from him.

But he wants to, he needs to, immediately set things right, no matter what it takes. Boomer is his dog, and he will see to it that Brian regrets having taken him. Whether or not Brian is also a murderer doesn't factor in to his thinking.

"They're moving," Willie says, watching the GPS device.

"They left the motel?"

"Yeah, they're on the road."

"Okay. I'm still going in the direction of the motel. You tell me how I should change the route."

Willie informs me that they're heading for the Garden State Parkway, which makes sense if Brian wants to go south and get farther away from Paterson. He doesn't seem to be driving particularly fast, a smart move since the last thing he would want is to be pulled over by a cop for speeding.

I don't want to be stopped either, but I'm more willing to risk it than Brian, since I am not wanted for murder. So I drive ten miles over the limit, and in the process we manage to make up a lot of ground on Brian and Boomer.

We're down near the Asbury Park exit when Willie says, "They've stopped."

"Did they turn off the road?"

"Doesn't look like it," he says. "Maybe he's going to the bathroom, or getting something to eat."

It's only about three minutes later when Willie says, "They're just about a half mile from here."

About twenty seconds later we see a rest area on the right of the road. I only see one car parked there; I have no idea if it's Brian's or not. My guess is that he managed to rent a car, possibly with a fake ID. Who knows where he got that.

Any question about whose car it is gets answered a few seconds later. There is Brian, near the side of the rest area building, walking Boomer on a leash. I turn off the highway and drive toward the building. There is no way to sneak up on him, so I might as well just drive toward them.

Brian looks up and sees our car approaching. I can see the look of alarm on his face, but he doesn't react physically. He just waits until Willie and I get out of the car and approach him.

"How did you find me?" he asks.

"There's a GPS in Boomer's collar," I say.

He smiles and pets Boomer on the head. Boomer in turn smiles and accepts the petting, apparently not understanding the seriousness of the situation. "So Boomer got me out of jail, and he's getting me back in."

"We're not here to arrest you, Brian. We're just here to take Boomer back."

He nods. "It's better for him. Take care of him; he's a great dog."

He leans down and pets and hugs Boomer. Then he hands the leash to me, and says, "I didn't kill them, Andy."

I don't answer him right away, which is just as well, because he couldn't possibly hear me anyway. That is because the area is suddenly filled with the deafening sounds of sirens, as three cars come racing toward us, blinding lights flashing. Two are police cars, and the third might well be also, though it is unmarked.

It is shocking, and while the humans in our group don't move, Boomer has a different reaction. He pulls away, ripping the leash from my hand and running toward the oncoming cars.

Brian seems to yell something, though that's just a guess, since I can't come close to hearing anything. He runs toward Boomer, who now stands frozen in the path of the cars. Brian grabs him just in time and yanks him out of the way, safe from harm. They both fall to the ground as the cars screech to a stop and the cops jump out.

There are six officers in all. Five are in uniform, guns drawn. The one not in uniform, with no gun in sight, is Pete.

They walk over to Brian, still on the ground with Boomer. Boomer, no dummy, senses they are not arriving with good intentions, and he growls at them, causing them to stop. Pete turns to me and says, "Take the dog."

I walk over and take Boomer's leash. "Come on, buddy," I say, and Boomer allows himself to be led away. I hand the leash to Willie, who pets him to calm him down, and then I walk back to Brian.

By this point, the officers are cuffing his hands behind his back, and Pete is reading him his rights. When he's finished, he turns to me and says, "Didn't know where he was, huh?"

I ignore that and speak directly to Brian, who has been brought to his feet. "You okay?"

He nods. "Did you lead them here?"

"I'm sorry; I must have, but I didn't intend to."

"Okay," he says.

"Don't say a word to anyone. Not one word to anyone other than me. You understand?"

He nods again. "Are you my lawyer?"

My turn to nod. "I'm your lawyer."

I'm really annoyed with myself. This does not exactly qualify as a major news event, as I am frequently annoyed with myself. For example, it happens every time I bet on the Giants and they lose by twenty.

But this time, I really blew it, and I spend the ride back with Willie mentally beating myself up. It never entered my mind that Pete might have me followed, or be following me himself. I didn't entertain the thought that he might not believe me when I said I didn't know where Brian was, especially since when I said it I was being truthful.

I'm also annoyed with Pete for assuming I was lying. Of course, had I known where Brian was at the time, I certainly would have lied, but that isn't the point. Pete is my friend; if you can't bullshit your friends, who can you bullshit?

Legally, Pete was within his rights. He wasn't in any way invading attorney-client privilege, because he had not obtained any information that intruded on it. Of course, no such information existed anyway, since Brian hadn't told me where he was.

What Pete did was smart police work, and what I did was stupid lawyer work.

Hence my annoyance.

Willie is mostly silent on the way back; he's being respectful and letting me think things through. Boomer, sleeping in the backseat, hasn't been very talkative either.

We're about twenty minutes away from home when Willie says, "What happens to Brian now?"

"He'll be taken back to the prison, and probably put in solitary, at least for the time being. They'll charge him with the murders, and throw in the escape charge as well."

"He did escape," Willie says.

I nod. "Yeah, it's pretty hard to deny that."

"You think he did the murders?"

"I don't know," I say. "It's certainly possible."

"You going to represent him?"

"I don't know that either. But I'll definitely take him through the arraignment. And if I don't continue on, I'll make sure he gets a good lawyer."

"As good as you?" he asks.

"Don't be ridiculous."

He laughs. "You'll take the case right to the end."

"Why do you say that?"

"You know why," he says, with as much smugness as Willie can demonstrate.

Of course, he's right, and we both know what we're talking about. "Those cars were bearing down on us, sirens blasting," I say. "He was about to be captured and taken back to prison, and what does he do?"

Willie smiles. "He saves Boomer, even though he could have been run down himself. So you figure a guy who would do that can't be all bad."

"He can't," I say.

"Which is why you'll stay in it to the end."

What Willie doesn't understand is that as a trained attorney and an officer of the court, I will examine all the relevant legal issues and make a thoughtful and reasoned analysis of my potential role in this case.

What Willie does understand is that I'll disregard that analysis and wind up taking the case because Brian risked his life to save Boomer.

The beneficiary of Brian's heroism, Boomer, is still sound asleep in the backseat. "Are you going to take him back to the foundation?" I ask.

"Nah, I think I'll take him home. He's had a rough couple of days, and Cash can use the company."

Cash is the dog Willie and I found the day we won a ten-million-dollar wrongful arrest judgment for Willie after he was released from prison. Somehow the name seemed appropriate, and Cash went from a stray street dog to a life as a pampered mutt sucking down designer biscuits.

There's no sense in me going to the prison now. It will take time for them to reprocess Brian, and I think he's smart enough to follow my instructions not to say anything.

I usually like to see an arrested client at the earliest possible moment. They are scared and bewildered by what is happening, and have to adjust to new and intimidating surroundings. I try to calm and reassure them that I am there to help.

But in this case, Brian is not facing anything new; the prison has been his home for quite a while. He'll be fine, and I can see him in the morning. It will give me time to think things through. Tomorrow I can find out his side of it.

All he had a chance to say to me today was, "I didn't kill them."

That's a start.

'm generally okay with most holidays. My favorite is Thanksgiving, a special combination of excellent food and televised football, which kicks off a weekend of excellent leftover food and more televised football. As far as most of the other holidays, my view of them has always been mostly positive, probably because their arrival usually means a day in which courthouses are closed.

I've never liked New Year's Eve; there's always too much pressure to have fun. Trying to have fun in those kinds of situations just isn't fun. At New Year's Eve parties, you hang out with the same people you're with all year, but suddenly you're supposed to wear paper hats and blow on ridiculous plastic noisemakers. The only factor on the plus side is the knowledge that once you get past the Eve part, New Year's Day is wall-to-wall college football.

But the one holiday I absolutely hate is Halloween. I don't mind the kids part; I'm fine with them getting dressed up and getting candy and stuff. I did that myself, in what seems like another lifetime. If the holiday ended there, I'd be good with it.

It's the adult portion of it that I can't stand, and it never lets up. The morning news shows set the table, since all the announcers are costumed as they sit behind their desks. You've got people wearing mouse ears and a bushy tail reporting on a plane crash.

I just don't get it. I assume they have research that says that viewers like it, but I would sure hate to get trapped in an elevator with those viewers.

Everywhere you look, adults are in ridiculous costumes. Tollbooth operators, tellers in the bank, cashiers in the supermarket . . . they all spend the day looking ridiculous in some misguided attempt to be funny.

When I, Andy Carpenter, ascend to my rightful position as undisputed ruler of the world, I will decree that no adult can ever wear a mask, unless that adult is robbing a liquor store.

While I'm at it, pumpkins are hereby banned from the kingdom. I don't like the way they look. I don't like their pies. I don't like their lattes at Starbucks. I don't like the faces people carve into them. I don't like their soup. I don't like their seeds. So they're out of here; no exceptions.

As long as I'm issuing holiday edicts, I think I'll throw in a couple of December ones. Christmas music is to be allowed for one week only, starting on December eighteenth and ending at midnight on the twenty-fifth.

Also, and this is an ironclad rule, newscasters are prohibited from pretending to be tracking Santa Claus's flight from the North Pole. I have no idea why they do it; one certainly doesn't have to check the comScore numbers to know that news show demographics do not include people of Santa-believing age. And who in their right mind would think it's funny, year after year after year?

I know some people are going to disagree with some of my decisions, but if they don't like them, they shouldn't have elected me ruler.

Today is unfortunately October thirty-first, so I'm bombarded with Halloween stuff from the moment I wake up. The difference is that with Ricky in the house, I can't walk around complaining about it. He's excited by the holiday, and pumped by the Ironman costume that he and Laurie have come up with for his trick-or-treating tonight.

Since it's Saturday, Ricky will be home all day and he and Laurie are going to carve a pumpkin. She knows my feelings about the fruit, or vegetable, or whatever the hell it is, so she isn't going to ask me to participate. I couldn't do so anyway, because I have my own fun day planned.

I'm going to the prison.

When I arrive, I go to the reception area to arrange to see Brian. The woman behind the desk, Carole, is someone I know very well, the result of unfortunately having a number of clients behind bars.

"He's in solitary, Andy."

I'm not surprised to hear that; wardens take a dim view of prisoners who leave their facilities without permission. But I am surprised at what she says next.

"And the dog program has been suspended."

"That's ridiculous," I say.

She nods. "Tell me about it. I always looked forward to it. Everybody did."

She arranges for me to see Brian, but it takes about forty-five minutes. There's nothing longer than a waiting-time minute at the prison; it's the equivalent of ten at a doctor's office or the DMV. Prisoners, guards, visitors, lawyers . . . there is not a single person happy to be there, and the depression wears on you.

When I finally get to see Brian, it's in an anteroom that only has a metal table and two chairs. He is handcuffed to the table . . . this is a far cry from our previous meetings. His attitude is also completely different; he barely looks up as I come in.

"You doing okay?" I ask, immediately securing the "stupid question of the year" trophy. He's in jail, facing additional murder charges, in solitary confinement, and handcuffed to a table. And his wife is one of the murder victims. I'm sure he's doing fine.

He doesn't answer me, which is probably the appropriate answer in this situation.

"We need to talk, Brian. It's the only way I can defend you."

It takes a few seconds, but he finally looks up at me. "Don't defend me."

"I know you're upset, but that's not the best approach in a situation like this. You have rights, and it's in your best interests to exercise them."

He doesn't answer.

"To start, there's an arraignment coming up. You'll be asked to plead."

"Guilty," he says.

"I thought you said you didn't kill them."

"I didn't pull the trigger. But I might as well have killed Denise."

"How is that?"

"I encouraged her," he says. "It's my fault that she's dead."

"Can you be a little less cryptic?"

"Okay, how's this? I did it; just say I killed them both."

"You said before that you didn't."

"Andy, do me a favor? Just plead me guilty and get the hell out of here."

Since I'd rather be carving pumpkins than spend another second in this room, getting out of here is exactly what I do.

I don't get to go trick-or-treating with Ricky. Either Laurie or I had to stay home, so we could give out stuff to the kids that come to our house. Our Paterson neighborhood is a particular favorite of the costumed set, and the doorbell doesn't stop ringing.

Our golden retriever, Tara, who happens to be the greatest living creature in the history of the world, and our basset hound, Sebastian, also quite great, absolutely love this night. Every time the doorbell rings, which is about every twenty seconds, they run to the door to accept petting from the new visitors.

I'm giving out bags of M&M'S, and I'm eating about one bag for every fifteen I give out. It's getting late, and the number of visitors is slowing down, so I should be able to up that percentage. But I do want to save room to eat some of Ricky's candy when he brings it home.

When Ricky and Laurie finally return, they're laughing and still enjoying what apparently was a very fun time. They tell me all about it in great detail, and then set about going through Ricky's bag to see what he's gotten.

It's a time-consuming process, as Laurie scrupulously checks every piece to make sure it isn't somehow dangerous. Any question and the item is jettisoned, and Laurie is the unquestioned decision maker. It's a far different situation from when I was a kid, when all my parents told me was to make sure to spit out rather than swallow any razor blades.

When we're finished sorting and checking and eating, Ricky goes to bed and I take Tara and Sebastian for our nightly walk. It's something that I really look forward to; it clears my mind, and I love watching the dogs enjoy it so much.

I get back to find Laurie already asleep; this motherhood thing must be really exhausting. But she wakes up when I enter the bedroom, and asks me to update her on what happened with Brian.

"So he's blaming himself for the murders without admitting to them?"

"That's right, though it seems like he's only talking about Denise. He says he encouraged her, whatever that means."

"What did you take it to mean?"

"That he maybe said something that put her in the position she was in, that made her vulnerable. But I could be completely wrong about that. Maybe he killed her but is in some sort of denial. Or maybe he's just lying to me, though if he's pleading guilty anyway, I don't know what he'd have to gain by it."

"What is your obligation as his attorney?" she asks.

"What do you mean?"

"Can you let him enter a guilty plea if he says he's innocent?"

"I've been thinking about that, and I'm sure I can. There's a Supreme Court case, *Alford v. North Carolina,* that speaks to it. In fact, when a client says he's innocent but pleads guilty, it's called an 'Alford plea.' All the court needs is some evidence of actual guilt." "There's plenty of that," she says.

"That's for sure."

"So that's your answer."

I shake my head. "That's 'the' answer; it's not 'my' answer."

"Because you want to know if he really did it."

"Right," I say.

"Why would he plead guilty if he wasn't really guilty?"

"He's depressed; his wife was just killed, and he's facing life in prison. Maybe he just doesn't want to fight anymore."

It's not until three hours later that I wake up from a sound sleep, the answer somehow clearer now. I'm not sure why I think better asleep than awake. I sit up, no longer tired, because of what I've realized.

Laurie wakes up herself and sees me sitting there. "What is it?" she asks. "Too many M&M'S?"

"Brian's not guilty."

"How do you know that?"

"When he told me he didn't do it, he said that he 'didn't pull the trigger' but that he was responsible."

"So?"

"So they were stabbed. He didn't even know how they died."

"Maybe 'pulling the trigger' was just a figure of speech," she says.

"I don't think so. I think if you murder someone you'd be damn precise about how you did it. I think he just assumed they were shot."

"So what are you going to do?"

"I'm going to find out what the hell is going on."

'm not in a huge hurry to see Brian again. The arraignment is not until tomorrow afternoon, and since it's just a formality designed to file charges and elicit a plea, there's really little preparation that needs to be done for it.

Brian's not going anywhere, that much is certain, so I can let him sit and think about his situation before I visit him again. In the meantime, I want to learn as much as I can about his original case. I know very little about it, because he was Nathan's client, and I've only been handling the parole application.

I call Sam Willis, who handles two main functions for me. He's my accountant, and even though I'm ridiculously wealthy, that is not a challenging job. My investments are pretty straightforward, and my tax return isn't that complicated.

The other role Sam has assumed is somewhat different. He has taken to referring to himself as my "director of investigative information." Sam is a genius on the computer; he can find whatever he wants on the Web, and everything is out there. He also has the ability to hack into anything he wants, no matter how secure the target thinks it is.

Much of that hacking is illegal, but we don't often let that stand in our way. Our rationale is that we use the information to further the causes of truth and justice, and sometimes that's even true. I'd hate to have to argue that rationale in court, so I'm frequently re-minding Sam to be careful.

"We got a case?" Sam asks after answering the phone, as per usual, on the first ring. He always starts our conversation with that question, since he likes investigating a hell of a lot more than accounting.

"We might."

"Let's crank it up, baby," he says.

" 'Let's crank it up, baby'?"

"It's an expression, Andy."

"You need to come up with some different expressions, Sam."

"I'll work on it."

"Good, but work on this first." I proceed to ask him to find me any and all information on Brian's life, his former company, and his criminal case.

"I'm on it," he says. "When do you need it?"

"Yesterday, if not the day before. And I also want to know who Gerry Wright called the week of his death, as well as who called him." Sam can break into the phone company's computer with ridiculous ease.

"I hear you," he says. "Starting on it right away."

"Just crank it up, Sammy."

My next call is to Edna, my secretary/assistant. She's filled that role since I started my practice, and even though she's now well past retirement age, she hasn't hung up her typewriter. Apparently, when you have a job that pays well and requires you to do absolutely no work, retirement is not that appealing a prospect.

Edna is a crossword puzzle wizard and spends pretty much all her time preparing for crossword tournaments. Our not having any clients fits in quite nicely with her schedule.

I can hear the fear in her voice when she answers the phone; obviously her caller ID has told her it's me calling. Her preference would be to limit our contact to my mailing her checks. "What is it, Andy?"

If a voice can cringe, that's what hers is doing. "Great news, Edna. We've got a client."

"Another one?"

"It's the first one in almost a year," I say.

"Time flies. Are you going to plead it out?"

She has no idea who the client is, or what crime he or she is accused of, but she's openly rooting for a plea bargain. "Is that what you'd recommend?" I ask.

She ignores the question. "What do I have to do?"

"I need you to go to the office and—"

She interrupts. "The office?" It's twenty minutes from her house, and she hasn't been there in a while.

"Yes, my office, the one where you work," I say. "Go into Nathan Cantwell's files and pull the one on the Brian Atkins case, and then bring it to the house. Call me if the trial transcript is not in there."

"That's it?" she asks. Apparently this isn't quite as bad as she anticipated.

"For now."

It comes as no great surprise that Sam arrives at the house before Edna. He shows up with a large folder filled with stuff he's printed off the Internet. I could have had him hack into the courthouse and get the trial transcript, but there's no sense breaking the law when it's not necessary, and Edna hasn't called to say it's not there. Of course, Edna may not have summoned up the energy to look yet.

Much of what Sam has brought me are media reports both before and after Brian's fall from grace. For a while, he was a business star, if not superstar. In a partnership with the now-deceased Gerald Wright that began when they were roommates at Dartmouth, he built Starlight Systems, a small but very successful technology company.

The company reinvented itself a couple of times, but they hit pay dirt about five years ago. Basically they built computer routers and servers powered by software that was simply faster than their competitors. Their customers were Wall Street firms, who were voracious in their quest for speed.

Stock trading, which once had been done by runners with slips of paper on the exchange floor, has completely changed over the years. Now it is done by computers, amazingly fast computers, which accomplish trades in milliseconds. It is a business conducted at warp speed, and to the fastest goes the advantage.

So Brian became a very wealthy man, and must still be so today, even after making restitution and paying a large fine. His descent came when he was accused and convicted of embezzling funds from his firm.

Gerald Wright was a key witness against his partner, despite publicly professing sadness at having to assume that role. Brian's five-year sentence was a very light one, a testimony to Nathan's effectiveness as his attorney and to Brian's never having been accused of anything previously.

The information suggests that Brian was the business guy, while Wright focused more on the technology. But apparently Brian had significant capabilities in the tech end as well, and the allegations are that he used his computer expertise to facilitate the embezzlement.

Edna shows up a couple of hours after Sam, file in hand.

She's a real dynamo.

It was the french fries, Your Honor. I did it for the fries." That's what I would say to a judge to explain my motivation for committing whatever crime I might someday be accused of. If I got lucky and the judge had been to Charlie's, he'd understand and let me off with a warning.

Charlie's is the perfect restaurant. Not because it has twenty-two flat-screen televisions that allow viewing access to at least four of them from every table in the place. Not because the hamburgers come charred on the outside and pink on the inside, alongside pickles that have mastered the art of crunching. Not because the beer comes ice cold in glasses that are even colder.

No, it is the french fries that have Charlie's sitting alone as the only five-star restaurant in the Andy Carpenter Guide to Fine Dining. They have no trace of oiliness or grease, and the chef will even cook them to taste. He long ago learned that I want mine burned to such a crisp that an autopsy would have to be done to prove that they were descended from potatoes.

So while I am pissed off at Pete for following me and thereby capturing Brian, I am not going to avoid him, because he spends every night at Charlie's. And that is because Charlie's, as I may have mentioned, has rather excellent french fries.

Pete is at our regular table when I arrive, sitting with Vince Sanders, who is here so often I think he might be nailed to the floor. Vince is the editor of our local paper, and although he could be classified as a close friend, I don't think I would recognize him if he didn't have a sneer on his face and a beer in his hand.

It's opening night of the NBA season, and Vince is a die-hard Knicks fan, so he's staring at their game on one of the TVs. They're down twenty in the second quarter, which means they're in mid-season form.

"Well, look who's here," Pete says when he sees me.

"You're surprised?" I ask. "Didn't you have me followed?"

"No, but I'm going to tail you when you leave. Maybe you'll lead me to John Dillinger, or Al Capone."

"I'm looking forward to getting you on the stand," I say, a pathetic comeback that Pete simply laughs at.

It does get Vince to look away from the TV for a moment. "Your boy is going to plead not guilty?" Vince couldn't care less what happens to Brian, he is simply interested in getting a scoop for to-morrow's paper.

"Off the record? Absolutely," I lie.

"Off the record?" asks Vince. "That's not a phrase I'm familiar with."

"He's bullshitting, Vince," Pete says. "Either that or he wants to go to trial so he can make a big fee. Money talks."

"Speaking of money, my days of picking up the check in this establishment are over." Since I am far richer than either of my obnoxious friends, it has become standard for me to pay the checks at Charlie's.

"On the other hand," Pete says, "everyone is entitled to the best defense possible. Innocent until proven guilty, I always say."

"Really?" I ask. "I can't recall you ever saying that."

Vince nods vigorously, the panic at possibly having to pay showing clearly. "He says it all the time. Right after he says what a wonderful attorney and human being you are."

"You guys are pathetic," I say.

Pete nods. "I can live with that." Then, "Are you really going to trial with this?"

"I am," I say. "So far you've got nothing." It's too early to have gotten discovery documents, so maybe I can get some information from Pete, which will help me advise Brian, should he decide to listen to my advice.

Pete laughs. "Right. He escapes from jail, on camera, and two hours later is found leaving the murder scene. And the victims are his estranged wife and the partner who sent him to jail." He laughs again. "Where is Sherlock Holmes when we need him?"

"You got a murder weapon?"

"We'll find it."

"DNA?" I ask.

"All in good time."

"You can't even prove he was at the scene," I say.

"The neighbor saw him."

"Maybe the neighbor did it."

"Andy," Pete says. "You're a good friend of mine, so I want to give you some advice, so that you won't embarrass yourself. Go home, think this over, and have your client plead guilty. But first pay the check."

Vince nods. "He's right, Andy. Definitely pay the check."

've never really approached an arraignment like this before. It's not that I've prepared differently, since arraignments take little preparation. It's mostly a formality, and whatever burden there is on the lawyers rests with the prosecutor, though there's very little of that. Unless there are some unusual issues to discuss, it's basically the defense attorney's job to look pretty and watch his client plead.

That, of course, is what makes this situation different. I'm not sure how Brian is going to plead, or what I'll do about it when he says whatever he's going to say.

I usually just have a short meeting with the client before court convenes, but in this case I've arranged for Brian to be brought a bit earlier. We meet in an anteroom adjacent to the courtroom, and I'm already inside when Brian arrives with a guard. He's handcuffed, so the bailiff leaves him with me and assumes a position outside the door.

"How's it going?" I ask.

"Wonderful," he says. "Everything is really terrific."

I ignore the sarcasm. "Okay, well I know you've been through the arraignment process before, but it's basically the prosecution's show. All you'll be asked to do is plead."

"Guilty as charged."

I nod. "That's your call. But they're going to want some information, some details to demonstrate that your plea is truthful." I'm lying about this, but I can live with that.

"Like what?" he asks.

"I'm not sure; it's up to them to decide what to ask. But for example, what did you do with the gun after you shot them?"

"I stopped and threw it in a Dumpster a few miles away."

"Which Dumpster?"

"I don't remember."

"What kind of gun was it?"

"I don't know; guns aren't my thing."

"Did it have a really sharp point?" I ask.

"What do you mean?"

"I mean that the victims were stabbed. Which makes you full of shit, and also makes you innocent."

He looks at me and doesn't say anything for at least thirty seconds. Then, "There was a lot of blood."

I nod. "That often happens when knives are plunged into human bodies."

He doesn't say anything, so I continue. "You can plead guilty, Brian. But if you do, I'm going to ask the court to let me withdraw as your attorney, because I don't agree with the plea. But don't worry, you'll find a lawyer that will go along."

"Andy, I've had enough. Okay? I've just had enough."

"Feeling guilty isn't the same as being guilty, Brian. I'm spitballing here, but it seems like you're blaming yourself for somehow putting Denise in a dangerous position. So you're trying to get the state of New Jersey to punish you."

"I would say that's accurate, whether or not you think it's justified."

"So in the process, you're preventing the state of New Jersey from punishing anyone else."

"What do you mean?"

"You didn't kill her, but somebody else did. Somebody who knows that they used a knife, and not a gun."

"So?"

"So doesn't that person deserve at least as much blame as you? Do you think the police are going to hunt down that real killer if you've already admitted to the crime?"

"So I say I'm innocent, like last time, and they convict me anyway. Then what, are the police going to keep searching for someone they don't think exists?"

There is a quick knock on the door, and then it opens. It's the bailiff, with a simple message. "It's time."

"Just a second," I say. Then, to Brian, "Why did you run?"

"What do you mean?"

"After you found the bodies, why did you run? Why not call the police?"

"Because I knew they would think I did it," he says.

"So what? You're going to plead guilty anyway."

He thinks for a minute. "I thought that if I surrendered, I'd never be able to find out who really did it, and get revenge." .

"Well," I say, "this is your chance."

We head into the courtroom, which is as crowded as I expected. This is a case in which wealthy people were murdered, and the accused is wealthy himself. Throw in the jilted-husband aspect, as well as a prison escape, and it's close to a perfect media storm.

The presiding judge is Henry Henderson, nicknamed Hatchet by all the lawyers who have had the misfortune to try a case in his courtroom. Hatchet hates lawyers and makes no effort to hide it. He hates wiseass lawyers most of all, which has put me directly in his sights.

The prosecutor is Norman Trell, who has long been considered an up-and-comer in the department. If he has tried a case this important before, I'm not aware of it, and his getting the assignment may be a sign that the state thinks Brian will plead guilty.

Of course, if Brian's own attorney has no idea how he will plead, it seems unlikely that New Jersey has any special insight.

Hatchet asks both sides if we are ready to proceed, and we both say that we are. I'm dreading where this is going. If Brian pleads guilty, then a person I know to be innocent will be punished for a crime he did not commit. Even worse, the person or persons who did commit it will remain free.

If he pleads not guilty, then I'm stuck in a murder trial that I don't want to be a part of and that I have a small chance of winning.

It's the definition of a lose-lose. I'd rather be home carving pumpkins.

Hatchet goes through a bunch of housekeeping details, and then he has the prosecution present the charges. Finally, he asks Brian and me to stand, and asks how he will plead. This only relates to the murder charges; we've already copped to the escape charge.

I think there's a chance I got through to him, but he hasn't given me any indication either way, so all I can do is wait like everybody else.

"Not guilty," Brian says, his voice surprisingly firm and determined.

"Well, gentlemen," Hatchet says after telling the clerk to record the "not guilty" plea, "looks like we have a trial to schedule."

Yes, we do. It's going to be wall-to-wall work, and I have only myself to blame.

The real question is: How am I going to tell Edna?

Do you think the judge will grant the change of venue?" Laurie asks.

The question surprises me. "I wasn't planning to ask for one," I say. "You think I should?"

"Well, since you're going to be in Florida anyway, I thought you might want to try the case there."

"Oh, damn. I forgot." We have an upcoming family vacation to Disney World planned, and it totally slipped my mind. Trial preparation and the trial itself will make it impossible. "Now what?"

Laurie smiles. "Now we move the trip to spring break. It's not your fault, Andy."

"You think Ricky will be okay with it?"

She nods. "As long as we go. We promised him."

"We'll definitely go. Should I talk to him?"

"I'll do it; he'll be fine. This way we'll be home and he can get presents under the Christmas tree."

"The tree?" I was hoping that the vacation would remove the need to have a tree. I've got nothing against Christmas trees in theory; it's the setting up I don't like. Laurie becomes an artiste when it comes to us putting up lights and trinkets; it took less time to create Mount Rushmore.

"No trip means a tree," she says. "I'll buy the lights this week."

Canceling the Disney trip is my first taste of feeling like a rotten parent; I have a hunch it won't be the last. But in this case, work comes first, giving me still another reason to eliminate work from my life.

I turn on the news and see that the murders are prominently featured. The local ABC affiliate has gotten an interview with Sarah Maurer, the neighbor who discovered the bodies.

She tells the reporter that the police asked her not to speak about the case, then proceeds to speak about the case. She describes how she saw Brian running from the house, and then found the dead bodies. She starts to sob as she talks.

The fact that the prospective jury pool is out there watching this is a nightmare, and makes me think that maybe I should ask for a change of venue. Orlando might be a good choice; maybe I should tell Laurie to hold off on the lights.

I head back down to the jail to speak to Brian. He seems down, which is obviously the appropriate way for someone in his situation to be. Before I see him, I confirm with prison officials that he will soon be removed from solitary and put back in with the general prison population.

"It's not a big deal either way," he says, when I tell him. "I don't have too many close friends here anyway. It's not like we hang out around the water cooler, you know?"

Brian didn't testify in his own defense during his first trial, so my reading of the transcript didn't tell me much about his side of the story. Sometimes lawyers can get a client's point of view in front of the jury without having the client testify, but Nathan was not successful in that regard.

Having a client take the stand is always risky, and most lawyers, myself included, try to avoid it whenever possible. Just reading the transcript, it seems that Brian's testimony was necessary, but since I don't know what he would have said, I can't be sure.

Though my reading told me quite a bit about Brian's case, I question him as if I'm starting from zero. I ask him to take me through the original embezzlement charge, and he starts off by proclaiming his innocence, a position he has never wavered on.

The case against him was convincing, as the prosecution showed clear evidence of money leaving the firm's accounts improperly and of that same money showing up in personal accounts of Brian's that were set up in secret, some overseas.

"I had nothing to do with any of that," he says. "Someone else did it in my name."

"Why and who?" I ask.

"The why part is obvious," he says. "To get me in here, or at least to get me out of the company. The who part is a little tricky."

"What do you mean?" I ask.

"Everything was done by computer," he says. "I wasn't accused of breaking into the company vault and carrying out the money in a bag. All the transactions were done by computer. So it could have been Gerry, or it could have been some guy sitting at a terminal in Bangladesh. Distance doesn't matter; it's all about access." The Gerry he is referring to is Gerald Wright, his now-deceased ex-partner.

I don't bother to ask how some outside party could have access, since I know that Sam Willis can access anything he wants. "So you think it might have been someone on the inside of the company, like your partner?"

"Gerry's my best guess, since he was the one most likely to profit from my leaving. But it also could be someone he was doing business with."

"Like who?"

He shrugs. "I don't know. But our products were remarkable, and we were making improvements in them daily. In the wrong hands they could be even more valuable than they are when used legally."

"Who will take over the business now?"

He shrugs. "I'm not exactly part of management anymore, so I can only guess. But there's a board of directors, and they'll appoint someone. Probably either Ted Yates, who is the CFO, or Jason Mathers."

"Who is he?"

"Head of the technology division. He and his team are the ones that make the place go."

"Who would you bet on?"

"Yates. He's more political; he knows how to work the system. He'll convince the board that Mathers is a war criminal."

Brian goes on to tell me about the company's "products," very little of which I understand. They make servers and routers, through which computer data travels. They are apparently very fast, which is why Wall Street companies use them, since speed is crucially important to gaining trading advantages.

"Wall Street companies needed us for the speed, and that's what we provided. But I don't know where the company is now; I've been gone for three years, which in tech is forever. Other people might have found other uses for what the company can do, and it might not be legal."

"Anybody in mind?" I ask.

"Yeah, one person in particular, someone who I know was involved with Gerry. He was the reason I broke out of jail."

"Who is that?" I ask, feeling an uncomfortable sensation that a bomb is about to be dropped.

"Dominic Petrone," he says.

Kaboom.

D ominic Petrone is the scariest anachronism on the planet. In an era when organized crime families are in decline nationally, Petrone has successfully fought against that tide. He's adapted to changing times, bringing modern business techniques to loan sharking, drugs, gambling, and prostitution.

He even looks the part of a successful CEO: he is a graying sixty-two-year-old whose suits cost enough to pay for a decent used car. But at the core, his business model is based on fear, intimidation, and murder.

I've had dealings with Petrone on a few occasions in the past, and I've done well in that I've managed to at least partially align my interests, and those of my clients, with his. For the most part I've accomplished my goals, the primary one being to remain alive.

But I have never had any dealings with him when I was not petrified, and I am not looking forward to going another round. Worse yet, this time we could well be adversaries.

It's hard for me to speak coherently and panic at the same time, but I manage to do so when I ask Brian, "What does Petrone have to do with this?"

"Most people don't know this, but Denise and I had decided to end our marriage before any of this happened. Before I was even accused."

Based on what he just said, I've got a feeling he's going to take the long way to get around to Petrone.

He continues, "The timing just seemed to people like she left me because I was arrested, but that wasn't it at all. We had recognized that it wasn't working, and we were ending it as friends."

I can't take it; the suspense is killing me. "We were talking about Dominic Petrone," I say, to move him along.

"I'm getting there. Denise used to come see me here all the time, and we got to the point where we talked about restarting our life together when I got out. It was as if my misfortune was making us closer, was making us realize what was important.

"Then, about a year ago, things started to change. It was the way she talked to me, and the fact that she communicated with me less. She didn't say it, but I knew she was seeing someone else. I wasn't angry; I was upset because I had come to realize how much I still loved her. But I didn't blame her."

I'm not going to interrupt with any more questions; it will just slow down the time it will take to get to Petrone.

"She never told me who it was, never even admitted that there was someone. But I knew it had to be Gerry; the three of us grew up together. She went out with him before me, and I knew he always resented that I beat him out. They saw each other every day at work, so it just wasn't surprising."

He pauses awhile, as if remembering. Then, "Finally she told me that it just wasn't going to work for us, that she wanted to go through with the divorce this time. She was crying and sorry, but that didn't change the bottom line. She wanted out. I was upset, but I gave her my blessing.

"Then about three months ago, she told me that she was getting concerned about something. She said that she had overheard some things and that she thought Gerry was involved with some dangerous people. She wondered if it might have anything to do with my case."

I think I have an idea who one of the dangerous people might be.

He goes on. "She said things were getting really weird, and that she was going to dig around and find out what she could, that maybe there would be a way to help me. I should have told her not to, to just stay out of the whole thing. I should have told her that I was going to be out of prison soon anyway. But I didn't." He pauses for a moment, then shakes his head and repeats, "I didn't. The next day, she told me she was scared. That someone named Dominic Petrone was involved, and that Gerry was leaving town, to try and figure out what to do. He said that she needed to go with him, that nobody was safe. She wanted to know if I still had the cabin."

"What cabin is that?"

"I owned a place in Maine, way up near Belgrade Lakes. But I sold it long ago; I tried to call and tell her that, but she wasn't answering her phone. That's when I decided I had to escape; I was scared for her, and I panicked. Whatever she was facing, I couldn't let her do it on her own. Not after I used her like I did."

"So you concocted that escape plan almost in the moment?" I ask.

He smiles. "Not really. It's a fantasy I had; probably all prisoners have it. I planned a way to do it years ago, not ever thinking that I would. This place is not exactly Alcatraz."

"So you broke out and went looking for them," I say.

"For her . . . yeah. But I was too late."

"What were you going to do if you weren't too late?"

"I have no idea, but I just couldn't let her face it alone. She sounded scared to death. It was my responsibility."

It's amazing to me that a smart guy like him put himself in this situation because of what amounted to chivalry. Chivalry toward a woman who dumped him. "You could have come to me," I say. "I would have helped."

He nods. "Well, now's your chance."

Lenny Butler's plan was to move into a much nicer place. Not that his Englewood house was a dump, not even close. But now he could afford more, and he saw no reason why he shouldn't go for it.

Well, there was one reason, but it was a short-term one. A sudden sign of affluence on Lenny's part could prove to be a detriment to his health.

They had warned him once, and he had considered himself lucky to have gotten off easily. In a way, that was a good thing: it impressed upon him the need to be more careful. And he had taken heed and conducted his business in such a manner that they would remain in the dark.

Lenny smiled just thinking of darkness. This was his favorite time of year; the clocks had just been adjusted to the point where it got dark before 5:00 P.M. He loved the dark, literally and figuratively.

This was Tuesday, a night that Lenny conducted much of his business. He did so carefully, making sure he wasn't followed, and meeting his clients in places that he knew to be secure. He made more money this night, and every recent Tuesday night, than he had ever made in a month holding a real job.

Real jobs were for suckers.

When he got home, they were waiting for him. He didn't know

that their names were Tony and Richie; they hadn't told him that when they warned him the first time. He also didn't know how they had gotten into his house, since he had an alarm system that he thought was effective. It must not have been, because Richie and Tony were sitting on his couch, smiling when they saw him enter.

"Hello, Lenny," Richie said. "Where you been?"

They couldn't know; there was no way they could know. So he had to assume they didn't and bluff, because if they did know, then all was lost. "Out having a few drinks. What are you guys doing here?"

"You pay cash for those drinks?" Richie asked.

"Yeah. Twenty bucks. Why?"

"Empty your pockets on that table."

"Come on, you guys. What's going on? I haven't done anything wrong."

"Your pockets," Richie said.

Panic setting in, Lenny walked to the table. They knew what he had done, and if they didn't then it would be clear when he emptied his pockets, or they emptied them for him. He probably had six thousand in cash, way too much to explain away.

The answer was in another pocket, not the one the cash was in. He had a .22 in there, and he would kill them with it. He was opting for the lesser of two very bad evils. If he did it, his life would never be the same. He would have to start running, and might never stop.

If he didn't do it, he would himself be killed.

That made the decision fairly easy.

Lenny walked over to the table and started to empty his pockets. Richie walked toward him while he did so, but Tony maintained his position on the couch. First Lenny emptied a pocket of some papers and change.

Then, using his body to shield what he was doing, he took out his handgun. Finger on the trigger, he turned slowly, in a manner designed not to provoke any reaction.

The bullet entered Lenny's forehead before he had a chance to fire his weapon. It came from Tony's gun, the sound cushioned by the silencer. He was dead before he hit the floor. He was dead before he even starting falling to the floor.

Richie finished the job of searching Lenny's pockets, finding the money and keeping it. Tony, meanwhile, was searching the house for an appropriate weapon. He found it in Lenny's bedroom, a baseball bat signed by a member of the New York Mets.

He brought the bat back into the room and proceeded to crush Lenny's arms and legs with it. They could have done it while Lenny was alive, but then there would have been all that screaming. Besides, Richie and Tony were hit men, not torturers.

The bat wielding was only necessary because the word would get out about it. People would assume that it was done while Lenny was alive, and the thought of it would deter "future Lennys" from doing what he did.

But there would be others, there always were, and they would pay the same price that Lenny did.

I need to accept that what Brian is saying is true. It very well may not be, but at this point I get nowhere by questioning it. If he's lying, if he broke out of jail and stabbed those two people to death, then I will come up empty in my investigation, and he will go down. Our only chance is if he's telling the truth, which means there's something out there to find.

My preliminary assumption is that the answer has to involve Starlight Systems, the company that Brian and Gerald Wright founded and built. If someone framed Brian, the likely reason I can see for doing so would have been to get him out of the company.

Starlight provides equipment that Wall Street companies needed, and that I assume helped them make barrels of money. When it comes to motivations for murder, money always ranks high up on the list. It's on a par with sex, but without the sweating and panting.

Also, Starlight is a company that specializes in computing, and if Brian is right, then his arrest and conviction were accomplished through computer sleight of hand. That is another reason to think that the company is at the center of this whole thing.

Of course, Gerry Wright had the computer expertise and the financial incentive to put his partner away. He also appears to have been interested in Brian's soon-to-be ex-wife. All of this gives Wright a reason to have framed Brian and gotten rid of him.

Unfortunately, that would also have given Brian a motive to kill Gerry. So Brian could well be not guilty of the embezzlement but guilty of the murders.

Ugh.

I do what I always do in these situations and call a meeting of our legal and investigative team. We'll convene in my office tomorrow morning, so I can tell them all that I know so far, which isn't a hell of a lot.

The thing I do first is visit the scene of the crime. I clear it with Pete Stanton, who really has no choice but to allow me in. He knows that if he doesn't, I can have a judge order him to, and he'd look bad for refusing.

Since Ricky is in school, Laurie is able to go with me, as she always does. And as an ex-cop, she knows her way around a crime scene better than I do.

On the way there, she says, "Ricky really seems to be into football."

I nod. "Like father, like son."

"Today he asked me about the line on the Giants game this Sunday. I asked him if he meant offensive or defensive line."

Uh-oh.

She continued, "But he meant the betting line."

I don't say anything, because in the moment nothing comes to me. I've got a hunch that if the moment lasted until next August, nothing would come to me.

"Andy, I don't believe in pushing a child into a career path, but I would be unhappy to see him become a bookmaker. It would hurt his chances to become president."

"I'll talk to him," I say.

"What are you going to say?"

"Trust me. I'll take care of it." She doesn't look terribly trusting, so I say, "What are you worried about?"

"That the two of you will switch our vacation from Disney World to Vegas."

We arrive at Gerry Wright's house, and the area looks much different from the last time I was here. Then there were all kinds of police vehicles, cops everywhere, and neighbors milling about trying to get a look at what was going on. Now there is just one police car, one cop standing on the front porch, and not a neighbor to be found.

Pete has cleared the way for us to enter the house, but it probably wouldn't have been necessary. The cop on the front porch greets Laurie like a long-lost best friend, though he sneers at me. Her former colleagues on the force cannot seem to grasp the concept that she is married to a defense attorney. It's a shame she may never live down.

Everything about the inside of the house says luxurious living, from the clearly expensive furniture to the fine art hanging on the walls. I know zero about vases, but there's one sitting on a stand that I would bet could be traded in for a Porsche.

This is a room that was meticulously and carefully designed; great thought must have gone into every piece, and money was no object. The kind of money represented here makes me think about Brian, Wright's partner and former business equal, who has spent years living in a seven-by-ten-foot cement cell. Of course, at this point, given the chance, I'm sure Wright would happily trade places with him.

All of this poshness makes the bloodstains all over the floor even more incongruous than one would expect. They are still more jarring because the carpet is so white. Two people died violently in this room, but the considerate killers seemed not to have disturbed so much as an ashtray.

I always find it weird and very disconcerting to be at the spot where lives were snuffed out, but when I turn to mention something like that to Laurie, I notice that she's not in the room. "Laurie?"

"In the kitchen," she responds, and while I have no idea where the kitchen is, I move toward an open door, since that seems to be the direction her voice was coming from. Sure enough, my detective skills are intact, and I reach the kitchen.

Laurie is on her knees, near another open door. I walk over and see that the door is to a walk-in pantry. Plenty of people live in apartments smaller than this pantry.

"What are you doing?"

"The female victim—"

"Denise," I say.

"Denise was hiding in here. They went and found her, and brought her into the other room, where she was killed."

"How do you know that?"

She holds up her hands, with something apparently squeezed between her fingers. "Was she blond?"

"I don't know."

"I'll bet she was, though it's not her natural color. I found at least five hairs; I'd bet they grabbed her by the hair."

"Couldn't five hairs be there because she lived here, or spent a lot of time here? Brian is sure they were having an affair."

"Possible, but forensics would have already picked up a lot of them. The fact that five were left behind means there were many more. And this door was open, which is not consistent with how neatly this house was kept. And look at this."

She points to a small streak or stain of some kind on the floor.

"What is it?"

"I'd bet it's from her shoes. She was dragged."

"That backs up Brian's story," I say.

"How?"

I think Laurie knows the answer to her own question, but it's a technique she and I have come up with, without ever acknowledging it. We get each other to talk about stuff, even when it's obvious, because the act of discussing it seems to help us think more clearly.

"If Brian was the killer, he would have killed her where he found her. There would have been no reason to drag her in there. Especially if he was in a jealous rage."

"Why would the killer have wanted to kill them together?" she asks.

I shrug. "Hard to know. Maybe he wanted to get information out of Wright, and he threatened to kill Denise to get him to talk."

"Why do you think the killer used knives? To make it look like a crime of passion and set up Brian as the patsy?"

I shake my head. "Doesn't seem possible. As far as anyone knew, he was in prison. That's a pretty good alibi. It's more likely he just didn't want neighbors to hear the gunshots." I don't mention it, but the use of knives has troubled me because it doesn't fit with my theory. It is not the way Petrone's people normally operate.

We don't talk for a couple of minutes. I'm digesting the horror of what went on in this room, and I suspect she's doing the same.

She breaks the silence and says, "This guy is the definition of a cold-blooded killer. Not the way you think of cybercriminals, or computer nerds."

I nod. "Let's find him."

It's my turn to walk Ricky to school. Laurie and I basically alternate doing so, though she probably winds up doing it two-thirds of the time. I'm going to utilize this morning's walk to have my talk with Ricky, and I'm a little nervous about it.

"Rick, do you know what gambling is?" is the way I start.

"Sure, it's what you do on football. If your team wins, you win money."

"Right, but I can also lose."

"I know," he says. "You lose when you take the Giants."

"Rick, gambling is not a good thing."

"Why not?"

"Because people can lose money that they need."

"Do you lose money that you need?" he asks.

"No. But it's still not a good thing."

"Then why do you do it?"

"It's a bad habit I picked up." This is not going well, and it's aggravating. The truth is I don't bet very much on games; it's just a way to keep me interested. But having this conversation is making me feel like Jimmy the Greek. "But you'd be better off going outside and playing sports, rather than staying inside and watching them."

"So you can't stop?" he asks.

"I can stop."

"So it's a bad thing, and you can stop, but you keep doing it?"

Mrs. Dembeck is right; this is one smart kid.

"I'll tell you what: Let's both stop," I say. "No more gambling for us."

"Is this Mom's idea?"

"Nope," I lie. "It's mine. We have a deal?"

He shrugs. "Okay. But can we still watch football together?"

"Absolutely," I say, sticking out my hand. He shakes it and the deal is done.

I am not pleased.

I drop Ricky off and head down to my office for our initial case meeting. Laurie arrives as I do, and we walk in together. Everyone is there: Sam Willis, Willie, Edna, Marcus Clark, and Hike, the other lawyer in my firm.

They are sitting at the long table in what serves as my conference room. The way they are situated makes the table look like a park seesaw. Marcus is at one end, and all the others are at the other end. Everyone here is afraid of Marcus, which makes perfect sense, since Marcus is one scary human being.

Hike is in the middle of one of his rants, talking to anyone who will listen, which as far as I can tell is no one. Hike is a complete and total pessimist, as distinguished from a worrier, since a worrier fears the worst but recognizes the possibility that it might not happen. Hike does not allow for the chance that there will ever be a good outcome of anything.

Hike's discourse today is on alien life and the certainty that it's out there. "You know how many planets there are? Three trillion. You think they're all just sitting out there with no one on them? Come on."

I'm not sure why nobody at the table answers him. It could be one of two things. Either they are not listening at all, or they don't want to encourage him to continue speaking.

Unfortunately, he doesn't need any encouragement. "You can be sure they're coming here," he says. "And they're not coming to hang out, you know? Before they even get here, they'll send a weird virus into our atmosphere. By the time they arrive, we'll all either be dead or have sores all over our bodies and a body temperature of a hundred and twelve. It's going to make Independence Day look like a Saturday-morning cartoon."

On the one hand, I'd like to see how long Hike can go on with absolutely no encouragement from his audience, but I need to interrupt. "On the off chance that the invaders don't get here before the trial, we probably should prepare," I say.

I bring everyone up to date on the basics, starting with Brian's escape, which they already know about from newspaper accounts. When I tell them about Pete's following Willie and me and capturing Brian, I look over at Marcus expecting disapproval at our carelessness. I don't find any; he is expressionless, either unconscious or asleep or both.

Willie jumps in to mention that Brian risked his life to save Boomer, and Hike and Edna nod, understanding that this is why we are taking the case.

"I think the answer lies in their business," I say, "and Sam, we're going to need your expertise in this area. I know nothing about computers and all that technological stuff . . . my eyes start to glaze over when I hear it. So you're going to have to study their company and educate me in a way that I can understand it."

"I'm on it," Sam says, though I think he's disappointed he won't get to shoot anybody.

"If I'm right, then we are dealing with people capable of framing Brian using computer expertise, and also of stabbing two people to death in cold blood."

"Denise Atkins worked at Starlight as well, didn't she?" Laurie asks.

I nod. "According to Brian, she's been there from the beginning;

she was a technology whiz in her own right. Brian says that his being there kept her from advancing too far; the board was concerned about nepotism. She works in the technology area."

"So you don't think she was at least one of the targets in these killings?" Laurie asks.

"I don't, but I don't want us to take that for granted. My guess is that she was in the wrong place at the wrong time. I think Brian and Gerald Wright were the two intended victims here, and what they had in common was the business that they ran. Denise was probably collateral damage. But, as always, I could be wrong."

Nobody jumps in to disagree with my comment that I can always be wrong, so I continue. "The wild card in all this is Dominic Petrone. It's hard to know where he figures in it, if at all. But Denise mentioned him to Brian, so that certainly points to his involvement."

"Doesn't sound like his kind of thing," Hike points out.

"True," I say, because dealing with computers and large corporations is not something Petrone has traditionally focused on. "But maybe Petrone is branching out. We need to keep an open mind, while treading very carefully."

I give out the initial assignments. Sam is going to focus on the business end, learning just what the hell that company does. Hike will attempt to speed up the turning over of discovery documents to us, and will also prepare a change-of-venue motion. I don't think it has a chance in hell of succeeding, but it's something we should pursue anyway.

Laurie will head up the investigating team, and Marcus will work for her. He likes her, and she's the only one of us not petrified to be near him, so that will work fine. Edna will hang around and answer the phones, if she can find the time. Willie has no responsibility at this point, but he usually comes in handy.

When the meeting breaks up and the others leave, Laurie asks me if I talked to Ricky.

"I did," I say.

"And?"

"And we're on the same page."

"Which page might that be?"

"Neither of us is going to gamble anymore," I say.

"You told him that?"

"We shook on it."

"Wow," she says. "You know you have to keep your word, right?"

"I do?"

"He's your son, Andy."

"You can't lie to your son? Who made that rule?"

"I did," she says. "A while back. I'm surprised I didn't mention it you."

Oh.

Sarah Maurer is shaken up. I can tell because when she greets me at the door her eyes are all red and she's holding a wet ball of tissue, which she uses to dab at those red eyes.

When I had called her she was reluctant to meet with me. I persuaded her with a generous dose of my Andy Carpenter charm, and also by mentioning that if she didn't agree to have a casual chat with me, we'd have to do a deposition with a roomful of lawyers.

That was a lie; I don't have the power to force her into a deposition. But I sometimes find that lies and threats help to supplement the aforementioned Andy Carpenter charm. And I'd certainly rather deceive her than head into a trial without having interviewed the main witness against my client.

Her house is simultaneously the closest to Gerald Wright's and yet almost a quarter mile away. If you're going to peek into a neighbor's window in this area, you'll need to use the Hubble telescope.

"Hello, Ms. Maurer, thank you for seeing me," I say when she opens the door.

She just nods and says, "Come in."

Her house is much more traditional and less modern than Wright's, though the layout isn't all that different. I can see a swimming pool and tennis court through the glass doors to the back;

I hadn't seen that at the murder scene, but I would assume that there was at least a pool somewhere on the grounds.

She leads me into the den, where a man is waiting. He's a big guy, dressed in an Oklahoma sweatshirt, sweatpants, and open-toed sandals, which look ridiculous on his very large feet. He is not smiling; it's more like sneering.

"This is my friend Jack," she says. I don't know if "friend" means "boyfriend," but at least it's not "husband."

He doesn't offer his hand, just says, "Don't you think she's been through enough?" The guy is instantly annoying, so I don't answer him. Instead, I turn to Ms. Maurer and say, "I'll try not to take too much of your time."

"You got that right," Oklahoma Jack says.

"Is it okay if Jack stays while we talk?" she asks.

I smile and say, "No."

"That's a lot of crap," Jack says.

She seems taken aback, while Jack seems positively flabber-gasted. "Oh," she says. "I thought it would be all right."

I smile again. "It isn't; Jack needs to leave. Or, we can do this at my office, and Jack won't even be allowed in the building." I'm just being obnoxious; the success of this interview does not hinge on Jack's leaving. I want him gone simply because he wants to stay.

Jack doesn't seem intent on leaving, so Ms. Maurer says, "Jack, please. I want to get this over with."

He seems about to argue, then changes his mind and walks out. He does so slowly, as if he has a choice and can stop at any time.

Once he's gone, and probably has his ear on the door, I say, "Thank you. I just find these conversations are better one on one."

She nods her understanding, so I continue.

"Can you describe what happened the day of the murders?"

"Well, I was just going for a walk. I do that every day; I prefer being outside to being on the treadmill."

"You were alone?"

She nods. "Yes, always. Jack doesn't like to take walks."

"How far do you walk?" I ask.

"Three miles exactly. A mile and a half out, and then back."

"How can you be so precise?"

She holds up her wrist and shows me a black band or watch; it might be an Apple watch. I assume it measures distance.

"How long does it take you?"

"Forty-five minutes," she says. "I'm a fast walker. It's the only exercise I get."

I ask her to continue, and she says, "I was on the way back when a car passed me. I didn't recognize the car, and that's a little unusual, because this road is so private."

"Were you coming back when you saw the car, or leaving?"

"Coming back; I was at the first corner. The car turned left onto our road. When I got near Gerry's house, I saw that the car was parked in his driveway, and the front door was open."

"Did this worry you?"

"I wouldn't say worry; it just struck me as unusual."

"Then what happened?"

"Then I saw Brian Atkins come out the front door. He looked a little strange."

"Strange? How?" I ask.

"I don't know. Excited? A little crazy? Scared? It's really hard to tell."

Unfortunately, Sarah Maurer is going to make a good witness; she's believable and appears intelligent and in control. "You recognized him?" I ask.

"Yes. I knew Brian well from back in the day, before he had his problems. I was surprised to see him; I thought he was still in prison. So I called out to him."

"Did he answer you?"

"No, at least not at first. He looked at me, but it was like he looked through me. All he did was run to his car and drive off."

"You said he didn't answer you 'at first'?"

"Right. He went down the street and turned around so he could leave the way he came. But he stopped when he passed me, and spoke through the open window. He said, 'Call the police.' Then he drove off."

Finally, a piece of good news. "Did you call them?"

"I didn't have my cell phone with me. I should have gone home and called, but I saw Gerry's open door so I went to it. I called his name a few times, but nobody answered. I stepped in, just a couple of feet because I was scared, and then I saw what I thought was blood, at the door to the den. So I ran home and called."

She again starts to dab her eyes with her tissues, an act that will endear her to juries. Even I am feeling bad for her.

"You never saw the bodies?"

She shakes her head. "No. Thank God."

I ask her a few more questions, but basically I've gotten all the information I can from her. Her role in this has been limited. She will testify to it truthfully, and the jury will believe her.

I thank her for her time and open the door to leave. There is Jack, standing a few feet away and not looking pleased.

"You can go in now," I say.

Joseph Russo saw the towering Vegas hotels through the plane window. Then the plane turned slightly, so that those hotels could only be visible from the opposite side of the plane. That would not represent much of a problem; Russo was on a private plane with two other passengers, both of whom worked for him. So he could have any seat he wanted.

But Russo had no particular interest in seeing Vegas. He didn't like the place, even though the last time he had been there was twenty years earlier. Actually, were Russo to suddenly develop some introspection, he would realize that he didn't much like anywhere other than where he had always lived. He was a Jersey boy, through and through.

A white limousine that seemed to Russo to be the length of a basketball court was waiting on the tarmac as the plane slowed to a halt. Russo's two men walked down the steps first, both as a way of protecting their boss, and possibly to also make sure the steps were sturdy enough. Russo was three hundred and forty pounds, down from a high of three forty-two, before he began dieting. So his two men, weighing five hundred and twenty between them, were a satisfactory test.

The steps held, and the arriving trio was taken in the limousine to the Mandalay Bay Hotel, where their meeting would be held in an enormous suite on the top floor. Russo viewed that fact as a less-than-amusing conceit on the part of Charles Capuano, the man with whom he would be meeting.

Russo knew that Capuano did not have an ownership interest in the hotel, nor did he make it his home. He was using the suite to show off in front of Russo, which meant his money would have been better spent at the blackjack tables. Russo was not easily impressed.

Even if Russo cared about the suite and the trappings, that would not have benefited Capuano. Russo was there as a representative of Dominic Petrone, so regardless of what Capuano said or did, it was Petrone's instructions that were going to be followed.

Even though they had never met, Capuano greeted Russo with a big hug, as if they were reunited old friends. This was the fourth such meeting that Russo had attended, and in each case the greeting had been the same. It was a sign to Russo that he held the power, and he would use it.

Within minutes, Russo's and Capuano's men melted away, leaving the two to talk in private. "So what brings you here?" Capuano asked.

Russo had no doubt that Capuano knew exactly what had prompted the meeting, but he knew he had to play the game. "I'm afraid that things have not been going well here," Russo said, and then followed up that truism with a lie. "It's the only city that is not performing up to expectations."

"That's not what I hear," Capuano said.

"Then you are not listening carefully."

Capuano was taken aback by Russo's disrespectful attitude, but he held his anger in check. "You are asking us to change the way we have done business for fifty years. Such a thing is not accomplished overnight."

Russo smiled, got up, and looked out the window at the lit-up Strip. "You know, I haven't been here in a very long time. The last time I was here, women walked around the casino with coin dispensers attached to their belts, changing bills into nickels, dimes, and quarters."

"So?" Capuano asked.

"So this time when I walked through the casino, nobody was using coins. It was all electronic; I never once heard the sound of money coming from the machines."

"So?" Capuano repeated.

"So times have changed. Technology has caused the people who make and own the slot machines to move on. Technology is making all of us move on. It's the way of the world."

"Petrone and technology are reducing my take by sixty percent."

"The remaining forty percent is for doing very little—just some minor enforcement where necessary."

"Without my people for that enforcement, you would soon have nothing."

"Your people are businessmen. If we pay them enough, they will become our people. And then you will be without people, and without forty percent."

"Are you threatening me?" Capuano asked. He was not used to being talked to this way, but he was also not used to being in this position.

"I would never do that," Russo said. "I am patiently explaining the situation, because you seem not to understand it very well. The fact is that we want to be in partnership with you, but we don't need to be in partnership with you. It is a decision that you will have to make for yourself."

Capuano didn't cave in the moment; that was not the way these things were done. But Russo knew that he would toe the line; he had no choice. Petrone held all the cards, and would play them as necessary.

What Capuano didn't know, what nobody knew, was that Russo would be playing the cards differently if he could. That he believed the cards were unnecessary, and only temporarily constituted a winning hand.

But there was a chance that no one would ever know what Russo was thinking; he knew that and was fine with it.

For now, he had the limousine take him directly back to the airport.

He wanted to get home.

If Ted Yates is at the center of the storm, it hasn't so much as mussed his hair. He's the CFO of Starlight, a company that currently has one founder in jail and the other just recently stabbed to death. Yet when I called to ask to meet with him, he agreed immediately. Just now, when I showed up at his office for our meeting, he smiled and seemed so casual and at ease that I felt like we were about to have piña coladas by the pool.

We're in the company's headquarters in Paramus, and Yates's office is on the tenth floor of the twelve-story building. It is spacious and modern, exactly what you would expect at a successful, cutting-edge technology company.

After we exchange pleasantries, I ask him about the large taped-up boxes lining the walls of his office. "Are you leaving?" I ask.

"Only this office. I'm heading upstairs."

"This one seems pretty nice," I say.

He nods. "It is. But the board of directors just made me interim CEO, and they think it more appropriate that I be upstairs. I disagreed, but the board overruled me." He smiles. "I'm sure it won't be the last time."

"You're moving to Gerry Wright's office?"

He shakes his head. "No way; far too soon for that. I'm moving into Brian's old office; it's been empty since he left." Then he adds, "This has been a rather difficult time for the company."

If he's having trouble coping with the difficult time, he's hiding it well. Having chitchatted long enough, I ask Yates if he has any theory as to who might have killed Gerry Wright.

He shakes his head. "No idea. But I do have a theory about who didn't do it. And that would be Brian Atkins."

"Why is that?"

"Because I know Brian, and I simply don't think him capable of that."

"But you thought him capable of embezzlement?" I ask.

"Where did you get that idea?"

"You testified against him at trial."

He reacts and leans forward; I seem to have struck a nerve. "Did you read the transcript?"

"I did."

"Then you should know that all I did was recite the evidence, the unauthorized transfer of money out of the company and into private accounts maintained by Brian."

"You don't view that as testifying against him?" I ask.

"No. They used me to insert the evidence. I simply stated what happened. They never asked my opinion as to who was responsible, and I never gave it."

"What was your opinion?"

"That someone defrauded the company. Either Brian, which I doubt, or someone intent on making it look like Brian was guilty. I have no idea who, and at this point it doesn't seem to matter."

"Did you think it could have been Gerry Wright?"

"Mr. Carpenter, what I do is come to work and do my job. Every day. One day at a time."

Brian had told me that Yates was the money guy, and that the head of the technology division, Jason Mathers, was the guy to talk to about the core product of the company.

"I'd like to speak to Jason Mathers. Is he in today?"

"He was," Yates said. "But he isn't now."

"Will he be here tomorrow?"

Yates shakes his head. "It would be surprising if he was. He resigned this morning."

"Why?"

"He said it was to pursue other opportunities. And he will certainly have those. He is a technology genius."

"Why do you think he left?"

"I think he was disappointed that the board chose me to be the interim CEO. I think he felt it meant he would not ultimately get the job."

Brian had predicted this would happen; he said Yates was far better at internal politics than Mathers. "Are you going to get it?" I ask.

He smiles. "I certainly hope so."

Joseph Westman didn't have to tell anyone he was leaving early. It wasn't a coincidence that he worked for a hedge fund called the Westman Group. He had founded it and built it from infancy into a thriving operation, managing over six billion dollars in assets.

At sixty-two, Westman did not work the kind of hours he used to put in. He no longer got in at five thirty in the morning, not leaving until eight o'clock. There was no need for that anymore; he had an experienced, highly competent management team under him. The truth is the place could run quite well without him, though it was Westman's prestige that was vital for bringing in new investments.

It's not that Joseph was not busy; there never seemed to be enough hours in the day. He was on three boards of directors and was one of Manhattan's leading philanthropists. In fact, he had just announced a hospital donation that would result in a building to be named after his wife, Linda. Linda had survived a battle with cancer three years earlier and rightfully credited the doctors and hospital with saving her life.

So there was no need to tell anyone he was leaving early, either in the office or at home. His two kids were grown and successful in their own right, though they had obviously benefited from family wealth and prominence.

But they were good kids, worked hard, and succeeded in their chosen professions, medicine and the law. Certainly no one had ever said of them what Ann Richards had famously said of George W. Bush. Joseph Westman's kids were not born on third base, thinking they had hit a triple.

Westman always drove to work. It was certainly not out of necessity; in addition to public transportation, he obviously could have afforded a driver. He just liked the feel of being behind the wheel of his Porsche.

On this afternoon, Westman got into his car, pulled out of his private parking space, and headed north. But instead of going to his apartment on Central Park West, he drove farther west and got onto the Westside Highway. Then he continued north until he entered the Saw Mill River Parkway, taking it well out of the city.

His destination was Elmsford, a particular spot along the road that he had scouted out before, around the time the idea had first occurred to him. For a while, he thought he would never go through with it, but it became more real as time went on.

And, finally, it became necessary.

The area along the road was tree lined, a peaceful and serene setting that Joseph considered among the most beautiful he had been to. Some of those trees were majestic, and were in place long before anyone had ever imagined such a thing as cars driving by them. Westman sometimes wondered how many had been erased to make room for the road; he was glad he was not around to see it happen.

There was almost no traffic at that time, as Joseph knew there would not be. He was able to go at whatever speed he wanted, and he gunned the Porsche up to almost ninety miles per hour. He didn't see any police around, but it was the last thing he would have worried about if he did.

Up ahead, the two trees that he had watched all these years stood along the road, even sturdier and more powerful than their neighbors. Joseph Westman pressed his foot farther down on the gas pedal and slammed into them head-on.

In the split second before he died, he prayed the trees would not be damaged permanently, but if they were, they would have died for a good cause.

Finally, at long last, they had brought Joseph Westman peace.

T he first discovery documents are here," says Hike, calling from the office. "How do they look?" I ask.

"They look like they're still in the carton," he says. "They just got here."

"Okay, I'll be down within the hour. Maybe you should open the carton."

"We got a knife or something? It's taped up pretty good."

"Ask Edna."

"It's nine o'clock in the morning. You think Edna's here?"

"I think there's a letter opener in her top drawer; it's pretty sharp."

"I could cut myself and bleed to death in here before Edna shows up."

"That's always a possibility, Hike, but look at the bright side. You'd miss the alien invasion."

I put leashes on Tara and Sebastian to take them for their walk, and as we're heading out the door, Willie Miller pulls up. He's got Boomer with him. "You going for a walk?" Willie asks.

"What tipped you off?"

He doesn't bother to answer the snide comment, but instead just starts to walk along with us. Boomer, Tara, and Sebastian all seem fine together.

"He's a great dog," Willie says, referring to Boomer.

I nod. "Sure is." I know exactly where this is going.

It goes there immediately. "I'm thinking, maybe Sondra and I will keep him until Brian gets out. You know, because of how much he loves him."

I shake my head. "Not a good idea, Willie. It's a nice thought, but a bad idea."

"Why?"

"Because he's not getting out anytime soon. He has to serve the rest of his sentence, then more time for the escape. And if we lose at trial on the murder counts, he's never getting out."

"You'll win," Willie says, at once overrating my talents and our chances.

"Maybe, more likely not. But it doesn't matter; he's still in prison for a long time."

"So we should place him?"

"Definitely. Otherwise it's not fair to him; he should get in a permanent home right away."

"Okay," he says. "I hear you."

"Good. You know I'm not going to be at the foundation much, right? I'm sorry about it." Whenever I'm on a case, the burden of dealing with the dogs always falls on Willie and Sondra, and I always feel guilty about it.

"That's cool," Willie says. "We're on it." The next time Willie complains about my not doing my share will be the first.

I cut the walk a little shorter than usual, because I'm anxious to get down to the office. I'm also dreading getting there, and not just because Hike is waiting for me. The discovery documents we've received will begin to lay out the prosecution's case against Brian. I want to see if there is other bad news in there, in addition to the very bad news we already know about.

When I arrive, Hike is immersed in the documents. In addition to being a very depressing individual to be around, Hike is also a brilliant attorney. He can inhale information and process it in a logical order, which is what he's doing now.

"How does it look?" I ask.

"Depends whose side you're on."

"Let's start with our side."

"Oh. Then awful. If we take this to trial instead of pleading it out, we should be disbarred."

"Our client doesn't want to plead it out. He'd spend the rest of his life in prison."

Hike shrugs. "Whatever."

Hike takes me through what he's learned so far, although we're just scratching the surface. The actual facts are not as bad as his assessment, which is usually the case. There isn't much more than what we already know, just some additional witnesses who will say that Brian hated Gerry and blamed him for everything.

That's the good news, and the other good news is that Dominic Petrone is not mentioned anywhere. We're going to have to find an alternative bad guy to present to the jury, and for self-preservation reasons I'm hoping that it's not Dominic Petrone.

The bad news is that what we already knew they had is more than devastating enough to convict Brian six or seven times over.

Dominic Petrone had no trouble getting a dinner reservation at Enzo's. It's not because he had a regular table, or because he owned that table, or because he owned the entire restaurant. All of that helped, but ultimately wouldn't matter. No maître d' in his or her right mind would ever say, "Sorry, Mr. Petrone, we're booked up. Perhaps you'd like to come another night? Or try and grab a seat at the bar?"

The food at Enzo's is extraordinary; there are only six entrées on the menu, but each one is as good as could be found anywhere. Of course, sometimes Petrone wanted something that wasn't on the menu, a request that was always greeted with a "certainly, Mr. Petrone."

Petrone had become more insular of late, going out far less than he used to, spending most of his time at home. He once fancied himself a prominent citizen, and in fact he had donated substantial money to various charities. But ironically, as he attempted to expand his business empire, he withdrew personally from the world.

But Petrone continued to eat at Enzo's three nights a week, every week. He sometimes varied the weeknights, for security reasons, but he could reliably be found there every Saturday night. He also varied his dinner companions: sometimes family and sometimes business associates. All Petrone's friends fell into one of those two categories.

On this particular Saturday night, there were no members of Petrone's family near enough to smell the garlic. He was dining privately with Joseph Russo, who was updating him on his recent successful trip to Las Vegas.

Only three other tables in the restaurant were occupied, and all by Petrone's men. All members of the public who had called to make a reservation had been told that the place was completely booked, and there were no tables available. That was clearly not true.

There was not a single person in the world that Dominic Petrone completely trusted. It wasn't that he assessed people and determined they were not trustworthy; it was more a philosophy of life. There was nothing to be gained by having complete faith in a person, but there was much to lose.

But Joseph Russo came closest to having Petrone's full confidence. He had been in Petrone's organization from the time he was a young teenager, and time and time again, he proved himself to be smart and completely reliable.

His devotion to Petrone over the years had been demonstrably total, often coming at great risk to his own health. Russo had once literally taken a bullet for his boss and later had gone to prison to protect him. Stuff like that is a rather good way to measure loyalty.

The two men had just finished their entrée and were having an after-dinner brandy when Russo's cell phone rang. He answered it with, "Yeah?" and then did not say another word.

When he hung up, he simply said to Petrone, "Time to go."

Petrone nodded, put down his brandy, and stood up. Two men at a nearby table stood up as well and walked with him into an office he used behind the kitchen. When they arrived there, Petrone went into the office, and the two men took up positions at the doorway.

It was exactly seven and a half minutes later that two men walked through the front door of Enzo's, hands in their pockets.

Their eyes scanned the room and registered surprise at
Dominic Petrone at any of the tables.

It was the last thing their eyes registered. They each too
let to the chest and one to the head, before they even had a
to get their own guns out of their pockets.

Once they hit the ground, one of Russo's men took the guns
of the dead men's pockets, while leaving the guns in their han
Another called the police, to alert them to the shooting that ha
just taken place.

Before the police arrived, Russo received another phone call,
reporting that the man who had sent the two killers to Enzo's,
Angelo Mazzi, had himself been shot and killed leaving the Bronx
restaurant where he often dined.

All in all, thought Russo, it had been a very productive evening,
even if they didn't get to finish their brandy.

Vince Sanders, in typical low-key style, has a huge two-word headline on his front page: "Mob War!" Laurie is reading the paper at the kitchen table, while having breakfast with Ricky, when I come down in the morning. I can see the two words dominating the front page from across the room. It seems like an anachronism, like something out of the thirties.

"What the . . ." is my clever opening comment.

Laurie looks up and says, "Quite a bit of action last night."

I walk to the table and look over her shoulder at the front page. Ricky does the same, and says, "What's a mob war?" I don't know why they have to teach these kids to read so fast.

"It's when two different groups of bad men have an argument and fight," she says.

"Is it always men?" Ricky asks.

Laurie nods. "Always."

"What's a 'hedge perv'?" Ricky asks, apparently not finished checking out Vince's high-class headlines.

Laurie hands me the paper, dropping the problem effectively in my lap. I look at it and see that Joseph Westman, a wealthy hedge fund executive, deliberately drove his car into a tree. The "perv" part comes from the fact that he was apparently about to be accused of consuming and disseminating child pornography.

"It's not clear," I lie. "Let me get back to you on it, Rick."

"Is it hedges like in front of the house?"

"Most likely," I say.

We wait until Ricky goes up to his room to keep talking about the Petrone story. I quickly read the article, after which Laurie says, "Looks like Petrone has more to worry about than your case."

The story says that there were two separate murder attempts on heads of organized family, almost simultaneously. The attempt on Petrone failed; the one on Angelo Mazzi succeeded.

The men who tried to kill Petrone are dead, and the ones who actually killed Mazzi got away. The authorities are not commenting, if they even know, whether Petrone and Mazzi were at war with each other, or whether a third party was after them both.

A number of men have been arrested, including Tony Costa, one of Mazzi's top lieutenants. They are being held on a variety of charges, though none of them sound too serious. Since this was most likely an interstate war, the FBI is involved, and I assume they have engineered the arrests in the hope of getting some of the arrested to talk.

Good luck with that.

This is a fairly shocking development; things like this just don't seem to happen anymore. In recent years these people have been too busy trying to preserve their domains and stay out of jail to fight with each other.

I'm interested in this news mostly because if Petrone should be killed, then he would be less likely to kill me. And I'm always in favor of that.

I don't dwell on it, because it is extremely unlikely that it has anything to do with my case, and that is where my focus has to be. That is why I am driving into the city to see Robby Divine.

Robby is a mind-bogglingly rich investor whom I happened to sit next to at a charity dinner a few years ago. We hit it off, and I occasionally call on him when I need insight into the club of the rich and richer. My pathetic thirty-five-million-dollar nest egg wouldn't get me past the bouncer that stands outside that club.

Robby's business is money; he makes huge investments in companies and often buys them outright, but not because he is particularly interested in their businesses. He is only interested in their ability to increase his wealth. It's how he keeps score.

But he is also smart, and every one of the many media articles written about him is quick to point that out. He doesn't make emotional decisions, but rather he thoroughly learns the intricacies of the businesses he invests in and uses that knowledge to make fortune after fortune.

He is Warren Buffett with a Chicago Cubs cap.

I bring up baseball when I walk into his office, and I mention that everyone is saying that this could be the year the Cubs break through and win their first World Series in forever.

"Don't say anything to jinx it," he says. "If you jinx it, I will have you killed."

"You believe in jinxes?"

"What else can explain it? You know how long it's been? Do you know what happened the same year that the Cubs last won it all?"

"I don't."

"The Montreal Wanderers won the Stanley Cup; they beat the Toronto Trolley Leaguers. William Howard Taft was elected president. The first Model T was built."

"That was a long time ago," I say, trying to go along.

"Really? You think so?" he asks. "You know who won the Cy Young Award that year?"

"Nope."

"Nobody won it," he says. "You know why nobody won it? Because Cy Young was still pitching."

"That was really a long time ago," I say, my only goal being to end this trip down memory lane. He's getting worked up about it.

"How could it take so long if there is no jinx involved?" he asks. "Why else would we not have won?"

I shrug. "The Saint Louis Cardinals?"

He glares at me, then speaks with a quiet intensity. "Never mention the Saint Louis Cardinals in my presence again. They are the source of all that is evil in the world."

I've always considered the Cardinals a classy organization, but I don't mention that. Instead I nod and take out an imaginary pen and paper, pretending to write. "Source of all evil . . . got it."

"Good," he says. "Now what can I do for you this time?"

I ask him about the routers and servers that Starlight makes, and how they make trades faster than other servers.

"You mean how the thing actually works?" he asks. "What goes on inside the machines? I have no idea; doesn't interest me."

"I thought faster trades would be important to you."

"Of course they are, but I just want to know that I have access to the fastest technology. I don't need to know how that technology physically works."

"How much faster is it?" I ask.

"A millisecond . . . a nanosecond . . . not sure what you call it, but it's a really small amount of time."

"Why is that a benefit?"

"You ever watch Jeopardy?" he asks, and then proceeds when I nod. "You know how sometimes they'll show a question, and all three people will press their buzzers? But only one of them gets to answer, because that person was the fastest to buzz in?"

"Right."

"Suppose you were one of those contestants. How big an advantage would it be to see the answer just a little faster than the two people you're playing against? Just enough to let you buzz in faster."

"I'd still wait until Alex Trebek read the clue."

"That's why you're poor," he says. "It would be a huge advantage. Equity trading isn't guys on the floor running around with a piece of paper anymore. Trading is computers moving fortunes around at the speed of light. Speed is the key, and those servers are the key to the key. I don't care how they work, as long as they work. And as long as they are working for me."

Boomer got adopted," Willie says, when I pick up the phone. "That was fast," I say.

"Yeah, it all just fell into place. Young couple, nice house, no kids . . . love at first sight. They have another dog that Boomer got along really well with."

"And Sondra approved?" I ask. Willie and I both think that among the three of us, Sondra is the best judge of how good a dog home a prospective adopter represents.

"Totally. She thinks it's the perfect home for him."

"Great," I say. "Thanks for not pushing back on this, Willie. It really is what's best for him."

"Yeah, you were right. By the way, you mentioned something at that meeting the other day about Dominic Petrone," Willie says.

"Right. His name has come up in this case. I'm not sure if it's important yet or not."

"You want me to talk to Joey?"

Willie is talking about Joseph Russo, Petrone's number two man. Willie and Russo had occasion to be in prison at the same time, but under very different circumstances, a major difference being that Willie was wrongly accused and Russo was very rightly accused.

They didn't really know each other, until one day when three fellow prisoners tried to make a name for themselves by sticking makeshift knives into Russo's rather large belly. Willie saw it about to happen, and the sight offended his considerable sense of fair play.

Willie intervened, using all of his significant intervening skills. He put all three attackers in the hospital, earning Russo's apparently undying gratitude in the process. We have taken advantage of their relationship a couple of times in the past, as Willie has spoken to Russo and gotten favors that have benefited us. It has helped that in those cases, Russo and Petrone's interests, if not coinciding with ours, didn't conflict either.

But that was then, and this is now. "Not this time, Willie," I say. "This time I think we're on opposite sides."

He nods. "Okay. Just let me know."

"I will, but I doubt it will happen."

Willie's question makes me realize that I should be paying more attention to Petrone's potential involvement. All I have so far is that Denise mentioned to Brian that she had reason to believe that Gerry Wright was involved with Petrone. It scared Brian enough that he broke out of prison to protect her, or at least that's his story.

But she could have been wrong, or she could have been right without it having anything to do with the murders. It is clearly something I need to find out about.

When I get off the phone with Willie, I go inside and call Pete Stanton. "Always a treat to hear from you," he says.

"The pleasure is mine. Which one of your law enforcement colleagues knows the most about Dominic Petrone and his operation?"

"Why? You looking to defend the two guys who tried to kill him last night? If so, I have bad news for you. They're dead, but maybe you can still collect a fee."

"Any chance you can just answer the question?"

"Nobody here would be that current on it. It's the state cops that ride herd on him."

"So who can I talk to over there?"

He thinks for a moment. "Barry Leonard. You know him?"

"I've cross-examined him a couple of times, and I saw him at your birthday party," I say.

"Right. He's a good friend."

"Perfect," I say. "Can you get him to meet with me?"

"Why would I want to do that?"

"Continued free beer?"

"Fair enough. But why would he want to do that?"

"He doesn't like beer?" I ask.

"Now that I think about it, he does. But not as much as he likes going to Giants games. Unfortunately, like me, it's almost impossible to go to a game on a poor police officer's salary. And by a game, I mean a game like this Sunday's game against the Eagles."

"I'm taking Ricky this Sunday." Pete knows I have season tickets to the Giants games, and he's always angling to get them.

"Then ask Ricky about Petrone," he says.

This is not much of a dilemma for me. I can give Pete the tickets in return for getting Leonard to talk to me. Then I'll just go on StubHub or one of the resale places and buy two more tickets for Ricky and me.

It's not a tough call, but it's very annoying. "You're an asshole, Pete."

"I am aware of that; it's part of my charm."

"Set up the meeting."

"It'll take a while. Last night's multiple murders might be occupying a lot of his time."

"It better be before Sunday, or you and Leonard can watch the game at your house, while you drink your own beer and moan about your poor police salaries."

"God forbid," Pete says. "Call him in an hour."

Sam Willis is one happy camper. He's coming with me as I interview the next potential witness, and can't seem to stop grinning. "This is really cool," he says, as the elevator door closes.

"What is?"

"You know . . . working the street."

"We're just going to talk to someone," I point out. "This is his apartment; we won't be on the street."

He nods. "Got it. We going to play 'good cop, bad cop'?"

"We're not going to play any cop," I say. "We're going to play lawyer, computer nerd. I'll be the lawyer."

Another nod. "Got it."

"And Sam," I say, "no shooting."

Sam is with me because I'll be talking to Jason Mathers, who until a few days ago was head of the technology division of Starlight. The CFO, Ted Yates, indicated that Mathers had quit because the board of directors had bypassed him and made Yates acting CEO. Brian had predicted that would happen.

I'm not planning to get into that much technical stuff; for my purposes, it shouldn't be necessary. But since my understanding of it is so limited, I felt I should have Sam with me just in case. As I watch Sam salivating over the prospect of "working the street," I'm starting to regret the decision.

The particular street we're working is River Road in Edgewater. The river the address references is the Hudson River, and across the Hudson from Mathers's apartment is Manhattan.

His apartment is on the twenty-eighth floor of a twenty-eight-story building, and as he lets us in, the first thing I see is the wall facing the river. It's a wall of glass, and the view, even in daylight, is breathtaking.

Mathers looks to be in his midthirties, dressed casually in worn jeans, sneakers, and an Arizona State sweatshirt. He looks completely relaxed; this is not a guy feeling the typical stress of unemployment. "Hey, guys, come on in," he says, when he opens the door, sounding as if we're a couple of fraternity buddies coming over to watch football.

We sit down in the den, brightly lit from the morning sun coming from the New York side. "That is one great view," I say.

He nods and smiles. "You should see it at night. And the dopes on the other side are paying twice as much, and all they look at is New Jersey."

I don't think that Sam has even noticed the view; his eyes are on a computer setup that Mathers has on the other side of the room. There are four monitors and a bunch of consoles, keyboards, and speakers that mean nothing to me, but certainly have captured Sam's attention.

"Thanks for meeting with us on such short notice," I say.

"No problem. Anything to help Brian."

"You testified on his behalf at trial."

He nods. "Yeah, for all the good it did. I didn't have any of the facts, so all I could be was a character witness. The jury wasn't impressed."

Time to get down to business. "Mr. Mathers—"

"Call me Jason."

"Jason, can you think of anyone who might have had a motive to kill Gerry Wright?"

"He was a pain in the ass, but kill him? I don't know people like that."

"Have you heard the name Dominic Petrone?"

"I saw that stuff about him on the news this morning," he said. "But I heard of him before that, sure."

"What about in relation to your company?"

He laughs a short laugh. "No. If I did, I would have been out of there a hell of a lot quicker."

"You can't think of any way in which criminals could take advantage of the products you provided?"

"Not unless they trade stocks. The key thing that we offered was speed, and the difference is in nanoseconds. In stock trading, nanoseconds are important."

"Can you think of any other transactions that would depend on speed?"

He thinks for a few moments. "Not really. Maybe if some huge concert was about to happen and online tickets were going on sale at a certain time, you'd want to get in before other people." Then he shakes his head. "Nah, forget that. Not the kind of speed we're talking about."

Sam seems about to ask something but hesitates, so I nod that it's okay for him to speak up. "When these trades go through your servers," he asks, "are you just a conduit? Or do you maintain a record of them?"

" 'Maintain a record' isn't quite the way I would put it," Mathers says. "Technically the trades can be retrieved, but the company never does. There would be no reason to; once the trades are executed, they become a matter of public record anyway." He pauses. "So yes, they could be retrieved, but there are billions of them, and there's nothing done in secret."

My turn. "Is there any literature that you could provide that would help us understand the capabilities of the machines?"

"Nothing that isn't proprietary," he says. "I wouldn't be able to give it to you, even if I still had access to it, which I don't. As you can imagine, the company keeps a tight lid on it."

I nod. "Makes sense." Then I make a mental note to ask Brian if he can get any of it for us. "Who is going to replace you?"

He shrugs. "I don't really give a shit, but my guess would be Stacy Mullins. He was my number two. He knows the systems, and he's very smart. They could bring someone in from the outside, but there would be a big learning curve."

"What are you going to do now?"

He shrugs and smiles. "Beats the hell out of me. But I'm not much in the mood to work for someone else again. I'd like to try something on my own, but I don't know what."

"You don't seem worried about it."

"I have no reason to be," he says. "I did very well working for Starlight. Worst comes to worst, I can just sit here and stare."

He points to the river and Manhattan.

Enough said.

've been skirting the edges of this thing. By that I mean I've been in learning mode, trying to understand the players and the issues, without developing a strategy or a point of view. That's not self-criticism, nor am I second-guessing myself; without getting up to speed, there was no way I could do anything else. But it's time to move into phase two, because phase three will be here all too soon.

Phase three takes place in front of a judge and jury.

Demonstrating reasonable doubt as to Brian's guilt is going to be a very difficult task. He's an escaped convict with a motive who was found at the murder scene. We could impanel a jury made up of members of Brian's family, and even they would lap up that kind of evidential scenario with a spoon.

But one foolproof way to show reasonable doubt is to present a credible alternative killer. By definition, if the jury considers someone else a possible second candidate for having done the crime, they can't also be certain that the accused is guilty.

I don't yet know enough about Gerry Wright to know who wanted him dead. Sam has been digging into his life, and will soon be telling me what he's learned. Maybe something will pop up then; maybe we'll find some long-term, implacable enemy of Wright's who recently threatened him.

But I've gone an entire career without getting that lucky, and

I don't see my streak ending anytime soon. So right now, I have to stick with what I have, and that all boils down to one name.

Dominic Petrone.

Miraculously, New Jersey State Police lieutenant Barry Leonard has agreed to meet with me. The meeting is taking place today at nine o'clock on Friday morning, just fifty-five hours before he and Pete will be sitting in my seats at the Giants-Eagles game.

We're meeting at an out-of-the-way diner in Englewood. My guess is that he was not anxious for his fellow cops to see him playing host to a defense attorney, which is probably why we aren't at his office.

I get here first, and five minutes later I see him walk in and look around for me. He knows who I am; about three years ago I cross-examined him at trial. It did not go well for him, but I've seen him a couple of times since, and he didn't seem to bear a grudge.

We exchange a few semipleasantries, and the waitress comes over to take our orders. He looks at the menu and then turns to me. "You are buying, I assume?"

"I am."

He nods and proceeds to order enough food for three people. I order French toast and coffee, and the waitress leaves us.

"So I wanted to talk about—" is how I begin, before he interrupts me.

"Wait a minute; before you start, I just have to tell you about this incredible coincidence. Right after I agreed to meet with you, I got a call from my friend Pete Stanton. He invited me to the Giants game on Sunday."

"Isn't that nice," I say.

"That's not the amazing part. We're actually going to be sitting in your seats. What are the odds against that?"

"Astonishing . . . gives me the chills."

He nods. "Yup, it's true. If someone didn't know better, it would almost look like you bribed me with the tickets to have this talk.

But that couldn't be, because I don't take bribes, and if you tried it, I would have to arrest you."

"So you're saying I shouldn't pay for your breakfast?"

"Breakfast is fine. Lunch would be a problem; you try and buy me lunch and you'll find yourself in handcuffs."

"A man with principles. Now can we get to this?" I ask, and he finally agrees.

Leonard is a smart guy; before meeting with me he would certainly have done his homework and learned who it is I am representing. So there is no reason for me to hold back on it; he would see through it anyway.

"As I'm sure you know, I am defending Brian Atkins on a double murder charge. Dominic Petrone's name has come up in my investigation."

"Come up how?" he asks.

"I can't say; it's privileged."

He frowns and leans forward. "Look, I've been trying to get Petrone for a very long time. I'll tell you some things, if it doesn't hurt my position to do so. But if you know anything that will help me, I need to hear them. This is not going only one way, tickets or no tickets."

"Fair enough," I say. "But I can't break a privilege; I know where the line is."

"Just make sure you draw it in the right place," he says.

I nod my agreement, and we move on. "Starlight is the company Gerry Wright and Brian Atkins founded. They struggled for a while and then hit it big by creating servers and routers that were faster than everyone else's. Their primary use is in equity trading, and they give an advantage to companies using them. I don't quite understand how it works; I'll never understand how it works. But it's real."

"Keep talking," he says, though I had planned to anyway.

"So Brian was gotten rid of by someone framing him and sending him to prison." Leonard gives me a skeptical look, but I disregard it. "Now his partner has been killed, and, like I say, Petrone's name has come up. What I want to know is if a guy like Petrone would want to move in on a company like that, or whether he would need what they're selling."

"I am not aware of Petrone having a particular interest in the stock market, although I would assume he invests," he says. "As a rule, the mob steers away from highly regulated industries; they prefer to fill vacuums. But of course it is not an ironclad rule."

"What about technology?"

"What about it?" he asks.

"Have they adapted to take advantage of it?"

He nods. "They have, but cybercrime is not their primary focus, and never will be. Their strength is in the person-to-person dealing, the intimidation and force tactics. I don't see them as morphing into nerds who sit in their basement and try to rule the world."

"Do you see Petrone moving into that world at all?"

He thinks about it, then shrugs. "He seems like the type; he fancies himself to be smart and capable of adapting, and he's probably right about that. But he's also old school in a lot of ways, so it's hard to say."

I'm just swinging blindly, hoping to get lucky and hit something.

I take another swing. "Why was Petrone shot at last night? And why did they miss?"

"Petrone knew they were coming; he wasn't even in the room when they got there. Mazzi didn't have such good intelligence, which is why he isn't living anymore. Chalk up a big win for Petrone."

"So they were after each other?" I ask.

"Either that, or it's a bigger coincidence than my having your Giants tickets."

"I need a road map here," I say. "Petrone is somehow involved in my client's case, and I don't know what rock to look under. Help me out, and anything I get is yours."

He hesitates before responding, then, "Look, what I'm about to tell you is off the record, and I'll tell you going in that I see no connection to your case."

It's not exactly a positive preamble, but I'll certainly hear him out.

He continues. "Petrone has been engaging in some unusual activity lately. At this point we don't know what he's doing, or why, but there is something going on."

"Unusual how?"

"Well, for one thing, his people have been making a series of trips to other cities, to meet with Petrone's peers, the heads of those local families. Petrone himself has not traveled; he's become more of a homebody in his old age."

"What cities?" I ask.

He shrugs. "No pattern. The ones we know of are San Antonio, Cleveland, Vegas, Chicago, and Baltimore."

"Could he be trying to get a piece of their action?"

"We don't know, but we have reason to believe he's not making any friends. If he's trying to expand, it's very uncharacteristic. He's always been completely local; he likes it that way. Invading other territories turns the system on its head."

"So maybe the Bronx was just another area he's trying to move in on?" I ask. "And that's why it went down the way it did last night?"

He shrugs again. "Always possible."

Whatever Petrone is doing, I'm not seeing how it could have anything to do with the double murder that Brian is accused of. I probe Leonard with some more general questions, but I get nothing, and I don't think he's holding back anything having to do with Brian's case.

By now we're finished eating, and the waitress comes over with the check. "It's breakfast, so he'll get it," Leonard tells her, pointing to me. He stands up, not even waiting for me to pay it. "The Giants seats any good?" he asks.

"Forty-five yard line. Club seats."

He nods. "That should do."

've got a couple of things I think you'll like."

Sam says that as soon as he walks in the door to my office, and as conversation starters go, that ranks way above "hello." Hike is there with him, and if Sam was willing to sit with Hike until I got here, he must really want to tell me something important.

Edna is not here, but that's not quite alarming enough to send out an all-points bulletin.

"Have you heard this news?" I ask Hike.

"Yeah."

"What do you think?"

"If it's true, it's okay. If not, it's a waste of time."

Now I'm really excited, because that assessment coming out of Hike's mouth is an unqualified rave. I sit down across from Sam and say, "Let's hear it."

"Well, you told me to look into Gerry Wright's life, his finances, acquaintances, that kind of thing."

"Right," I said.

"So I did, and I didn't find anything very interesting. He was rich, we already knew that, but even richer than I would have thought. Of course, he was the head of a privately owned company, so he could pay himself whatever he wanted. I'd have to dig a lot more, but I have my doubts I'll find anything we can use."

"That wasn't the good news part, was it?" I ask.

"No. Everything I found in his finances is in this file; I'll leave it with you."

"Can we move this along, Sam?" He has a tendency to draw these things out in a way that makes me want to kill him. Hike is rolling his eyes, though that doesn't mean much, since Hike's eyes are always rolling.

"I'm getting there. I also checked his phone records for the week before he was killed."

"And?"

"Well, the business phone records do nothing for us, because there's no way to know who within the company made each call. Wright had a private line, but he didn't seem to use it."

"Sam . . ."

"Instead he used his cell phone, so I got those records, as well as his home landline. He made quite a few calls"—he looks at his records—"a hundred and fourteen in that last week. Most of them seem as if they could have been business calls, you know, money guys. Some of it was more trivial kind of stuff. Like ordering in food, that kind of thing."

Sam does not realize it, but he's two boring sentences away from strangulation.

"But two of the calls stand out, one more than the other," he says.

"With the next words out of your mouth, I want you to tell me who those calls were to," I say.

Sam nods. "One was to a guy named Steven Thurmond. I checked him out; friends call him Stevie. He got out of prison three years ago."

"What was he in for?"

"Hacking. He's a master at it."

"As good as you?" I ask.

"If he was as good as me, he wouldn't have gone to prison. Anyway, I think it's interesting that Wright would be talking to him. Because of his background, and because of other stuff."

"I agree. What other stuff?"

"Well, Thurmond lives in Harbor Towers, but he doesn't have a job."

Harbor Towers is an exclusive apartment building in Fort Lee. "Maybe a rich uncle died and left him money."

"Then the uncle keeps dying. Thurmond has three hundred and seventy-five grand in the only bank account I checked, and it comes in twenty-five grand at a time, through untraceable wires."

"You hacked into his bank account?" I ask.

"I shouldn't have?"

It's obviously illegal, but no more so than many of Sam's other activities on my behalf. "I approve wholeheartedly. Who is the other guy he called that you were about to mention?"

"Tony Costa."

"The Tony Costa I just read about?" I ask. Tony Costa was Angelo Mazzi's right-hand man, before a bunch of bullets made Mazzi no longer require either right- or left-hand men. The paper said that Costa was one of the men arrested and held by the FBI.

"The very one," Sam says. "He made a call to Costa on the day he died. Of course, I have no way to know what he said."

"Sam, it took a while, but you came through."

I'm going to want to talk to Thurmond, but I'm not sure that will come to anything. Gerry Wright was in the technology business, so dealing with a computer expert, even a convicted hacker, falls into the realm of the possibly legitimate.

But Wright talking to Tony Costa is far more significant, and more interesting to me. It connects Wright to organized crime, and organized crime is full of people that a jury could reasonably see as killers.

I want to talk to Costa, and I think I might have a way in.

C indy, great to hear your voice. How long has it been?" I'm calling Cindy Spodek, the second in command of the Boston office of the FBI. Cindy is a friend, more Laurie's than mine, but she has helped me on a number of cases. She'd never admit it, but I've helped her as well.

"Well, let's see," she says. "The last time we talked was the last time you needed a favor. And the time before that was the last time you needed a favor before that. I could go back farther, but I think you see the pattern."

"Then I've got to start needing more favors," I say. "Because I really miss our little talks."

"What do you need this time, Andy?"

"Don't you want to chitchat first?"

"No. I speak to Laurie every week, so I know how she and Ricky are doing."

"Does she talk about me much?" I ask.

"Less than you might think. I'm busy, Andy. Can we get to it?"

"Absolutely. You, meaning the FBI, are currently holding a guy named Tony Costa. He's the right-hand man of the recently deceased Angelo Mazzi, and was apparently present when Mazzi was shot to death in the Bronx the other night."

"I'm in Boston, Andy. This may come as a surprise, but the

Bronx isn't in the Boston territory. If it were Queens or Staten Island, I could help you."

"I'm aware of all that. But my hope is that because of your vast influence within your organization, you can persuade your colleagues in the Bronx to get me in to talk to Costa."

"Why would I, or they, for that matter, want to do that?"

"Because I'm going to bring down Dominic Petrone."

"By talking to Costa?" she asks.

"It's a piece of the puzzle. I can't tell you more right now because it's privileged," I lie.

"People that we detain aren't open to the public. We can't have people just walk in and chat. And he wouldn't have to talk to you if he didn't want to."

"He'll talk to me. Just have them tell him I want to talk about Dominic Petrone."

She sighs. I know she doesn't want to get involved, but down deep she knows that our deals have proved beneficial in the past. Unfortunately, I have much less to bargain with this time. Fortunately, she doesn't know that.

"The FBI is a large organization," she says. "Isn't there someone else you can bother with this stuff?"

"If there was, I would. And maybe they would even be properly grateful."

"Sit tight," she says. "I'll get back to you."

I'm not really sure how one "sits tight," but I use the time to go through the information that Sam brought me. It's mostly financial, and as Sam said, Gerry Wright was a rich man. I notice that all of his personal investments were with a particular hedge fund, and I've got a hunch that his trades went through his own company's servers. He's done well in the market, but not extraordinarily so.

Three hours after Cindy instructed me to sit tight, she calls back. "He's being held in the federal jail in the Lower Manhattan courthouse. For some reason, he's willing to talk to you."

"I'm a good conversationalist."

"Yeah," she says. "A real treat. Be there at nine o'clock in the morning."

"Cindy, believe it or not, I do appreciate this."

"Show your appreciation by giving us Petrone. We want him badly."

Her comment, and especially the tone of it, surprises me. "Why?" I ask.

"Because he's a criminal. We like to catch criminals."

"Oh."

If you want to impress someone, but live in New Jersey . . . Okay, I get it. If your goal in choosing a place to live is to impress someone, then you wouldn't be living in New Jersey at all. But if you did, then you'd do well to choose Harbor Towers.

It's forty-one stories of modern elegance, sitting about a mile upriver along the coast from former Starlight technology head Jason Mathers's apartment, with a view of New York that is every bit as good.

It's the perfect location to get into the city or to the shopping malls in Paramus. And if some future governor of New Jersey again decides to close the George Washington Bridge to traffic, residents of Harbor Towers will once again have a great view of the whole thing.

You don't just walk into a building like this; you have to pass muster with the doorman. This particular one doesn't smile; his demeanor is that of a bouncer at the hottest nightclub in town. The people who live in this building are better than the visitors, he reasons, and because he is their representative, he is also of a higher class.

I could have called ahead and asked Steven Thurmond to meet with me, but I always prefer not to give people that much lead time to prepare. I recognize I might not get past the doorman, but I figure I'll give it a shot.

"I'm here to see Steven Thurmond."

"He expecting you?"

"No. I'm here on a legal matter."

"Is that right?" he asks. "You wouldn't by any chance be the police, would you?"

It's an interesting conversation starter, that's for sure, and one to be pursued. "No, but I'm a lawyer, and I sure know a lot of cops." I don't mention the fact that except for Pete, they all despise me.

That seems to have made at least a modest impact; I can see him considering his options.

"Does Steven Thurmond have a lot of dealings with the police?" I ask.

"Not enough. Hey, don't I know you from somewhere?"

"Maybe. My name's Andy Carpenter; you've probably seen me on television." A number of my cases have been high profile, so I have been prominent in the media pretty often. It often can work in my favor to open doors, a timely benefit since I'm trying to get by a doorman.

"You think the police should be paying more attention to Steven Thurmond?" I ask. "Maybe I can help with that."

"He throws loud parties, the neighbors complain. I call the cops, they talk to him, and nothing happens."

"I'll see what I can do," I say, which is, of course, complete nonsense. But nonsense spouted by someone who is always on television can sometimes seem credible. If you don't believe me, watch the Sunday-morning news shows.

"You want me to call up and tell him you're here?" he asks.

"Actually, I'd rather take him by surprise." I smile, but avoid winking. That would seem a bit over the top.

He returns the smile. "Twenty-six B," he says.

"You sure? I don't want you to get in trouble," I say.

"Don't worry about it. It's not the first time I've surprised him and sent up someone he doesn't want to see. Just say I wasn't here when you came by."

"Nice not to see you again," I say.

I take the elevator up to the twenty-sixth floor, and Thurmond's apartment is the second farthest down on the left off the elevator. It's not the corner apartment, but it's close.

I ring the bell, expecting someone on the other side to warily ask who's there. Since the process is usually for the doorman to ring up, I would think that unannounced visitors must be few and far between.

Instead the door just opens, and a man who couldn't be more than thirty stands there, holding a half-eaten apple. He's wearing either a sweat suit or pajamas; it's hard to tell which. His hair is longish, and he's got an earring in his left ear. This cannot be a guy with a connection to Dominic Petrone. He may not even have a connection to reality.

"Who are you?" he asks.

"My name is Andy Carpenter. I'm a lawyer, and I want to talk to you about a case I'm working on."

He shrugs, apparently indifferent to the entire matter. "What kind of case? Come on in."

I enter an apartment that will never be featured in *Better Homes and Gardens* magazine. It is a filthy mess; I'm a slob, and it makes my office look like a hospital operating room.

"You want anything to drink?" he asks. Without waiting for an answer, he points to what I assume is a couch buried under discarded clothing, and says, "Just sit anywhere."

"No, thanks," I say, which is an answer referring to both the drink and the seat. "How did you know Gerry Wright?"

The change in attitude is immediate; it's as if someone went over him with an "indifference remover."

"Who?"

"Gerry Wright."

"I don't know him."

"That would have been a good answer if I had asked, 'Do you know Gerry Wright?' But what I asked is how you knew him. I already know that you did."

"I helped him with some computer stuff," he says, admitting in the process that he lied about saying he didn't know him. If there is a God, he will let me cross-examine this person in front of a jury.

"What kind of computer stuff?" I ask. "And why you? He owned a company full of nerds that could have helped him."

"I got nothing to say to you."

"Does the name Dominic Petrone mean anything to you?"

He reacts, almost doing a double take, but simply repeats, "I got nothing to say to you."

"You're going to be talking to me in court anyway, so it might make sense to start now. You know, give you an idea of what you're going to be faced with."

"Why did the doorman let you in?"

"You have a doorman? Wow, ritzy building. You must have a really good job to afford an expensive place like this. Or maybe you get money from somewhere else."

"Get outta here."

"You've been in prison once, Steven. The way to avoid going back is to talk to me."

He walks over and opens the door, just in case I hadn't gotten the hint. But I had, so I smile my most winning smile and leave.

This is a solemn occasion, part of a decades-long passing of the torch. I am taking Ricky to a Giants game, the third one we have attended together this year. The season tickets have been in our family forever, and it seems like yesterday that my father was taking me. But, of course, it wasn't yesterday. Not even close.

The first time I brought Ricky, he was dazzled by the entire experience. The massive crowd, the incredibly green field, the noise and intensity when an important play was about to take place . . . it literally left him openmouthed in amazement.

But now he's an old-timer, and it's much more about the game than the experience. He's become a passionate Giants fan and, like the rest of us, dedicated to their success but intolerant of their failures. They are one and one in the two games he's attended, so he's already experienced both.

Since Barry Leonard and Pete have my regular seats, I've purchased tickets on the open market. We're on the thirty yard line instead of the forty-five, but Ricky seems fine with the new location. It's a four o'clock start, so it's going to be quite cold by the time we get to evening, and we've dressed warmly.

The Giants are playing the Eagles, a team I would have trouble rooting for if they were playing Al Qaeda. Pretty much the nicest thing I can say about the Eagles is that they are not as evil as the Cowboys.

"You think we're going to win?" Ricky asks, once we're settled in our seats.

"Absolutely."

"What's the spread?"

I cringe at the question; I have created a nine-year-old bookie. I can say that I don't know the answer, but he'll know I'm lying. "Giants by two and a half," I say.

He nods wisely. "It's a lock."

Unfortunately, he forgot to clear his lock prediction with Eli Manning, who throws two interceptions, both of which the Eagles capitalize on. At the half the Giants are down twenty-one to ten, still within range but with a pretty big hill to climb.

Ricky and I head to the concession stands to get sustenance for the second half ahead. We're both going to get hot chocolate, while he has chicken fingers and I have a hamburger.

My seats are in the club section, which has its own private concession stands, but today's seats are not, so we find ourselves on a line at least ten people deep. Ricky wants to go back to the seats himself so as not to miss the start of the second half, but there's no way I'm letting him out of my sight.

"Looks like a long day, huh?"

I don't recognize the voice, so I look back and see that the man behind us is talking to me. He's at least six three and two hundred and forty pounds, and looks to be in great shape. The Giants could have used him at middle linebacker in the first half.

"So far," I say.

"Your son a Giants fan?"

Something about the way he says it gives me a bit of the creeps, which is somehow enhanced when I notice that he's not alone, and that he is standing with a friend who is at least as large as he is, though not as well proportioned.

"We both are," I say, and look away, hoping to end the conversation. My instincts are alerting me to a problem, and I generally like to trust them.

"Hopefully you can both be Giants fans for a long time. All you got to do is make sure you don't bother the wrong people."

I now have no doubt this was not a chance meeting, and my hand protectively goes on Ricky's shoulder. "I'll take that into consideration," I say, and turn away as he replies, "You do that. You better do that."

It takes about five minutes to reach the front of the line, though it seems like five hours. I'm in a bit of a panic here; I think it has just been a warning to deter my future actions, but I can't be positive.

We reach the front of the line and place our order. The guy behind me has been talking to his friend about how we're ignoring him, in the process mocking my fear. I take my phone out, and get it ready. When we get our food, I wait a moment, leaving the tray on the counter. I turn and raise the phone. "Smile," I say, and snap a picture of the guy who has been talking to me.

"What the . . ." he starts to say, but I grab the food and usher Ricky back to our seats. It's not easy to get there, because my legs are shaking.

Once we get to the seats, I call Laurie and describe everything that has just taken place. I have to talk softly, so that Ricky can't hear me, and I have to pause occasionally when the crowd cheers and makes communication impossible.

After I've told her everything I can remember, I say, "I could be wrong about this, but I really don't think so."

"Doesn't matter," she says. "We have to assume you're right."

"Should we leave now?"

"No, then you'd be alone in the parking lot, and they might want to send you a stronger message. What gate do you use to leave the stadium?"

"Gate C."

"Okay. Look for Marcus; he'll be waiting there for you."

The rest of the game would have been enjoyable, if I wasn't so scared. The Giants put together a great second half, Manning throws for three touchdowns, and the defense comes up big. They win thirty-four to twenty-four, and Ricky is positively euphoric.

As for me, my legs do a lot of shaking, and it's not from the cold. I spend the time hoping teams will call time-outs in order to give Marcus more time to get to the stadium. I've been scanning the crowd for some sign of the two goons, but I don't see them. My fear is that they see us.

A bigger concern is that they could be waiting for us near our car. We weren't in our regular seats, so if they knew where we were sitting, they must have followed us to, and into, the stadium. That means they know where we are parked.

Usually we'll leave with a couple of minutes to go in the game, if it's out of reach one way or the other. This time, however, we stay until the final gun, and then file out along with the mass of people.

Marcus is there waiting for us at Gate C, a fact that delights both me and Ricky. "Uncle Marcus!" he yells. "Dad, Uncle Marcus is here!" Ricky shares Laurie's lack of fear of Marcus, and is actually crazy about him.

Marcus comes over and picks Ricky up, holding him in the air as if he were a paper cutout. He then puts him down, and whispers to me, "Show me."

"Okay," I say. "Not sure if they're still here."

We're parked all the way at the far end of the lot. I like to do that so that it will be easier to get out when we're leaving. I'm sorry I did that today, especially since it's now dark out, but I'd be a lot sorrier if Marcus wasn't with us.

We walk the long way with Ricky between us, and each of us with a hand on one of his shoulders. The entire time I'm scanning the people around us, looking for the two goons, but I don't see them. I'm not great at recognizing faces, but with their physical size, I have no doubt I'd know who they were.

As we reach our car, the crowd has thinned out almost totally, since everyone else has already gotten to their cars, which are closer to the stadium. All of a sudden there the two of them are, standing against a car about forty feet from mine, which I assume is their car. Watching us.

"Marcus," I say, and make a motion with my head in their direction.

He looks over at them, says, "Yuh," and makes a motion of his own toward Ricky, and then my car. I assume he wants me to get Ricky inside. Marcus is not the most talkative guy in the world.

I start to do that as Marcus walks over to the two guys. It's a little hard to see in the dim light, but they seem to straighten up as he comes over. They don't seem at all worried, since it's two against one, but they recognize the need to be prepared.

I get Ricky in the car, but I stand outside. It seems somehow cowardly to hide in the car myself, though I can't imagine I will have much value to Marcus wherever I am. At least this way, I can see what happens and call 911 if things go badly.

Marcus walks right up to them, ultimately standing maybe a foot or so away. They separate slightly, so that one is closer to Marcus's left, and one to his right. I assume they think it gives them a tactical advantage, which means they are not familiar with

Marcus. For them to have a tactical advantage, they'd have to have a nuclear weapon in the trunk.

I have no idea what they're saying, though if I know Marcus, there are very few syllables involved.

I can't see that well, but it seems as if the confrontation gets more intense, and the guy who did the talking to me makes some kind of sudden move.

Whatever he's doing, or planning to do, provokes an interesting response from Marcus. Marcus kicks his leg up into the guy's groin with a force that, if he were inside the stadium kicking a field goal, would probably be good from sixty yards. Then he raises his arm, with his fist on the end of it, in an uppercut into the guy's chin. It sends the goon back against the car, and then onto the ground, though I doubt he's awake enough to feel his fall.

It takes his partner a split second to swing into action, which is a split second too long. Marcus comes across with his right elbow, hitting the guy either in the throat or the side of the head. I'm guessing it's the head, because I don't hear any retching, and the guy just drops like a stone.

I look around to see if any people have seen this. I don't think they have, or at least no one is reacting. The whole thing was like watching a silent movie, albeit a violent one.

Marcus casually walks over to us and says, "Home."

"You need a ride?" I ask, not knowing how he got here.

"Nuh," he says, and waits there until we pull away. He's got his eyes on the fallen goons, lying in dark shadows next to their car, but they don't seem to be able or willing to move.

I call Laurie to tell her that we connected with Marcus and that we're okay and on the way home. Ricky hadn't seen Marcus dispose of the two guys, so I don't want to describe all that just happened.

She's waiting for us at the door when we enter. She asks Ricky how the game was, while hugging him so close that his mouth is pressed against her so hard he can't talk. When that's finished, she hugs me in a similar fashion, and I am not inclined to object.

While she puts Ricky to bed, I take Tara and Sebastian on our evening walk. The day's events have really shaken me. I have always been a coward, but my fear when Ricky was threatened dwarfed anything I've felt in the past. It also makes me angry, an anger that washes over me as we walk. I want revenge, though Marcus already took care of that pretty well.

Tara seems to sense that something is going on, because instead of spending her time sniffing the surroundings, she holds back and stays at my side. Sebastian is oblivious to me, but does seem surprised that Tara is not joining him. He keeps looking back at her, as if to say, "There's great stuff to sniff over here . . . what's going on?"

When I get home, Laurie is waiting for me with two glasses of wine. I describe in detail what happened when we left the stadium. "Let me see the photo," she says.

I take out my phone and show it to her, but she doesn't recognize the two guys. She suggests that I call Pete, which I do.

"I can get used to those seats," he says, when he picks up the phone.

"Thrilled to hear that," I say. "I'm going to e-mail you a photograph; tell me if you recognize the guys in it."

"Who are they?"

"That's what I want you to tell me. Call me back."

I send him the e-mail, and while I wait for him to call, Laurie and I discuss the situation. "First things first," she says. "We need to make sure you and Ricky are protected."

"I can take care of myself," I say, but since we both know better, she ignores the comment.

"Marcus will stay with you, and I'll be with Ricky. Once we find out who they are and what kind of danger they present, we can reevaluate if necessary."

"They have to be Petrone's guys," I say. "I've been asking around about him, and it's obviously gotten his attention. This wasn't a chance meeting; it took a lot of effort and planning. They followed us to the stadium, knew where we were inside, and got on the line behind us. They are serious."

"I'll talk to Marcus and see if he learned anything. But my guess is they just told him to get lost, and tried to enforce that when he didn't listen. They clearly had no idea who they were dealing with."

"They do now," I say.

The doorbell rings, which in the current circumstances is a frightening sound. Laurie stops at the closet on the way to the door and takes her gun out from the top shelf, where she keeps it well out of Ricky's reach. I see her loading it as she goes to the door.

"Who is it?" she asks.

"Pete."

Laurie opens the door to let him in.

"Are you unfamiliar with the concept of the telephone?" I ask.

"Sorry, but I just came upon a coincidence so great that I wanted to share it in person."

I know where this is going, but I play along. "What might that be?"

"The two guys in the picture you sent me were found unconscious in the Giants Stadium parking lot a couple of hours ago. And get this, it's the same Giants Stadium that you were at today."

"Talk about a small world," I say. "Who are they?"

"Names are Joey Manto and Luther Montrose. They're hired muscle."

"For Dominic Petrone?" I ask.

"I'm assuming that wasn't a lucky guess," he asks. "Now tell me what the hell is going on."

"Well, I saw these two guys at the game, and they looked familiar, but I couldn't place the faces, so I took a picture of them. I thought maybe they were in my high school fraternity."

"Wiseass," Pete accurately points out.

"Then, as Ricky, Marcus, and I were leaving the stadium—"

"Marcus was with you? Bingo . . . mystery solved."

"As we were leaving the stadium, we heard a commotion, but

we didn't know that anyone was hurt, or we would have gone over to help."

Pete turns to Laurie. "Tell him to stop the bullshit."

"I can't tell him what to do," she says, and then turns to me. "Stop the bullshit."

I nod. "I've been asking around about Petrone because he's involved in the Brian Atkins case. He sent these two guys to threaten me, so I took the picture to find out who they are. Then Laurie called Marcus, and I don't remember the rest."

I'm not about to throw Marcus under the bus, and Pete has no desire to have me do so. "I've got a hunch this is going to be an unsolved crime," he says.

"Certainly appears that way."

"Do I have to tell you to be careful? That if they went to the trouble of sending these guys that this is important to them?"

"I already told him," Laurie says. "They threatened Ricky also."

I'm not sure I've ever seen the look that comes on Pete's face when he hears what Laurie said. "They're going to be in the hospital for a few days at least," he says. "While they're there, I'm going to have a talk with them."

"What are you going to say?"

"That if they mess with Ricky, they will look fondly on what Marcus did to them in the parking lot. Because I'll put a bullet in each of their goddamn heads."

I learned something very important at the game, besides the fact that I might die soon. I learned that Denise knew exactly what she was talking about when she said that Gerry Wright was involved on some level with Dominic Petrone. I also learned that Petrone is worried about what I am doing and about what I might find out.

Those are facts, and they lead to my beliefs. I believe that Dominic Petrone is behind the two murders, because killing is part of his job description. I believe that the only way I can win this case is to get the jury to buy into that premise. And I believe that Petrone is going to do whatever he can to stop me.

And he can do a lot.

My first concern is Ricky. If anything were to happen to him, and I can't even bring myself to verbalize what "anything" might be, I have serious doubts I could survive it, or would want to.

"His safety has to be the first priority," I say to Laurie, which no doubt is the perfect example of preaching to the choir.

"Nothing will happen to him," she says. Her voice is so intense and determined that I'm glad I love her, because I'd hate to go against her in divorce court.

"What did you say in bed the other night?" I ask.

She thinks for a few moments. "You mean, 'Not tonight, Andy, I'm not in the mood'?"

"Besides that."

"I don't know. What did I say?"

"We were watching the documentary on the Cuban missile crisis, remember? Then we got to talking about Kennedy and presidential assassinations—"

She interrupts. "Now I remember why I wasn't in the mood."

"—and you said that if killers want to get to someone badly enough, even the president, they can do so."

"Andy . . ."

"You know what I'm getting at?" I ask. "Do you see my point?"

"It's not exactly subtle."

"Look, I know you would do anything to protect him, and I understand you can handle yourself in any situation. But, and you can call me selfish for saying this, I don't want you to take a bullet either."

"So what are you proposing?" she asks.

I think she's weakening under the onslaught of the Andy Carpenter logical mind.

"That you and Ricky go visit your Aunt Celia in Findlay." Laurie went back to her hometown in Wisconsin a while back and reconnected with family, especially her Aunt Celia. She and Ricky spent two weeks there this summer. "You know how Ricky loves her," I say.

"He's in school, Andy."

"She's a fourth-grade teacher! She can homeschool him for a month or so, just until we get a handle on what's going on. And you'll see all your old friends."

"What about you?" she asks.

"What about me?"

"You're in more danger than Ricky."

"I have Marcus. If Marcus was in Dallas back then, Kennedy would be doing Viagra commercials today."

"I need to think about this."

"Take your time," I say, then, "What did you decide?"

Laurie's not a big fan of talking and thinking at the same time. I know she's really upset about what happened at the game, but she needs some time to process it. Since my talking is rarely conducive to processing, I take Sebastian and Tara for another quick walk. I'm sure I shouldn't do it without Marcus guarding me yet, but I doubt that Petrone has had time to react to the Giants Stadium fiasco.

I stay alert and shorten the walk some, but as always I find it relaxing. Life is simple for Tara and Sebastian, and it's a little simpler for me when I'm walking and watching them.

I get back home, but Laurie doesn't seem to have come to any decision. I head into the den with the discovery documents; I will read them at least twenty times before and during the trial. I have to be able to draw on every piece of available information instantly, in the moment, when I'm in court.

The evidence doesn't get any less daunting with each reading, and I'm not getting any closer to countering it. When I'm done, I read the information that Sam brought me, in terms of Wright's finances and telephone calls he made or received the week of his death.

One of the names is familiar to me: it's Joseph Westman, the hedge fund guy who killed himself and was called the "hedge perv" on the front page of the newspaper. It would make sense that Wright would be talking to financial people, but Westman's violent death gets me to make a note to check and see if I can find any connection to my case.

It's almost eleven o'clock when I hear Laurie call me from the bedroom. I put the documents down and head upstairs.

Laurie is sitting in bed and reading when I get there. She looks fantastic; she always looks fantastic, but somehow bed is her best venue.

She puts the book down and pats the bed right next to her. "Come here," she says.

Oh, boy.

I almost fall on my face in my haste to obey, but I manage to make it to the bed intact.

"We have to talk," she says.

"Talk?" This is not a good sign.

"Yes. What did you think?"

"Well, since I was faced with deadly danger today, I was hoping that you'd have a reaction."

"What kind of reaction?" she asks.

"Well, I thought perhaps you'd want to ravage me. I can be very ravageable."

"I hadn't noticed," she says. Then, "I've decided to take Ricky to Findlay."

"Good; glad to hear it."

"I'll stay with him for a few days, and then come back here and work the case with you."

"Good. Tell me when you want to go, and I'll book the flights."

"This way I know he'll be safe."

"Yes, he will."

"And I'll be here to help you. And Marcus."

"It's a win-win," I say. "Now, we were talking about ravaging."

She doesn't say anything; just stares at me.

"What?" I ask.

"Actually, you do look pretty ravageable," she says. "How come I never noticed that before?"

"Better late than never."

In one way nothing has changed, yet I know that everything has changed. The fact that Dominic Petrone has threatened me does not impact the job I have to do; I have to defend Brian Atkins to the best of my ability. That is a given; I can wish I had never gotten involved in the first place, and I do, but that boat has sailed.

I will go about my business, and Marcus will protect me, and the legal chips will fall where they may. Representing clients is what I do, even if I keep trying unsuccessfully to stop doing it.

But the long-term picture is just as clear, and it doesn't bode well. Dominic Petrone is my enemy; we are on opposite sides. Making matters worse is the embarrassment he suffered at Giants Stadium. That is something he will not forget. Forgetting isn't his specialty.

Marcus cannot protect me for the rest of my life, and Ricky belongs at home. Yet there is far from a guarantee that a resolution of the case, even if it ends in Brian's acquittal, will eliminate Petrone's desire for revenge. So my fundamental goal has changed. It will no longer be sufficient to simply use Petrone as a way to convince the jury that they should have reasonable doubt.

I have to put him away.

Fortunately, my first stop this morning is to see someone who has already tried to put Petrone away, permanently. The fact that he failed to do so is a concern, probably more for him than for me, but I'm hoping we can use our common cause to get the job done.

Tony Costa was the right-hand man of Angelo Mazzi, the head of a crime family in the Bronx. Mazzi failed in his apparent effort to have his people gun down Petrone, and was himself killed by Petrone's people the same night. Costa was arrested by the FBI and is being held for a few days in an effort to get him to talk, but I doubt that's going well.

I'm hoping he'll talk to me, because we have identical interests: We both want to get Petrone.

Cindy said to be at the federal courthouse in Lower Manhattan at 9:00 A.M., so I leave the house at six thirty. Getting to Lower Manhattan from New Jersey during the morning rush hour is like climbing Mount Everest, without the snow and Sherpas. In terms of miles it's not that far, but it takes forever.

Laurie had told Marcus where and when I was going, but I don't see any sign of him. That doesn't worry me; Marcus is never seen unless he needs to be. If he's supposed to be watching me, then he's watching me.

I arrive thirty minutes early, which is good because I'm dealing with the Feds. Guards in local jails can be a pain in the ass, but the Feds wrote the book on it. I have to fill out four pages of paperwork, mostly identification stuff.

It twice asks me the purpose of my visit, and each time I write, "I'm hoping Mr. Costa and I can double date when he gets out." But I also shade the truth by describing it as an attorney's visit. I am an attorney, though not Mr. Costa's, but I want to be put in a room where our conversation is not listened in on.

By the time I'm processed and searched twice, it's almost nine thirty. I'm brought back to what is labeled an attorney's room, so it's possible my effort succeeded. Or not. It's not crucial either way.

I'm the first to arrive, and it's another ten minutes before a guard comes in with Costa. He's no taller than I am, and I can barely dunk a doughnut. My guess is he's about forty, and he doesn't look at all stressed out by his situation.

Which makes one of us.

Costa's hands are cuffed in front of him. The guard indicates that he should sit in the chair, and then tells me that he'll be right outside the door if I need him.

"Tony, I'm Andy—" is how I begin, but he cuts me off.

"I know who you are."

"I want to talk about Dominic Petrone."

"Tell me something I don't know."

"He killed your boss," I say.

"Yeah?" is his clever response. He's quite the conversationalist.

"I want to know why."

"What do you have to do with any of this?" he asks.

"In addition to killing your boss, he killed Gerry Wright and Denise Atkins, and my client is about to go on trial for those murders."

"Who the hell are they, and why would he kill them?"

"They were executives with a technology company. Petrone is moving in on territories all over the country, just like he was moving in on you and Mazzi. Mazzi didn't like it, so he's dead, and you're in here. Gerry Wright was helping Petrone, until Petrone didn't need him anymore."

"What does any of that crap have to do with me?" he asks.

"You spoke to Gerry Wright the day he died."

"Bullshit. Is that all you got?"

"That's all I'm going to share with you. But I'm going to get Petrone. I would think that would interest you."

"A lot of things interest me. Come back when you've got something real."

So I leave. All in all, it wasn't the most productive of meetings, but that doesn't mean I didn't find out anything. Costa was doing one of two things. He was either withholding information because he didn't trust me or using the meeting to gather information himself.

I think it was the latter. Costa agreed to meet with me simply because he was told I wanted to talk about Petrone. I think Costa wants to nail Petrone, but isn't convinced I have anything to help him do so. He's mostly right about that, so far.

I've had meetings go better than this one.

Among the challenges we're going to face will be the difficulty in getting our evidence admitted. It's not an urgent problem yet, since the trial hasn't begun, so at this point there's not even a jury to see our evidence. A slightly bigger hurdle is the fact that we don't happen to have any evidence to get admitted.

But when it comes to pointing the finger at Petrone, we will not be able to get by with theories. We are going to have to show a concrete connection between him and the two murders, or the judge will not let any of it in.

The fact that Brian says Denise mentioned Petrone, or the fact that I can claim that two of his goons threatened me, will not carry any weight at all. We are going to have to have substantive, provable facts, and they are going to have to directly tie in to the case before the jury.

Richard Wallace is a prosecutor I like. That is not as rare as you might think; I basically think they are decent people doing their job in the best way they know how. My father, in fact, was a prosecutor, and a damned good one at that.

What is much harder to find is a prosecutor who likes me; they could hold my prosecutorial fan club meetings in a phone booth, if phone booths still existed. Yet Richard, unless I am badly misjudging things, actually likes me.

Part of that is because Richard worked for my father; he learned from him. I got to know him back then, and we just always got along. My father would be proud of him these days; Richard has become a fair adversary who would rather get to the truth than get a conviction. I wish he was prosecuting Brian's case.

Richard and I have gone up against each other twice in court, once in the Willie Miller retrial, and I've won both times. As far as I can tell, he's never held it against me, which I hope remains true, because I need something from him.

Richard has become the go-to guy in the prosecutor's office for child pornography cases. Fortunately, it's not a full-time job, though there have been some successfully brought cases in recent years. But he has become an expert in that area of the law, so cases naturally fall to him.

He is also called in to consult in other jurisdictions, and is privy to all that goes on in the child pornography area through most of the metropolitan area. He has to stay on top of all of it, because he is now part of a tristate task force, created because that kind of garbage really doesn't respect artificial geographic borders.

I've asked to see him today to talk about Joseph Westman, the successful Wall Street guy who recently killed himself by plowing his Porsche into a tree at ninety miles per hour. According to the newspaper accounts, Westman feared that his involvement in kiddie porn was about to result in his arrest, and he took his own life so as not to have to face that fate.

The reason I'm interested in Westman is that he was on Gerry Wright's call list. Since they were both involved in equity trading in some capacity, his presence on the list is not so surprising. But his suicide is interesting enough that it makes me want to check this box off my list.

I had called Richard and asked if he was involved in the Westman case, and his answer was "to some extent." I'm not sure what he meant by that, but he agreed to meet me to talk about it. So here I am.

As he leads me back to his office, his colleagues stare at me as if I were Peyton Manning wandering uninvited into the Patriots locker room. If they could think of something to charge me with, I'd be in handcuffs already.

Once I'm in the safety of Richard's closed office, he gets me a cup of coffee and we chitchat about the old days. I generally think that as a rule the old days are overrated; they only seem great because we're comparing them to the new days, which are pretty crummy. But talking to him reminds me of my father, which is never a bad thing.

Finally, he says, "So you want to talk about Joseph Westman?"

I nod. "I do. What can you tell me about him?"

"Not much."

"The media reports were that he killed himself to avoid facing an imminent child pornography prosecution. His wife as much as admitted it; she referred to him as tormented and in pain."

"I know. But if he killed himself because cops were after him, he should ask for a do-over, because he wasn't on any of our radars. Of course, he is now."

"What do you mean?"

"Well, we never heard of him before he drove into that tree. But we saw the same reports you did, so we started an investigation. We want to see if we can connect him to other people, or to his source. Sure enough, he was guilty as hell; the garbage was all over his computer."

"Where was he getting it?"

"Normal places; there's no shortage of slime on the Internet," he says. "We run them down as best we can, but they can be any-where."

"What would make him think you were after him if you weren't?"

He smiles. "My reputation?"

"You got a second choice?" I ask. "Just in case that's not it?"

"Nope. Why don't you ask his wife?"

"You know her?" I ask.

"I do now."

"Will you call her and suggest she talk to me?"

He thinks for a moment. "What's your interest in this, Andy?"

"It could be connected to the Atkins case, but basically I'm fishing. But if it means anything, I'm fishing for Dominic Petrone."

For Richard, the prospect of nailing Dominic Petrone is game, set, and match.

"I'll call her right now," he says.

W here the hell have you been?" The caller is Jimmy Rollins, who is sort of my friend, and definitely my bookmaker. He's wondering why I haven't been calling to bet on football. "Everything okay with you? Laurie and the kid all right?"

Jimmy is not worried about his loss of revenue; I don't bet nearly enough for that to be the case. He's just genuinely concerned that my absence might mean there's something seriously wrong.

"It's a long story," I say, not wanting to get into the situation with Ricky, and my vow to set a good example. "But nothing to worry about."

"Good, because you're one of my regulars, and my regulars aren't so regular anymore."

"Why not?" I ask.

"Goddamn Internet is taking over the world."

"You mean that Costa Rica stuff?" Sports and casino gambling Web sites have been operating offshore for a long time now. Americans use them, though they are technically illegal. Gamblers don't get prosecuted, probably because of a recognition that the gambling laws in this country are hypocritical and insane.

For example, it's perfectly legal to bet on horse racing online, but not on other sports. Why one is immoral and dangerous, and the other isn't, has never been satisfactorily explained, at least not to me. Same goes for why sports betting is okay in Nevada, but not in the other forty-nine states.

So sports betting has gone offshore, where it operates with relative impunity, but without our government getting a piece of the pie in taxes.

"No, that's yesterday's news," he says, referring to the offshore betting sites. "I can deal with that. This is local."

Bells are clanging inside my head. I've been trying to figure out how and why Petrone could be using the Internet. Could it be something as simple as gambling?

"What do you mean by 'local'?" I ask.

"I mean local. And I think it's connected."

"Petrone?"

"That's the word on the street," he says. "My self-preservation instinct and I would ask that you don't quote me on that. I'm an independent operator; I don't swim in those waters."

"Jimmy, I need to talk to one of your customers that's left you, somebody who you think is using this local Internet thing."

"Why?"

"It may tie in to a case I'm working on," I say.

He thinks for a few moments. "I don't know, Andy. I doubt anybody's going to want to do any talking. They'll be afraid of trouble."

"How about for money?" I ask. "You got someone in this situation who can use a couple of thousand dollars? I'll pay for the information, and I can promise I won't tell anyone that they spoke to me."

"A lot of these guys can always use money."

"Good. I'll go as high as five thousand," I say.

"For five thousand, they'd rat out their mother. Let me see what I can do."

I tell him I need for this to happen quickly, and we hang up. It could turn out that Ricky's picking up on my gambling will prove to be beneficial to my case.

Ain't fatherhood great?

I'm now going to be anxiously awaiting calls from both Jimmy, to set up a meeting with one of his gambling ex-clients, and Richard Wallace, who is attempting to arrange a conversation with Joseph Westman's widow.

Both of these meetings are long shots to have anything to do with the murders, or even Petrone, but I've got nothing better at the moment, so in my mind they have more importance than they deserve. In fact, I think I'll spend some time fantasizing about the possibility that they'll crack the case wide open.

"We're ready, Andy."

So much for fantasy; the words that Laurie has just spoken are a cold dose of reality. She and Ricky are about to leave for Wisconsin, and although it was my idea, I'm dreading it.

The plan was to exercise an abundance of caution and not have me drive them to the airport. In case I am being followed, we would not want the bad guys to have any idea that Laurie and Ricky are leaving town.

So we put the suitcases in the trunk of the car while it was in the garage, thereby making it seem to anyone watching that Laurie and Ricky are not going anywhere special. I wanted to have Marcus follow them just in case, but Laurie vetoed it. She claimed, probably accurately, that she is experienced enough to detect if she is being followed.

I'm feeling both sadness and anger, and I think anger is winning out. This is my family, and they are being temporarily taken away from me by a bunch of assholes. Even worse, they are being deprived of the freedom to live their lives as they see fit. Add to that the fact that Laurie and I are being forced into worrying about the safety of our son, and I can't remember the last time I was this pissed.

For now I conceal these feelings, and prepare to say goodbye. I have to feign enthusiasm, because Ricky has no idea that he is being shipped out because of any danger; he thinks he's going on a fun vacation.

"Great!" I say. "Boy, you guys are going to have a terrific time; I wish I was going with you."

"We'll call every night, won't we, Rick?" Laurie says.

Ricky nods. "Sure will."

"Say hi to Aunt Celia for me," I say, and Ricky promises that he will.

I give Ricky a big hug, which thankfully he returns in kind. Then it's Laurie's turn, and we give each other a hug the likes of which it would be nice if it never actually ended. I can see that she is upset but won't let Ricky see it.

"I love you," Laurie says.

"And I you" is my response.

They go, and I watch my family leave, and it raises my anger level a notch higher.

I'm not a particularly tough guy, and my threats are usually empty, but this time I'm making a silent one that only I know about.

Someone is going to pay for this.

've decided to kill two public relations birds with one stone. I've been neglecting the PR aspect to the Brian Atkins case, which is uncharacteristic of me. I haven't spent any time talking to the public, a major mistake since residing in that public are the people who will make up the jury.

My other goal in utilizing the media is to exercise my self-preservation instinct, as it relates to the threat of Dominic Petrone. I fully trust Marcus, but just in case, I want to take out some insurance.

I invited Vince Sanders to lunch, since I want to break the story in his newspaper. I can't be sure that he'll think it's newsworthy, though I'm quite sure that if I gave it to some other outlet, he would berate me for betraying him.

He's fine having lunch with me because he's a friend and he knows I'll get the check. He would eat horseshit on a bun if he didn't have to pay for it. But that doesn't mean he has to be cheery; he's always going to be Vince.

When he walks in to the diner, the first thing he says is, "You ever tweeter?"

"Do I ever tweeter? You mean, do I tweet? Am I on Twitter?"

"Yeah."

"No, I don't and no, I'm not. Why?"

"The publisher wants me to include tweeters in my stories, like from the general public. So in the middle of the piece, I should include what some dope holed up in his room typing and eating cupcakes says about it."

"Why?"

"Two reasons. One, the publisher is an idiot. Two, he thinks it will make people feel like they're part of the story."

"What did you say?"

"I said they're not part of the story; they're barely part of the human race. But if you care what these idiots have to say, why don't you pay them and put them on staff?"

"What did he say?"

"He said why should he do that if he can get them for free?"

"What did you say?" I ask.

"I said he should take today's edition of the paper and shove it up his ass, and then I walked out."

"How much of what you just told me isn't true?"

"Only the part about shoving the paper up his ass. I just thought of that now."

"Good. Now, can we talk about what I want to talk about?"

"Let's order first," he says, so we do.

Once that's out of the way, he asks me why the hell I dragged him out of his office. "Are we off the record?" I ask.

"Off the record? Are you nuts? What the hell am I doing here if we're off the record?"

"You're being given a scoop, but you're not getting it unless it's on my terms," I say. "And if you don't like that, you can read it in the *Daily News,* and then you can tweeter about it. And you know what? *Daily News* reporters pay for their own goddamn lunch."

He sighs loudly for effect. "You're a pain in the ass. Okay, here's the deal. You say whatever you have to say, the full story, and then you can tell me at the end what's on and off the record, and what I can print."

"Deal. My investigation is showing that Brian Atkins did not murder those two people."

"Wait, let me run back and stop the presses," he says. "I can write the headline now. Legal Shocker: Defense Lawyer Claims Client Is Innocent."

I ignore him and continue. "And I'm going to tell the jury who ordered the killings: Dominic Petrone."

That shuts him up successfully, at least for the moment.

"And one of the reasons I know about Petrone is that he sent two goons to threaten me and tell me to back off."

"When was this?" he asks.

"Sunday, at Giants Stadium."

"The two guys they found unconscious in the parking lot?"

I nod. "Yes."

"Marcus?" he asks.

Another nod from me. "Marcus."

"Can I take Marcus to my next meeting with the publisher?"

I go on to tell Vince the whole story, while not revealing any privileged communications between Brian and me. The other thing I leave out is any mention of Ricky being at the game, or Laurie's and my concern about his well-being.

I tell him that he cannot publish Petrone's name, but he can make references that will make it clear to most people who I am talking about. He also needs to say that I have gone to the police and told them of the threat, the implication being that if I turn up dead, they will know who to go after.

When I'm done, he asks why I'm placing the story. "So the jury pool out there will understand there is another side to the story, and also so Petrone might hesitate to go after me once all this is public."

He thinks about it and says, "You may not be as dumb as you look."

"Thanks."

"It might work," he says.

"I hope so."

"But keep Marcus around just in case."

Jimmy Rollins was the first to come through. The name he gave me was Daniel Bowie, and when I asked if it took much convincing to get him to meet with me, he said it had not.

"What did you tell him?" I asked.

"That you'd bring money."

I don't like to pay for information, but in this case I am making an exception, for two reasons. One is that I figured it would be necessary to get Bowie to talk with me. And two, while taking money would compromise his effectiveness as a witness, I can't foresee a situation where I would actually call him to the stand. All I'm looking for is a road map.

When I called Bowie, he agreed to meet me at his house, but he set the meeting for eight o'clock. He sounded nervous, and I had the feeling that the time was set because it will be dark out when I arrive. Apparently the chance to be seen with the famous Andy Carpenter was not something that he found particularly appealing.

Bowie lives in Clifton, about a block and a half from Nash Park. My high school baseball career was littered with failure, but some of my worst experiences were at Nash Park against Clifton High School. My last pitch there was hit so hard and far that I think it might still be rolling.

It's pouring when I pull up, so I delay getting out of the car for a few minutes in the hope that it will let up. It doesn't, but I'm still glad I waited, because while I'm still sitting there Laurie calls to tell me they've arrived safely at Aunt Celia's.

The call gives Laurie a chance to remind me to be careful five or six more times. It has become her mantra, but I don't complain, because I know that she is upset she can't be here to watch over me.

Bowie seems nervous when he comes to the door, looking around at the street as if he fears someone might be watching. Hopefully the only one out there is Marcus.

Bowie is a smallish guy, maybe five seven and a hundred and fifty pounds. His hair looks like it hasn't been combed since February, though he doesn't have that much of it. He wears a Maryland sweatshirt, along with sweatpants that don't brag about being from any particular university.

He doesn't offer me anything to drink, but does say I can sit in one of the two chairs in the sparsely furnished living room. "You bring the money?" he asks, as a way of breaking the ice.

I nod. "I have a check."

"A check?" His disappointment in my chosen method of payment is clear.

"Right. A check."

He considers this for a moment, and then nods his assent. "Can I have it?"

"Once we talk."

"How come?" he asks, officially getting on my nerves.

"Look, Daniel . . . here's the way it's going to work. We're going to talk, and you're going to honestly answer my questions to the best of your ability. I will then keep your answers in confidence; no one will ever know we talked. I will also give you a check for five thousand dollars for your trouble. If that isn't acceptable to you, then tell me now, and my check and I will leave."

"No . . . it's okay. I'm just being careful."

"I understand. Now, Jimmy Rollins tells me that you've been placing sports wagers on the Internet."

"Yeah."

"This is not one of those offshore books?" I ask.

He shakes his head. "No. This is better."

"Better how?"

"That offshore stuff, you got to put money up to bet. Here you get credit, like with Jimmy."

Traditional bookmakers, like Jimmy Rollins, don't require money up front to place a bet. His customers bet on credit, and then at the end of the month, he and the player settle up. Having credit is preferred by gamblers because it enables them to bet more, and on more games.

"Why didn't you just keep betting with Jimmy?"

"This site has more action. Every kind of prop you can think of."

He's talking about proposition bets, which are different from bets on the outcome of the games themselves. For instance, a proposition bet on a football game might be whether Adrian Peterson gets more than 105 yards rushing in the game. They can get pretty obscure; you can actually bet on the coin toss. For players in need of "action," and my guess is that Bowie falls into this category, proposition bets can be pretty irresistible.

"Show me," I say, and he picks his laptop off the table. He sits at a chair away from the table and, using the word "laptop" literally, he places it on his thighs and starts pressing keys. Within a minute or so, he shows me the site he has gotten to.

I've seen offshore betting sites, and this one has less frills than most. It's a nuts-and-bolts betting site, which would be fine for someone like Bowie. He wouldn't care about the glitz; he'd only be interested in the action.

I copy down the link to get to the site; I want to show it to Sam. Then I ask, "Do you know who runs the site?"

He shakes his head. "Not really; just guys. Scary kinda guys."

"How do you pay and get paid?"

He smiles his first smile. "Get paid? I haven't found that out yet."

I nod my understanding. "Then how do you pay?"

"I put an envelope with cash in my mailbox when they tell me to. It's always at night. They pick it up."

"So you never talk to them?"

"No. They e-mail me. They called me once when I didn't pay on time. That's how I know they're scary."

"I'll need their e-mail addresses."

"But you'll keep me out of it?" he asks, obviously worried.

"I will."

"Okay," he says.

"So you haven't seen them? Could you identify them?"

"No, and I wouldn't if I could," he says.

"When are you due to pay next?"

"Tomorrow night. They said to have it in the mailbox before eight o'clock."

"And will you do that?" I ask.

"If your check clears."

I leave Bowie's house with no better idea whether or not Petrone is behind the gambling Web site he uses. Even if he is, I don't have a way to connect it to the two murders that Brian is accused of.

There are probably better ways to spend five thousand dollars.

MOB CONNECTION TO ATKINS CASE? That is the headline on the top of page one in Vince's newspaper, and I have to admit I couldn't have written it better if I tried. Based on the big block letters, Vince obviously thinks it will sell papers, and I hope and think he's right.

The article is filled with quotes from me, some of which I actually said, and some Vince made up. He had called and cleared the latter quotes with me, and I approved all but two of them.

Basically, the piece says that I have evidence that a local mob boss was behind the murders. I wouldn't name names, and my reason was that it was more appropriate for the jury to hear it first. Anyone who lives in New Jersey and has not been asleep for the last decade will assume that I mean Dominic Petrone.

The article goes on to mention that I've been threatened, without connecting it to the incident at Giants Stadium. I don't want any investigation into what happened to involve Marcus in any way.

I finish the article with a feeling of satisfaction. At least some future jurors will likely read it, which was my main goal. My second goal, that of dissuading Petrone from going after me because of the public attention, may or may not have been achieved. I won't really know that until all this is over; I'll either still be alive, or not.

I'm sort of hoping that I will.

Judge Henry (Hatchet) Henderson is pissed. To make matters even worse, I'm the one he's pissed at. Lawyers are scared to death of Hatchet, and those who have annoyed him have often never been heard from again. You might say that Hatchet is the legal version of Petrone.

But he's got me in his crosshairs, and I knew it was coming. I deliberately antagonized him in order to help my client. I took a bullet for the team.

Hatchet has called the prosecutor, Norman Trell, and me into his chambers for a pretrial conference. I'm the target, but I'm glad Trell is here. This way, he'll be able to tell my loved ones what happened, and where my body is buried.

"So I was reading the newspaper this morning over coffee," Hatchet says. "I like to read the paper; it's the way I learn what evidence I am going to admit at trial."

I don't say anything; one of the anti-Hatchet techniques I have learned is not to volunteer anything, but rather simply to answer questions he asks. He hasn't asked any yet. He will.

"Today's reading was particularly interesting. It said that you, Mr. Carpenter, are going to tell our jury about some mysterious mob connection. I assume you were quoted accurately?"

"More or less, Your Honor. But I never said you were going to admit it. I said I would present it. I meant present it to you, for you to consider. I'm hopeful that you will admit it; I think it is relevant and significant."

"You were talking to prospective jurors," he says.

"Yes, I was."

"You admit it?" he asks, clearly surprised.

"Of course. But I was doing exactly what Mr. Trell was doing when he called a news conference to announce my client's arrest. He was telling the future jurors that Brian Atkins did it, and now I was saying that he didn't. Mr. Trell's press conference was one of the reasons I asked for a change of venue, which Your Honor denied."

Trell sees an opening and says, "I was merely announcing an arrest. It is standard procedure, and is in the public's interest."

I nod. "And I didn't lodge a complaint, or protest in any way. What you did was fine with me, and what I did should be fine with you." I turn to Hatchet. "I believe what I did was proper, Your Honor."

"You are perilously close to annoying me, Mr. Carpenter."

"I'm sorry, Your Honor; that couldn't be further from my intention. There is not a person on the planet I would be less anxious to annoy."

"I'm not going to impose a gag order on this case, but be very careful what you say to the media, or you will wish that I had. And do not ever again force me to read about what is or is not going to take place in my courtroom."

Trell and I both express our agreement with this point of view, and then Hatchet adds, "Have you had settlement discussions?"

"No, Your Honor," Trell says. "My assumption was that the defense had no interest in plea bargaining."

"Oh, but we do," I say. "And now would be a good time, if it's acceptable to Your Honor."

"I would encourage it," Hatchet says.

Trell looks suspicious, as he should be. "I'm willing to listen, but he murdered two people in cold blood. What do you have in mind?"

"One year on the escape charge."

"That's it?" Trell asks. "No plea on the murders?"

"That's it."

"Why should we agree to that?"

"Because this trial is about the murders. We acknowledge that he escaped, and that he should be punished for it. But it will only clutter up the trial, and is unnecessary for the jury to deal with."

Hatchet nods. "Cleaner is better."

Trell is unconvinced. "The jury needs to know that he escaped from prison."

What Trell really wants to make sure is that the jury knows Brian was in prison in the first place. They will assume that the jury that put him there was correct, and that he is a criminal. But we were never going to keep that out anyway, so there's no sense fighting that battle.

"We'll stipulate that he was in prison, and that he escaped," I say. "Your Honor can announce that at the beginning of the trial."

Hatchet nods and says, "Mr. Trell?"

"I'm not sure about this."

"Look," I say. "We all know he escaped. Our position is he did so to prevent the deaths, and your position is that he did so to cause them. If you're right, then he's going away forever, and the year we're talking about doesn't matter. If we're right, and the jury agrees, he shouldn't have to spend an extra minute on the inside."

Trell thinks about it for a few moments, and then nods. "Agreed."

Hatchet smiles. "I'm glad we had this meeting."

I don't usually try to arrange "alone time" with Marcus. I've had to be with him in a car a number of times, including a couple of stakeouts, as well as a long drive to Maine on a case. A "Marcus minute" feels like an hour. It's as if there's a hand grenade on the seat next to me; it never says a word, and I'm always afraid it might explode and kill me.

Tonight we're alone in the car, because that's the only way this will work. We're parked on the Clifton Street where Daniel Bowie lives, with a sight line to the mailbox in front of his house. He said that the people he gambles with online will be there to pick up his cash payment for the money he has lost.

We're going to be here to watch it happen.

At ten minutes to eight, Bowie comes out of his house, an envelope in his hand. I'm sure he has cash in there, and that it came from the money I gave him to talk to us. It wasn't my proudest moment, but without having done so we wouldn't be here. It remains to be seen whether that is a good or bad thing.

Bowie puts the envelope in the mailbox, and then goes back in the house. For the next half hour, absolutely nothing happens outside or inside the car. I speak four words: "I hope they're coming." Marcus says one word, but I can't make it out. It sounds like "Drruh."

At about eight thirty, an SUV—it's a dark color but I can't tell in the darkness if it's black—comes down the road and slows to a stop in front of Bowie's house. It appears as if there is only the driver in the car, but it's hard to know for sure.

He gets out of the car, leaving it running with the lights on. He doesn't bother to close the door as he walks the few steps to the mailbox, quickly opening it and taking out the package. He does not look around as he does so, obviously not afraid that he is being watched. All he does is get back in the car and drive off.

And we follow him, for two hours, as he makes eighteen more stops throughout North Jersey. At nine of the stops he takes an envelope out of the mailbox, and at the other nine he puts an envelope into it. If half the people are winning on their bets rather than losing, they're better at it than I am.

We get close enough at one point to see the license plate number on the car, and I call Sam. I could have called Pete for the favor, but then I would have had to answer too many questions.

"Sam, if I give you a license plate number, can you get me the name and address of the car owner?"

"You insult me by even asking the question," he says. "I'll just get it off the DMV computer."

The access he has to this stuff amazes me. I give him the plate number and ask, "You want to call me back?"

"No, hold on a second," he says.

It takes more than a second, more like three minutes, but he gets back on the line. "Nicholas Winters, 551 Seventeenth Avenue, in Passaic."

"That was fast, even for you," I say.

"No big deal. I was on their computer this afternoon, fixing a speeding ticket. So I knew my way around."

"You can fix speeding tickets?"

"Sure. You got one?"

"Not exactly. I went through a stop sign," I say.

"Same difference; I'm on it."

"Before you do, can you find out whatever you can about Nicholas Winters? Let me know tomorrow."

"You got it."

There's no telling how many stops Winters is going to make tonight, but following him any more won't help us. We've seen all we need to see, and we have no way to get near him. When he makes one of the stops, if we pulled up he'd see us coming, and have time to react.

So instead we go to his home in Passaic. There's always a chance he won't return here tonight, but we're betting that he will. It's our only chance to get to him.

We park down the street, within sight of the house. Marcus gets out, leaving me alone in the car on the very dark street. It turns out that the only thing I like less in these situations than being alone with Marcus is being alone without Marcus.

Marcus mutters that he'll call me, and heads for the house. He disappears in the darkness, and I can't see him. At this point I am not having much fun.

Maybe a dozen cars go by in the next forty-five minutes, until finally I see Winters pull up to his house. He parks in front, rather than in his garage. I don't know where Marcus is, so I can't say whether that's a good thing or a bad thing.

Five frustrating and scary minutes go by without anything happening, or at least anything I know about. I hope Marcus is okay, even as I know Marcus is okay. He is, after all, the son of Jor-El.

Suddenly my phone rings. I guess the first ring of a phone by definition always happens "suddenly," but this one more so than most. It sounds so loud and shocking in my car that it feels like everyone with ten miles must hear it.

"Hello?"

It's Marcus, grunting something unintelligible into the phone. It could be anything from "come here" to "call 911"; I simply cannot make it out.

"You want me to come there?" I ask.

"Yunh."

I'm going to take that as a yes, but I'm going to press him for details. "In the car?" I ask, but he's already hung up.

It's decision time; I have to decide what to do. My first choice would be to go home and hide under the covers, but that's not feasible at the moment. I do not want to walk down this dark street alone, although I have no reason to think anyone would threaten me, since there doesn't appear to be anyone around.

I make up my mind and drive to the house, headlights off, and park in front of it. I get out and walk to the front door, since it is open. There are a few lights on inside the house, but I don't hear any noise.

I go inside, not because I want to, but because I can't figure out any alternative. I head to the room with the most light, and it turns out to be the kitchen.

And that's where I find them.

Marcus and Winters are in a large open area in the center of the room. They're not exactly sitting at the table having coffee and croissants.

Winters is a large man, considerably larger than Marcus. I wouldn't want to guess at his height, because he's not standing up. He's lying on the floor, on his back, hands spread out. On the floor next to him is a plastic bag, probably filled with the night's take.

Marcus is casually sitting on his chest, not straddling over him, but sitting with his legs to the side, as if he is on a bench waiting for a bus.

Marcus sees me and gets to his feet. Winters doesn't move or say anything, and that becomes more understandable when I see that he is unconscious. I don't see a welt or bruise on his face; it's possible that Marcus just scared him into oblivion.

"Is he alive?" I ask, but Marcus doesn't answer. Instead, he goes to the sink, and fills a glass with cold water. He walks over and pours it onto Winters's face and head. It doesn't jolt him into consciousness, so Marcus does it again.

While Marcus is attempting to revive the guy, I answer a phone call from Sam. He's searched for online information about Winters, and says he's found four separate stories that allege he works for the Petrone "family."

I'll have Laurie reconfirm this with her police sources, but I have no doubt it will turn out to be the case. I'm elated by it, because it is my first concrete proof tying Petrone to the online world, in this case running the gambling site that Bowie uses.

When I get off the phone, Winters still hasn't come to. Another five minutes go by, during which I'm wondering if I have a moral and legal obligation to call an ambulance. Finally I see some movement, and over the next five minutes Winters goes through various stages of grogginess until he regains coherence.

He focuses on me, even before Marcus, and starts to get up. That doesn't work out for him, because Marcus comes over and puts his foot on his chest, keeping him in place.

"Who are you?" he asks me.

"Doesn't matter," I say, not wanting to give my name. "What were you doing tonight?"

"None of your business."

Marcus must be increasing the pressure on his chest, because Winters moans and puts his hand up in a gesture of conceding. He gasps out, "Hey, man, I can't breathe."

"What were you doing tonight?" I ask again, even though it didn't get me anywhere the first time.

"Doing my job."

"Assuming you like breathing, you might want to be a little more responsive," I say. "What was the job you were doing?"

"I was collecting and dropping stuff off."

"For who?"

"My bosses."

"Petrone and Russo," I say.

"You said that, I didn't."

Marcus puts some more pressure on, and Winters says, "Come on, I don't know who's up the damn ladder. Some guys hire me to do this. I'm a messenger boy. I mention names and they'll kill me. You might as well kill me now."

"How much do messenger boys make these days?" I ask.

"Enough."

"You're starting to get on his nerves," I say, pointing to Marcus.

"Five grand a week."

"How many nights do you work?"

"Two," he says.

"Five thousand dollars for two nights?"

"Yeah. What do you guys want?"

I pick up the plastic bag and open it. "Five thousand dollars," I say. "A week's pay."

"I can't go back to them with less. You know what they'll do?"

"File a grievance? Cut off your health insurance? Not contribute to your 401(k)?"

"What the hell are you talking about? They'll beat the shit out of me."

"Then replace the money out of your own pocket," I say. "Because here's the deal: None of this happened. If you mention a word of it to your bosses, I will put out the word that you told us you were working for Dominic Petrone and Joseph Russo. Which will in turn affect your job security and your life."

Winters agrees to our terms, maybe because he understands the logic, or maybe because he wants Marcus off his chest and out of his life. Whether he'll follow through on the agreement is anyone's guess.

I'll find out soon enough. But whatever happens, I got my five thousand dollars back.

haven't been to see Brian as often as I should. That's mostly because he's not new in his surroundings, and therefore not as freaked out about them. Most clients of mine aren't prisoners at the time they allegedly commit their crimes. He's a smart, levelheaded guy, and probably needs reassurance and hand-holding less than most.

There's probably also a psychological component to my not being there often, and it's one I'm not proud of. I like to be able to convey some good news, some developments that can foster hope, but I really haven't had any to offer, so I subconsciously resisted talking with him.

"I'm glad you came," he says, when he's finally brought in. "I was going to call you."

"What's up?"

"That's what I want to know. I've been reading about you pointing the finger at a mob guy; I assume you mean Petrone?"

"Yes. I think he's behind it. But I'm a long way from having the evidence to present it to a jury."

He shakes his head, a little sadly. "Just like Denise said. And he threatened you?"

"He did."

"Be careful, Andy. He's a dangerous guy."

"Really? I wasn't aware of that. You got a pen? I'll make a note of it."

He laughs. "Always glad to help." Then, "What is Petrone doing in this? Why would he want to kill Gerry and Denise?"

"I've come to ask you the same question. Petrone is somehow using the technology your company had to make a profit. For one thing, he's running a gambling Web site."

"You mean sports gambling?"

"Yes, and casino games are possible as well. Why would he need Starlight for that?"

Brian thinks for a few moments. "He wouldn't. It's just not a big deal for computers to handle. Those sites have existed for years."

"But not locally," I say.

He nods. "That's because they would be easy to find and shut down."

"Would your servers make them any harder to find?"

"Not to my knowledge; we were just about speed. Nanoseconds shouldn't matter in gambling. But I've been in here three years; there could be developments I don't know about. Did you talk to Jason Mathers?"

"Yes, but not about this; I'm going to talk with him again. He doesn't work at Starlight anymore. He quit when Ted Yates got the top job."

Brian nods his understanding. "It's like I told you: Yates is a politician. If Mathers didn't quit, Yates would have found a way to get rid of him. Eliminating threats."

"Which also happens to be Petrone's specialty; they just use different tactics."

"But if Petrone was using Starlight's servers for illegal gambling, it still makes no sense that he would murder Gerry and Denise. There is no chance Gerry would have gone to the cops with what he knew; how could he have been a threat to Petrone?"

It's the question I've been asking myself, and all I have are a couple of possible theories. "If Gerry was in bed with Petrone on the gambling site, Petrone wouldn't have turned on him unless he didn't need him anymore and wanted to get rid of him. Or unless Petrone was expanding into areas Gerry wanted no part of."

"Could be money laundering," Brian says. "Criminals have used the Internet for that purpose before."

"How do they do it?"

"I'm sure there are a lot of ways, but, for example, they set up an online auction, and then overpay for the item themselves, or maybe the item never existed. The money moves, lots of it, but it's going from one of their pockets to the other."

It makes sense to me, but then the idea runs into a brick Internet wall. "But why would they need Gerry and Starlight?" I ask.

"Andy, I just don't know."

When I leave the prison, I call Jason Mathers and tell him I need to speak with him again. He's home at his apartment in Edgewater, and tells me I can come right over.

"I appreciate it," I say.

"Hey, I've got nothing better to do. I'm unemployed, remember?"

"I remember," I say. What I don't say is that I also remember when I was unemployed, just last month. I remember it fondly.

Carpenter has to be taken care of," Dominic Petrone said. He spoke in a casual tone, as if it were a minor issue, certainly not worthy of debate. Of course, very little of what Petrone said was subject to debate or disagreement.

But this was different.

Joseph Russo had been taking orders from Petrone literally since he was fourteen years old. He had reached a point where he occasionally could and did voice disagreement and try to reason with his boss. It didn't happen often, and he quite rarely succeeded in persuading Petrone to reconsider his position. Usually he just backed down and went along.

But this was different.

"Dominic, the guy just announced to the world that we were threatening to kill him. We do it now and they'll be all over us. We've got more important things to worry about now."

"He is a threat to us, Joseph, and we must deal with him as we deal with all threats. Down the road it may be too late; he might have learned and revealed too much."

"He knows nothing. And when the trial is over, he will disappear and move on to his next case. If we kill him, it will draw too much attention to us and what we're doing."

"We've had their attention before, and yet we're at the peak of our strength. Are you saying you can't get this done?"

Russo knew he could get it done. But what he also knew was that while Petrone's name would be front and center, Russo would be in the line of legal fire. He would directly order the hit, and his fingerprints would be on it, far more than Petrone's.

"Of course I can get it done. I'm talking about whether we should, not whether we can. Let me think about it, Dominic. Please."

Petrone smiled. "There was a time, not that long ago, that you left the thinking to me, and trusted that it would be right."

"Nothing has changed, Dominic, you know that. I trust your judgment completely. You are the boss."

"Then don't think about it," Petrone said. "Do it."

Jason Mathers doesn't seem to be pounding the pavement looking for work. He greets me at the door to his apartment wearing pretty much the same outfit he had on last time: jeans, sneakers, and a sweatshirt. Last time it was an Arizona State sweatshirt, and this time it's Stanford, so he's at least working his way up the intellectual ladder.

But his attitude is similarly casual and unstressed, the sign of a man who is enjoying the freedom that having lots and lots of money can bring. "What can I do for you this time?" he asks.

"I just need more information about the Starlight computer servers," I say.

"There's a limit on what I can tell you," he says.

"Why?"

"When I left I signed a confidentiality agreement. I had to do it in order to get my payout."

"You got a lot of money for leaving?"

He smiles broadly. "Ain't this a great country?"

I agree that the country is great, though it seems greater for Mathers than for somebody like, say, Brian Atkins. "I have reason to believe that certain people, utilizing the Starlight servers and routers, have set up a Web site to take sports bets."

He shakes his head. "No chance, unless they did it in the last couple of days. Otherwise I would have known about it."

"It's not possible?"

"Not possible."

"Hear me out," I say. "Assume for the moment that it happened, and is happening, and for some reason you didn't see it."

"Okay," he says, clearly dubious that this hypothetical is going anywhere. "Then what?"

"Then why would they need the Starlight machines? What would they do for them that they couldn't have done on their own?"

"Nothing. Anyone can set up a gambling Web site. You're going off on a tangent that is not going to get you anywhere. It doesn't make sense, and it didn't happen."

"I saw it myself," I say, "and I can show it to you."

He points to one of his computers. "Be my guest."

I sit down in front of the computer and type the Web address that Bowie showed me, and instantly a message comes up that the page can't be opened, because it doesn't exist.

"It existed a couple of days ago," I say. Since I promised Bowie I would keep our conversation confidential, I don't mention his name.

"A lot of these things are rip-offs," Mathers says, "so they appear and disappear all the time."

Mathers has nothing more for me; he swears that the Starlight machines could not have been used for gambling on his watch, that he would have known about it.

Before I leave, I say, "At some point I may need an expert tech witness to testify at trial. Would you be willing to do that?"

He doesn't hesitate. "If it helps Brian, then I'm there."

I leave and call Daniel Bowie; I want to set up another meeting and see if his computer can still access the site. He doesn't answer the phone, so I make a note to try again later.

I turn on the news and hear about an execution-style killing in Clifton, the body having turned up in Nash Park. Before they even mention the name of the victim, I know who it is going to be . . . Daniel Bowie.

The announcer says the police do not yet have a suspect or a motive, but I know who is most responsible for the killing.

I am.

I call Sam and tell him about the disappearance of the betting site. He tries it himself when he's on the phone with me and gets the same result. "They must have taken it down," he says. Then, "You sure you got the address right?"

"I'm sure. My technology ability extends to being able to copy down an address."

"Nothing I can do then," he says. "It could just be down, so I'll try it again later. Who gave you this address? I could talk to them directly."

"No, that's not possible right now," I say, leaving out the part about Daniel Bowie being the one who gave it to me, and then dying because he did.

As soon as I hang up, I get another call, and I see that it's Jimmy Rollins. It's a conversation that I'm dreading, but one I should have instigated by calling him first.

"Andy, you heard about Daniel Bowie?"

"I did, Jimmy. I was going to call you."

"Am I the reason he was killed?" he asked.

I thought he would be accusatory, and in fact he should be. But instead he's feeling guilty himself. "No, Jimmy, you're not."

"Are you?"

"I don't think so, but I don't know for sure. I know that I did not tell anyone he and I talked, and no one saw me talking with him. I'm positive of that. It's possible that he told someone that he shouldn't have; there's no way for me to know that."

"But even if he told someone, why should talking to you have gotten him killed?"

"Jimmy, if I knew that, I'd know everything."

I no sooner get off that call than I get another; I think I need a switchboard operator. This time it's Laurie, and once she tells me that she and Ricky are fine, I quickly start to bring her up to date on what has been happening, or not happening, as the case may be.

She stops me. "Andy, I don't have time now; you can tell me all about it when I see you."

"When will that be?"

"In about four hours; I'm heading for the airport. Can you meet me?"

"What about Ricky?" I ask.

"He's fine, Andy. He loves it here, and he loves Celia. Besides, she's got two neighbors that have boys Ricky's age. They get along great; he won't even notice I'm gone."

Laurie's plane is ten minutes early, and I'm at baggage claim when she arrives. I've known that I love her for a very long time, but I'm still struck by how I feel when I first see her. It's a feeling I hope I never outgrow.

I wait until we get in the car to bring her up to date on the case. When I get to Daniel Bowie, I say, "It can't be a coincidence that he was killed right after he spoke to me. I'm the reason he's dead."

"Don't go there, Andy. You didn't kill him."

"Here's what you can add to the list of things I don't understand. When Marcus roughed up the guy who was collecting betting losses—"

She interrupts. "Nicholas Winters."

"Right. We threatened him that if he told anyone about it, we would put out the word that he ratted out Petrone and Russo. He said he wouldn't."

"He was under some duress at the time, right? Like Marcus's kind of duress? Maybe he just said it to get you out of there."

I nod. "Very possible; let's assume he did. But how would they have traced it back to Bowie? We never mentioned Bowie, and Bowie was one of probably twenty stops Winters made that night. How could they have known that Bowie was the one we talked to?"

"Maybe he was under some kind of surveillance."

"But why would that be?" I ask. "The only way we came to Bowie was because Jimmy Rollins lost him as a client. It was random; there's no way Petrone's people could have known that. And betting sites need a lot of customers to make it worth their while to operate; they couldn't be watching all of them."

"Maybe your phones at the office are tapped, or maybe ours at home. We need to have it checked."

She immediately makes a phone call to a former friend on the police force who has helped us out before. He promises to immediately check out both sets of phones and report back if there is any problem.

As we're nearing home, Richard Wallace calls me to say that he has convinced Linda Westman, widow of suicide victim Joseph Westman, to talk to me. At this point it has the most tenuous connection to our case; Joseph Westman happened to speak with Gerry Wright a few times the week of the murders.

Richard says that I can head over there now, but to understand that Mrs. Westman is still devastated, and not particularly talkative.

When I hang up, I ask Laurie, "You want to go with me to comfort a grieving widow?"

She sighs, probably for effect. "It's good to be home."

It can be argued that Central Park West has it all. Stretching north for fifty-one blocks from Fifty-ninth Street, it is all residential, so those living there do not have to put up with the swarm of shoppers that other New Yorkers do.

But CPW is only one block from Columbus Avenue, two blocks from Amsterdam Avenue, and three blocks from Broadway, which means that shopping is convenient, and the excitement of the city is within an easy walk. You can live in an expensive, exclusive neighborhood, and still go downstairs at midnight and get a piece of pizza. Try that in Scarsdale.

If you throw in the fact that directly across the street is the grandeur and beauty of Central Park, an oasis of green in the cement city, CPW is, for many, hard to beat.

Of course, it wasn't quite enough for Joseph Westman. Though he lived in the Dakota, perhaps the most prestigious building in all of New York, on Seventy-second and Central Park West, he still came to the conclusion that he was better off smashing his car at high speed into a tree.

The Dakota has been home to countless celebrities, but its greatest and most dubious claim to fame is that it is where John Lennon lived and died, having been shot downstairs when returning home.

The Westman suicide is far less embarrassing for the building and its residents. Of course, if he had taken a nosedive from his eighth-floor apartment, that would have created more of a stir for the Dakota than driving into an upstate New York tree.

Laurie and I park in a ridiculously expensive lot on Columbus and walk to the Dakota. The doorman wears white gloves, which I guess is designed to make things classier. The amazing thing is that he keeps them white, even though I'm sure he helps with luggage and opening cab or limousine doors. He must have an extra glove supply stashed away that allows him to keep changing them.

Linda Westman has left instructions that it's okay to send us up, and as we head for the elevator, he calls to tell her we're on the way. When we get up to her eighth-floor apartment, she greets us cordially, but without enthusiasm. This is a woman who has had the energy sucked out of her by tragedy; one look at her tells us that she is grieving and in pain.

Laurie tells her how sorry we are for her loss, and Mrs. Westman's reply is, "I'm sorry it took so long to see you; things have not been easy. But Mr. Wallace said that it was important."

"Thank you," I say. "It may well be important; that will really depend on what we learn from you."

"I'll help in any way I can."

There's no easy way to say this, so I just go ahead and tell the truth. "The newspaper said that your husband was afraid he would go to prison because of his involvement in child pornography."

She nods. "Yes. My understanding is that he never participated in the creation of it, nor did he ever abuse any children." She takes a deep breath; this is obviously extraordinarily hard for her to talk about. "But he was a consumer of that trash; there can be no doubt about that."

"Do you know how long that went on?"

She shakes her head. "I don't. I know this may be hard to believe, but I only became aware of it the day before Joseph's death.

And even then I did not understand the extent of it." She starts to dab at her eyes with a tissue.

"I'm sorry," Laurie says. "I can only imagine how hard this must be."

"With all respect, I suspect it's beyond what you can imagine."

"Does the name Gerry Wright mean anything to you?" I ask.

"It sounds familiar, but I can't place it."

"Your husband never mentioned him?"

"Not that I can recall."

"Do you know what made your husband think he was a target of the police, or that they even knew about what he was doing?" I ask.

She shakes her head. "I don't. I only know that he sat me down and said that he had something to tell me, something horrible. And he told me, and he cried, and said he couldn't help himself. And that he had kept the secret for so long, from me and everyone else, and that it was not a secret any longer. He said that he believed he would go to jail for what he had done."

"That's all he said about it?"

She nods. "Yes. He was growing increasingly irrational those last few weeks. I should have seen it, but maybe I refused to. He was a troubled man, but he retained a talent for hiding those troubles until the end. And I obviously retained my talent for denial."

She pauses to do a bit more reflecting and eye dabbing. "Anyway, the day after he told me, he went off to work, and I never saw him again. The police confirmed that the trash was on his computer, but thankfully I never actually saw any of it."

We ask her some more questions, but she really has nothing more to offer. This is a woman whose entire world has just been shattered, but there is also a strength that comes through loud and clear. She'll get through this, but it won't be easy.

And if any of this is related to our case, I don't see how.

As we're getting ready to leave, she asks what it is we are trying to connect to her husband's death.

"He spoke to Gerry Wright a few times in the weeks before he died. Gerry Wright was himself murdered; perhaps you read about it."

She shakes her head to indicate that she had not. "Good luck," she says. "I hope I was helpful."

"You were very helpful," I lie.

I ask that you do one thing . . . follow the facts, not the words." That is now Norman Trell begins his opening statement to the jury. We've empaneled twelve people who wanted to be here enough that they didn't lie during voir dire to get out of it. There are seven men and five women, eight whites, three African-Americans, and one Hispanic. I agreed that each of them could be on the panel, and yet I don't have a clue what they might be thinking going in.

"The facts are going to be easy. As Judge Henderson has already told you, one of those facts has been agreed to by both the prosecution and defense. It is an undisputed fact that Brian Atkins broke out of jail three hours before Gerald Wright and Denise Atkins were brutally murdered. You don't have to conclude that, it has been stipulated to, so it is a given.

"There are other facts that we will bring forward that the defense will, of course, differ with. Those are the areas in which you will be called upon to exercise your reason and judgment. When you do so, please differentiate between hard evidence and mere words and theories.

"We will demonstrate, through clear and convincing evidence, that once Brian Atkins engineered his escape, he stole a car. Then he drove to the house of his former partner, Gerald Wright, where he found Mr. Wright and his own wife.

"Shortly after that, an eyewitness saw him leaving the house, rushing to his car, and fleeing the scene. That same eyewitness then entered the house and discovered the carnage.

"So this is not a whodunit, and it is not even a why-dunit. Brian Atkins was enraged, both at the partner who helped put him behind bars, and the wife who jilted him. But in this county, in this state, in this country, you don't get to kill people you happen to be mad at.

"So those are the facts you will hear, supported by the evidence. But you will also hear words, supported by theories. You will hear from the defense that a sinister, criminal element is behind all of this.

"Straw men will be created, to fool you into not seeing this for what it is: a convict bent on revenge, taking matters into his own hands, committing a horrible act.

"Words and facts. Facts and words. Please keep in mind, as I know you will, that there is a difference."

Hatchet asks me if I want to give my opening statement now, or wait until it's time to present the defense's case. As I always do, I opt not to wait.

I never write out my statements in advance; I find it's better when I simply know what points I want to make, without restricting myself to a set speech. That allows me to react spontaneously to what else has been said in the courtroom, which is what I do now.

"Mr. Trell is right that we agree on the fact that Brian Atkins escaped from prison. But he is wrong when he says that is the only thing we agree on. We also agree that facts matter more than words.

"But as it relates to why you are here, the murders of Denise Atkins and Gerald Wright, words are all he is going to give you. There is no eyewitness testimony to the killings. There is, in fact, no forensics evidence that Brian Atkins is guilty of this horrendous crime. Yes, let me repeat that, you will not see a single shred of forensics evidence pointing to Mr. Atkins's guilt.

"So you will be presented with facts and words, and you will have to determine which is which. That's your job; it's why you're here. But there is something you have, which everyone has brought with you today, that will help you make your decision.

"It is logic. No one asked you to check your logic at the door when you entered this courtroom. Your ability to reason is what makes you human, and it is what makes humans good jurors.

"Brian Atkins did not kill those two people. That is what I am telling you today, right now, standing here. When this trial has concluded, you may agree with me, or not, but I submit that you will at least have a reasonable doubt as to his guilt.

"So listen to the words, look at the facts, and use your logical minds to decide what weight to give all of it. That's all I ask. Thank you."

Brian smiles when I head back to the defense table. "Thank you," he says, and shakes my hand when I get there. He's feeling good, because someone has finally risen to his defense and said something supportive.

I'm glad he feels that way, but he'd better hang on to it, because it's going to be a while before he feels that way again. It's going to be downhill from here.

Hatchet turns to Trell and says the chilling words that are going to start our descent. "Call your first witness."

For the first time in as long as he could remember, Joseph Russo was worried. He had been in dangerous situations before; his work life was defined by dangerous situations. But somehow they always felt within his control, as though through guts or toughness or smarts he could survive and triumph. This time was different.

He wasn't panicked, not even close. He always survived and advanced, and he would again; this time was no different. But this time he couldn't yet see the path that it would take, and for the first time, he didn't have full confidence in the person choosing that path.

Russo had always had complete faith in Dominic Petrone. He never questioned his confidence in Petrone, never had come close to doing so, and it had ultimately served him well. Petrone was smart, brilliant in fact, and Russo had always been in awe of that. He felt Petrone combined smarts and toughness in such a way that he could have, and should have, been president of the United States, had he chosen a very different career path.

Actually, were Russo to think about that some more, he would have realized that Petrone could not have put up with the bullshit that went with the presidency. Too much trying to get other people to go along, too much compromise. That was not Petrone's way.

But Petrone's way was changing. He had always been content

to dominate within his sphere of influence, and let others do the same within theirs. But he had been presented with this opportunity and had grabbed it.

Part of his explanation and reasoning was that if he hadn't done so, someone else would have. It would have put Petrone in the same position that he is now putting others. But Russo didn't buy that, not for a second, and it made him uncomfortable to have these feelings of borderline disloyalty.

Worse yet, Russo had been made the front man for the operation. He knew that it was because he was the person Petrone most trusted and had confidence in, and in a way he relished the power and prominence it gave him.

But with the prominence came vulnerability; Petrone was making some serious enemies and Russo would be in their crosshairs. That's the way it had always been; the stakes were just much higher now.

Recently added to the equation was Andy Carpenter. Russo felt he should be ignored; he was a smart guy, but he'd never figure out what was going on. Sending the two guys to scare him off at the Giants game had been a mistake, and now it was a public one.

But now Petrone was telling Russo to compound that mistake. He didn't want Carpenter threatened, he wanted him dead. And Russo thought that was a terrible idea.

It led to Russo paying a visit to Willie Miller. Russo didn't have many soft spots, but he had one for Willie. Of course, Willie had earned it by beating the shit out of three guys out to kill Russo in prison. Willie was a stand-up guy, and Russo owed him big-time. That would never change.

Russo and two of his guys showed up at the Tara Foundation building in Haledon. They walked in and found Willie on the floor in the main play area, wrestling with six dogs and having them fetch balls and toys.

When he saw Russo, he lit up. "Joey, how's it going?"

"You still doing this?" Russo asked. "What the hell is it with you and dogs?"

"They're the best," Willie said. "When they're your friend, it's for life."

The dogs were barking loudly, and Russo said he wanted to talk to Willie alone, where they could hear. So Willie took him back to the office where potential adopters filled out their applications.

When they got back there, Russo said, "Willie, I'm telling you this because you're a good guy. Your boss is causing trouble."

"My boss?"

"Carpenter."

"Oh, he's not my boss. We're partners."

"Doesn't matter. He's causing trouble."

"What kind of trouble?"

"He'll know what I'm talking about when you tell him to lay off."

"He wouldn't listen even if I told him, which I won't."

"Don't get on the wrong side of this, Willie."

"I know Andy pretty well, and I've never seen him on the wrong side."

Russo looked at him, sizing him up, although he already knew what he was going to find. Willie Miller, unlike just about everybody else that Russo dealt with, was simply not afraid of him.

"Take care, my man," Russo said.

"You too, Joey."

Russo left the office and went into the main area, only to find his two men having assumed the Willie Miller role of playing with the dogs and throwing tennis balls.

"You got to be kidding," Russo said.

Trell starts off by making a tactical mistake. At least that's my opinion. He calls Donnie Thigpen to the stand, an unusual choice at best. Thigpen currently resides in the state penitentiary, and will be spending at least the next ten years there for aggravated assault.

Most prosecutors will first call witnesses whose testimony, if not crucial, is ironclad and immune to serious challenge on cross-examination. You want to give the feeling that you are confident in your case and that you have your act together.

Prison squealers are notoriously unreliable and unlikely to be trusted by juries. Just as Trell thinks the jury will look down on Brian for having been in prison, they will likely look down on Thigpen for the same reason. But Trell clearly wants to go with motive first, and that's why he made this call.

"Mr. Thigpen, where are you currently living?" Trell wants to be open and upfront about this, though he really has no choice.

"The state prison."

"Why are you there?"

"I was convicted of assault."

"During your time there, did you have occasion to know and speak to the defendant, Brian Atkins?"

"Yes, a bunch of times."

"Where did those conversations take place?"

"In the mess, the yard, the gym . . . a bunch of places."

"Would you describe your relationship as friendly?"

"Sure. Yeah. I guess so."

"Did you speak with Mr. Atkins in the days before his escape?" Trell asks, as if he didn't know the answer.

"Yeah, he said his wife had dumped him. She was screwing around with his ex-partner and he was pissed about it."

Trell keeps him on the stand for another ten minutes, breaking the indoor record for most consecutive times asking the same question, but Thigpen basically has nothing more to add.

He finally turns him over to me. Brian has told me that he doesn't remember ever speaking to the guy, and I assume that's true, though I don't know it for certain. Whether Thigpen is testifying truthfully or not, I can still challenge him.

"Mr. Thigpen, you said you were convicted of assault."

"Right."

"Were you guilty?"

He delays answering for a few moments. I doubt he's trying to remember whether he committed the assault or not; he's just trying to figure out which answer will play best and cause him the least harm.

"No."

"The jury was wrong?" I ask.

"They said what they thought."

"And what they thought, that you were guilty, was wrong?" I ask.

"Yeah. It was wrong." Hopefully this jury will be insulted on behalf of Thigpen's jury, but it's a small victory.

Thigpen continues. "And I've been a model prisoner; that's why they moved me to minimum security."

"Congratulations. All of us, except maybe the woman you threw down the stairs, are happy for you."

"Objection," Trell screams, propelled out of his chair.

"Sustained." Hatchet looks sternly at me. "Be careful, Mr. Carpenter."

"Certainly, Your Honor. Mr. Thigpen, you say that Mr. Atkins confided in you regarding his feelings about his wife."

"Yeah."

"So you were close friends? You shared intimate details about your lives?"

"We talked, yeah."

"What else did he tell you?"

"About what?"

"About his life," I say.

Thigpen is wary and clearly worried. "I don't know what you mean."

"For example, where did he go to college? Did he and his wife have any children? Was he married before? Before he was in prison, did he wear boxers or briefs? That kind of thing."

He shakes his head. "I don't remember him saying any of that stuff."

"What do you remember?"

"Just what I said."

"That's it? He approached you in the prison one day, having told you nothing about his life before, and volunteered that he was angry at his wife and ex-partner?"

"Right. That's what happened."

"Mr. Thigpen, did you testify at your own trial?"

"No, my lawyer wouldn't let me. That's why I got myself a new lawyer."

"So this is your first time testifying in front of a jury?"

"No, I've been in other trials."

"Is it true you've testified for the prosecution in three different cases, each time claiming that the defendant in those cases confided incriminating information to you?"

"Yeah, I'm an easy guy to talk to," he says.

"A regular Dr. Phil," I say. Trell objects, and Hatchet sustains. "No further questions."

They don't even get the Giants games on TV. They get the Packers," Ricky says. "And they wear these cheese things on their heads, and they think Aaron Rodgers is better than Eli Manning." Ricky is obviously still trying to adjust to life in Wisconsin.

"They know not of what they speak, Rick." I say this even though when it comes to the Rodgers/Manning comparison, they unfortunately know exactly of what they speak.

"Ask them how many Super Bowl rings Rodgers has," I say.

"How many does he have?"

"One. Eli has two."

"Great. That's a good one. What about the cheese on their heads?"

"That I can't help you with. Here's Mom."

I give the phone to Laurie; I really enjoy the morning calls from Ricky, especially since Laurie's friend has told us that our phones are not tapped.

Sending him to Wisconsin was a tough call, but it was the right one. Laurie has friends on the police force up there who are keeping an unobtrusive eye on him and have not reported anything unusual. In that small a town, strangers would stand out, especially the kind of strangers that would work for Petrone.

Hatchet has announced that he had a commitment that would

prevent court from starting until 11:00 A.M. today. It might be a doctor's appointment, though that would indicate that Hatchet is human, so it must be something else.

In any event, it gives me a chance to take Tara and Sebastian for a longer walk than usual. We pretty much cover Eastside Park, which is empty this time of year. It's supposed to snow later, and I hope it does. Watching them play and roll over in the snow is one of my favorite things to do. As always, I don't see Marcus, but I take comfort in the knowledge that he's out there, watching.

Though she would growl and never admit it if I said it to her face, having Sebastian in the house has made Tara younger and more active. I thought she might react badly to no longer being the only dog, but she hasn't. It might be because she knows she'll always be my favorite. Sebastian, for his part, seems okay with that.

When I get home, Laurie says that Willie called to report that Joseph Russo told him to tell me to lay off. I'm not happy about it, but I'm sort of surprised that Russo handled it in that manner. To me it seems uncharacteristically weak and ineffectual, and I know plenty about weak and ineffectual.

I go into the kitchen to feed the dogs, and I hear the doorbell ring. Laurie yells out that she'll get it, so I finish the feeding and then go to see who it is.

Marcus and Laurie are in the den, and on the table next to them is a bag about the size of a plastic grocery bag. It seems to be made of nylon, or some synthetic fabric. "What's going on?" I say. My hope is that Laurie will be the one to respond, since she's the only one of the two that I can understand.

She does. "After you left last night, Marcus went looking for Winters as he picked up and left betting winnings. A lot of the places he stopped were the same as the night you followed him, so he was easy to track."

As she talks, I realize that the bag looks like the one Winters deposited in some mailboxes that night.

"He put this in one of the mailboxes, and Marcus decided to

get a closer look at it. It isn't filled with money; it's filled with cocaine."

I walk over and take a look, though I wouldn't know cocaine from talcum powder. "I should have realized it," I say. "There was no way that many people could have been collecting winnings. That didn't make sense."

"So what does it mean to you?"

"Well, it's no surprise that Petrone is in the drug business as well as gambling. The real question is whether he's selling it on-line, and using the Starlight technology. I'm betting that he is."

"Can you use it?" she asks.

"Not so far. We could always set Winters up to be caught with the drugs the next time he goes on his route, but he'd have to be crazy to testify against Petrone. And even if he did, I don't have a connection to my case."

"What do we do with this?" Laurie asks.

"Might as well flush it down the toilet. It's already going to cause some chaos when the customer complains he didn't get it. The most interesting thing to me is that Winters is still on the job."

"Why?"

"It most likely means that Winters didn't tell Russo or Petrone that Marcus and I paid him a visit, and took the five thousand. Which makes it even less likely that Bowie was killed because of anything I did. It had to have been something else."

"Winters will suspect that you or Marcus took the drugs," she says.

I nod. "Probably. But he won't say anything, because he'd have to explain why he thinks it. That's not something he's willing to risk."

"So now what?"

"Now it's back to court."

Nancy Roosevelt is going to make a very good witness. She's attractive, which never hurts, but she also comes across as intelligent and levelheaded. She will give Trell exactly what he wants, and the jury will believe her. The only positive in all this is that what she is going to say will not be terribly damaging.

Trell takes a little time for the jury to get to know her, asking her where she lives and what she does for a living. She runs a popular thrice-weekly Web magazine called *A Sharp Eye,* doing much of the writing and editing herself, and he lets her explain it some before getting down to the reason she is here.

He prompts her to say that she was parked in a strip mall parking lot about a mile and a half from the prison on the day that Brian escaped. "I was sending a package," she says. "There is a UPS store there."

"What happened when you went out to your car?"

"I saw a man standing outside the store; I noticed him staring at me, so I walked a little faster toward my car. When I opened the door, there he was right behind me. He grabbed my arm with his hand."

"Is that man in the courtroom today?"

"Yes."

Trell gets her to point to Brian for confirmation, and just to beat it to death, he has her confirm that she's talking about the defendant.

"What did he say?"

"That I shouldn't scream, and that he didn't want to hurt me. He said he needed my car."

"Did he have a weapon?"

"He said that he did, but I didn't see it."

"Did you feel threatened?" he asks.

"Of course."

"For your life?"

She frowns slightly, as if annoyed by the question. "Of course."

"Can you describe his demeanor?"

"He looked desperate to me. Like he was in a hurry, but more than that. He looked scared, maybe panicked."

"So what did you do?"

"I gave him the key, and I backed away. He got in the car and drove off."

Trell turns the witness over to me. Her story is true, and I'm not about to shake it. "That must have been a frightening experience for you, Ms. Roosevelt," I say.

She nods. "It was."

"Did he say why he needed your car?"

"No."

"And he didn't threaten you with a weapon?"

"No, he did not."

"You never saw it?"

"No, but he said he had one."

"Did he say what kind?"

"No, just that he had a weapon. Looking back, I think he was saying that to get me to hurry up and give him the key. I have no idea if he actually had a weapon or not."

"Did he say anything after you gave him the key?'

"Yes. He said he was sorry, and that he wished he didn't have to do this."

"Thank you, Ms. Roosevelt. No further questions."

W hen court ends, I listen to a message on my cell phone. It's from Linda Westman, widow of the hedge funder who ended it all on the Saw Mill River Parkway. She sounds worried and says that she needs to see me right away.

I return the call with more dread than curiosity. The only connection Joseph Westman had to our case is that he had spoken to Gerry Wright on the phone, and when Laurie and I spoke to Linda Westman the first time, we got nothing out of it. It may sound harsh, but I don't want to spend time getting drawn into her world; I have enough problems in mine.

"Mr. Carpenter, thank you for calling," she says. "When can I see you?"

"What is this about?"

"I'd rather not say on the telephone."

"You think your calls are being listened to?" I ask.

"No, I just think this should be in person. And I have something to show you."

It's rush hour, and in the time it will take me to get to her apartment in the Dakota, I could fly to North Dakota. But I agree to drive there because I am Andy Carpenter, the Considerate and Caring One.

The George Washington Bridge is unusually crowded for the

inbound lanes at the evening rush hour; I can only assume the mayor of Fort Lee has once again pissed off Chris Christie. But once I get off, the West Side Highway is surprisingly quick, and the cross-town traffic is better than usual.

I'm sitting in Linda Westman's apartment by seven fifteen. I'm tired and very hungry. She offers me some little triangle-shaped things that look like lettuce sandwiches with a small piece of anchovy on top.

I'm not that hungry.

She thanks me for coming and talks about how difficult things have been for her, that Joseph was the one who took care of everything, etc.

I need to get things moving. "What did you want to show me?" I ask.

"Well, among the things that Joseph took care of was money. It was only natural; his business was to invest. And when it came to his own money, our own money, he was very prudent."

"I understand."

"But now I have to do everything, deal with his estate, get a handle on things . . . I'm embarrassed to say it, but it's very difficult for me."

This is taking so long that those sandwiches are starting to look good.

"I met with the accountant this morning, and he told me that he found some unusual things in our books and accounts. Joseph had been making large cash withdrawals in the three months before his death."

"How large?"

"At first in increments of $10,000, then $15,000, and ultimately $25,000. All together it came to $210,000. The man has been Joseph's accountant for years and says he can never recall him doing anything like this."

"What do you think was going on?" I say.

She hesitates for a few moments, then, "Drugs. I've discovered prescription drugs, a lot of them, painkillers and such, that I did not know Joseph used. I now believe he had a drug problem." She starts to tear up. "How could I live with someone for so long and not know him?"

"So you think he was using that cash to pay for drugs."

She nods, sadly. "Don't you?"

"Mrs. Westman, the next time I buy illegal drugs will be the first, but that seems like an awful lot of money to pay for them. I think there must have been something else going on."

"Like what?" she asks.

"First let me ask you, why are you telling me all this?"

"Should I not have?"

"It's fine that you did, I'm just not clear why you chose me to tell."

She thinks for a few moments, as if trying to understand it herself. Then, "I had no one else. It doesn't seem to be a matter for the police, and I don't want to destroy Joseph's reputation any more than it already has been. I feel like I can trust you, and you were interested."

"I'm glad to try and help," I say. "Mrs. Westman, did your husband have a personal computer that he used at home?"

"Of course."

"Here's the situation as I see it, and here is what I can do for you. I did not know your husband, or anything about his life. So I can't begin to say what these strange withdrawals mean. But I do not believe that he was using that much money to buy drugs." I don't add the words "unless he was also distributing them" because I don't think that's what was going on, and it sounds harsh.

"But I can do this for you. I can take his computer and have a member of my staff go over it for you. It's very possible that the answer is somewhere on there, and if not, you haven't lost anything. And I can promise that I will not tell anyone what we find out."

"You're a lawyer, so it would have to be confidential, right?"

I shake my head. "No, because I'm not your lawyer. You would have to take me at my word, and if you don't want to do that, I understand."

"Can I hire you as my lawyer?"

"Perhaps, but not now. I don't think this has anything to do with the current case I'm working on, but on the off chance that it does, taking you on as a client would represent a conflict. If we find out that it does not, then you can certainly hire me, and I would be bound by attorney-client confidentiality."

She seems conflicted; my guess is that she would like to find another way, but can't think of one, which is why she called me in the first place.

"I'll get his computer," she says.

After declining the sandwiches one more time, I leave with the computer. I call Sam Willis on the way home and relate all of what I know about Joseph Westman, up to and including the conversation I've just had with his widow.

"I have his computer," I say. "I'd like you to go over it, top to bottom."

"What are we looking for?" he asks.

"An explanation for why he might have been using all of that cash, and why he killed himself. I think the two are probably related."

"I thought he killed himself because of the kiddie porn?"

"That's true," I say. "But the cash might tie in to that. I think he might have been blackmailed. He thought he'd wind up in jail, but the police knew nothing about him. It could be that blackmailers were threatening to go to the police."

"Does this have anything to do with Atkins?"

"I don't think so," I say. "But you never know. That's one of the things I want you to find out."

Sam wants to get going on this right away, as I knew he would.

He tells me he'll meet me at home when I get there, to pick up the computer.

I don't know what can come from this, but at the very least I might be able to get Linda Westman some answers, and a little peace.

Wendy Watson's only connection to the case is that she was Denise Atkins's friend. Trell knows that as a prosecutor he is not required to prove motive, but he also knows that juries latch on to it when it is proved. That's why Watson is here.

"Would you say that you were Denise Atkins's best friend?" Trell asks.

I could object that the witness couldn't know what was in Denise Atkins's mind, and I'd get the objection sustained. But it would be a waste of time, and would make me look like I'm trying to prevent the jury from getting information. As a rule, I use objections sparingly.

Watson does it for me anyway. "I can't speak for Denise," she says, "but she was my best friend and I like to think she felt the same way."

Trell nods. "Fair enough. But is it accurate to say you had conversations that were intimate and revealing about each other's lives?"

"Definitely."

"I'd like you to think about the last two or three months of Denise Atkins's life. Was there anything unusual about her behavior? Was she acting strange or different in any way?"

"Yes, absolutely."

"How so?"

"She seemed nervous, tense. We would make arrangements to meet, maybe for lunch or dinner, and she would cancel at the last minute. She'd say she was busy at work."

"Where did she work?"

"Starlight. It's a computer company; Brian was one of the founders."

"What did she do there?"

"Some kind of technology stuff; I don't understand any of it. But Denise was a whiz."

"Did you ever find out what was making her so tense?" Trell asks.

She nods. "She was having an affair at work."

"Do you know who she was having the affair with?"

"She wouldn't say, but I think it was Gerald Wright. She did mention once that it's not a good idea to sleep with your boss. She and Gerald were very close, and I know he was pursuing her. She had been resisting for a long time, because she and Brian were talking about trying to save their marriage."

"Did she talk about Brian much?" Trell asks.

Watson nods. "Yes, she really cared for him, but she came to realize that their marriage was over. She worried about telling him, about how he would react."

"Did she finally tell him?"

"Yes; she said he was very upset."

"Angry?" Trell asks.

"She said 'upset.' That's the only word she used."

"When was the last time you spoke to her?"

"About a week before she died," Watson said. "She was rushed, and sounded nervous. She got on the phone and said she'd call me back, but she never did."

She pauses for a moment, getting visibly upset. "I told her I understood, and said goodbye. I didn't realize it would be for the last time."

Trell turns her over to me. She is a sympathetic, emotional witness who is obviously telling the truth, so I have to handle her with kid gloves.

"Ms. Watson, to the best of your knowledge, was Brian Atkins ever physically abusive toward his wife?"

"No."

"She never told you he struck her, or was physical with her in any way?"

"No. And Denise was a strong woman; she would not have put up with that. Not for a second."

"She never expressed a fear that he might become violent?"

"Not to me."

"You said that she was acting tense and nervous. Do you know why that was?"

"I did not know for sure; I thought it might be that she was dreading hurting Brian by telling him there was someone else."

"So you thought that she was nervous and acting strangely because she dreaded telling Brian that the marriage was over. After she told him, did that make her feel better? Did she begin acting more normally?"

"Maybe at first. You have to understand that she was busy at work, and I am busy as well, so I didn't see or talk to her that often. But after a short while she definitely was acting strangely again. I never really found out why; I wish I had."

There's nothing more for me to get from her. I don't think she was a particularly valuable witness for Trell, but she didn't have to be. He's got much more ammunition to nail us with, and it's coming.

Sergeant Luther Mitchell and his partner were the initial responders to Gerry Wright's house. Sarah Maurer had discovered the carnage that day and had immediately called 911. It was Mitchell and his partner who got there first, and Mitchell was the first to enter the house.

That's why he is here today, to help Trell set the horror scene as vividly as possible, in words and photographs. He's a huge man, very intimidating, but he and Laurie were close when she was on the force, and I've come to know him as a good and decent guy.

"So you responded to the 911 call?" Trell asks.

"Yes, sir."

"Describe your actions and what you saw when you arrived, please."

"Ms. Mauer had gone home to make the call, and when she saw us arrive, she came out to meet us. She told us that she had looked into the house, and there was blood everywhere. I requested that she stay way back, and my partner and I entered the house through the open front door.

"There was in fact blood everywhere, as Ms. Maurer had said. Farther into the house, I guess you could call it a den, were a male and a female. They were both deceased.

"We searched the house to make sure the perpetrator was not still present, and determined that he or she was not. We then left

the building, so that the forensics people could arrive and do their job."

"Did you determine how the victims died?" Trell asks.

"That is a coroner function, but it appeared to be from multiple stab wounds."

"You say the front door was open. Was there any evidence that the lock was damaged, or that there was forced entry?"

"There was not."

"Which might indicate that the victims knew their attacker?"

Mitchell is not about to let Trell put words in his mouth. "It simply indicated to me that there was no sign of forced entry."

Trell then introduces photographs from the crime scene and lets Mitchell identify them. They are gruesome and horrible, and the jury recoils from them, as they should. Trell wants that reaction; he wants them to feel like someone should pay for such a horrible act. Of course, the only person handy that they can make pay for it is Brian Atkins.

There is almost nothing for me to get from Mitchell when I start a cross-examination, so I ask a few perfunctory questions and thank him for his time.

If I'm going to throw punches, I want them to have a chance of landing. Otherwise I'm just flailing around, and the jury will know it.

Next up is Janet Carlson, the only coroner in America who could moonlight as a model for *Vogue* if she were so inclined. Janet is beautiful, and I mean Laurie kind of beautiful, and people who don't know her simply do not believe her day job is cutting up bodies.

But she is completely competent at what she does and is widely respected in her field. She is also an outstanding witness, and while I can try to get her to say favorable things, there's no way I can successfully attack what she says.

After presenting her credentials to the jury, Trell asks her what the causes of death were for the two victims in this case.

"Multiple stab wounds," she says.

"How many?"

"Seven in the case of Mr. Wright, nine in the case of Ms. Atkins."

"Did they bleed to death?" he asks.

"Extraordinarily unlikely; each victim received stab wounds into the heart, any of which would have been sufficient to cause death."

"So it's fair to say that the killer continued to stab bodies that were already deceased?"

"I would agree with that," Janet says.

"Would you say that is the sign of an enraged killer?"

"That is not within my province," Janet says, although Trell knows that the question was more important than the answer. The jury has heard it, and though Janet refuses to confirm Trell's theory, it no doubt makes sense to them.

Trell takes her through a few more of the gorier details, further horrifying the jury, and then it's left to me to try and repair the damage.

"Ms. Carlson, do you know who committed this terrible crime?" I ask.

"I do not."

"Can you tell us how tall the killer is?"

"No."

"Weight?"

"No."

"Male or female?"

"No."

"Do you know the motive?"

"No, I don't. That has nothing to do with my work."

"You testified that the killer stabbed numerous times, and probably continued after the victims were dead."

"Yes."

"In the heat of the moment, would death have been obvious?" I ask.

"I would doubt it."

"So unless he or she stopped to feel for a pulse, or listened for a heartbeat, there would have been no way to be sure the victim was dead?"

"That is very likely, yes."

"The jury has seen graphic pictures of the murder scene. Is it fair to say that the victims lost a great deal of blood?"

"No doubt about it."

"Arteries were severed?"

"Yes."

"Blood would have been spurting?"

"Definitely."

"As we have seen, the blood was all over the room. Would some have gotten on the killer?"

"I can't say for sure," she says, "but it would be hard to imagine otherwise."

"Thank you, Ms. Carlson."

There is nothing louder than a ringing phone at four o'clock in the morning. It ricochets around the room, deafening and heart-poundingly jolting to anyone who has the misfortune to be in hearing distance. I would estimate hearing distance of a 4:00 A.M. phone call to be about twelve miles.

In the long history of middle-of-the-night phone calls, there has never been one that brought good news. It just doesn't work that way. So I pick this one up with a mixture of dread and panic. Laurie sits up in bed, watching me, no doubt feeling the same.

Please don't let it be about Ricky.

It isn't; it's Sam. "Andy, I've got something you need to see."

I don't answer him right away; instead I turn to Laurie. "It's Sam." She slumps back down to the bed in relief and exhales; I think it's the first act of breathing she's done since the phone rang.

"It's four o'clock in the morning, Sam; you scared the shit out of us. What are you, a dairy farmer?"

"I'm sorry, but I wanted to get you before the court day started."

"The court day hasn't even started in Europe yet," I say. "But never mind that; what's going on?" Even though Sam can be a lunatic, if he's calling me at this hour it really may be something important.

"I found something on Westman's computer. But you need to see it."

"Where are you?"

"At the office," he says.

"Why aren't you at home?"

"I'll explain when you get here."

"Okay. It'll take me a little while."

"No problem," he says. "Bring coffee."

When I get off the phone, I relate the conversation to Laurie. She agrees that Sam must have found something significant and wants to go with me.

"He wants me to bring coffee."

"That's a very good idea," she says.

We shower and dress quickly, stop for coffee, and are at Sam's office, which is right down the hall from mine, in an hour. He opens the door to let us in, grabs the coffee from my hand, and heads back to his computer setup on his desk.

He's got his main desktop, and two other laptop computers off to the side. One of them looks like Joseph Westman's, but I can't be sure. "Come over here," he says, and Laurie and I do so.

"Sam, you didn't have to spend all night working on this," I say.

"I didn't plan to, but once I started I couldn't stop. Sit down," he instructs, pointing to two chairs across from the desk. This is obviously Sam's show, so we continue following his commands.

"I've completely gone over Westman's computer, starting with financial information. Fortunately, he kept records of his passwords on his computer, which is the absolute dumbest thing you can do."

I don't say anything, because the "dumbest thing you can do" is exactly what I do on my computer.

"That made it much easier to get around. Financially, his wife is exactly right, and the information the accountant gave her is accurate. He's been converting assets into cash, and there is no record of where that cash is going. He could afford it; the guy was rich as hell."

Sam continues, "He was also heavily into kiddie porn; it's hidden everywhere. Disgusting stuff; I won't show it to you. You can just take my word for it."

"We will," Laurie says.

"But that's not all his wife was right about," Sam says. "Come here and check this out."

Laurie and I come around and look at what he's pointing at. It's on Westman's computer, and there's a site on the screen that at first glance looks much like the betting site that was on Bowie's computer.

But it isn't.

It's a place to order drugs, prescription drugs, illegal drugs . . . I'm not an expert on the subject, but I can't think of one that is not on here. "Holy shit," I say, because the more shocked I get, the more eloquent I become.

"It's like Amazon for illegal drugs," Laurie says.

"Exactly," Sam says. "And the only reason I was able to find it was because Westman left his passwords where they could easily be found."

The implications of this are staggering, and I'll need some time to understand them.

I'm not going to get that time soon, because Sam says, "I haven't gotten to the important stuff yet. I could have told you about all this over the phone."

"What else is there?" I ask, mentally forgiving Sam for the 4:00 A.M. call.

He points to the other laptop on the desk. "I typed the address of that site into this computer. It came up as an entry page needing a password. There was no hint on that entry page what the site was for. No big surprise there; they want to be careful."

He continues, "So I used Westman's password and got in. They haven't shut off his account because he died; maybe they don't even know, or maybe they just forgot."

"They can't tell it's coming from a different computer?" Laurie asks.

"Technically they could, but it wouldn't matter to them. A client like Westman could use different computers. As long as he has the password, they wouldn't care. But I had to download a program to make it work on this computer."

"But here's the thing," he says, and pauses for effect. "When I tried to hack into this site, to find out everything about it from the inside, I couldn't."

"Why not?" I ask.

"Because it doesn't exist, at least not in any meaningful sense."

"You'll need to explain that," I say.

"It's almost an illusion. Sort of like a front. What comes into this feeds into their real site, but they have a way to route it so that it can't be followed. The same thing was true with Bowie's gambling site; it's why I couldn't find it."

I still have no idea what he's talking about, and I tell him so.

"When you go on a Web site, any Web site," he says, "the connection doesn't go from you directly to the site. It gets routed in what would seem to you like a crazy manner . . . all over the country, maybe all over the world. The Internet finds the fastest route, and it's never direct."

He continues, "They have found a way to direct the routing, to choose their own route, and send it through such a bizarre and complicated pattern as to make it impossible to follow and penetrate."

Sam can see the look of confusion on my face, so he tries harder to explain. "You know what the dark Web is?"

"No."

"Okay, well it's an area of the Internet that search engines don't access, that you need special configurations to get into. Law enforcement has a very difficult time penetrating it, so lawlessness can run rampant."

"Is that what this is?"

"No, that's what is so remarkable. This exists out in the light . . . just as impenetrable, yet at the same time available to anyone they want to get to it."

"If it's identical to Bowie, then Petrone has to be behind it. And it fits into Winters making the drug deliveries."

"So we know what they're doing, and how," Laurie says. "We just can't prove who is behind it."

"I still haven't gotten to the best part yet," Sam says, clearly gloating. "You ready?"

"Ready."

He hunches over the non-Westman laptop. "I use this computer as a spare just for situations like this," he says, tapping some keys. "Look at this."

I look and see that he has opened an application called an "activity monitor." He points to the screen. "You see that?"

"I see the screen," I say, "but I have no idea what I'm looking at."

"I don't either, Sam," says Laurie.

Sam nods and points. "Okay, that means that the computer is being used; there's a program running."

"So?"

"So I'm not using it. They are. My downloading the program has allowed them inside my computer. They now have complete access, and I'll bet they have the same access to Westman and everybody else they deal with. Most people wouldn't be able to detect it; they wouldn't even have reason to look."

He pauses to let all of this sink in. "They know everything about everyone they deal with. There are no secrets."

L aurie and I ask a lot more questions, and Sam tries to make it all clear. I get the gist of it, without understanding all the technical aspects, and I certainly know enough to know that it can have a tremendous impact on our case.

But I'll have to put it on the mental shelf and think about it later, because Hatchet would be unlikely to grant me a continuance for a "thought" day. And Trell is planning to start trotting out his key witnesses today.

First up is Sarah Maurer, Gerry Wright's neighbor. She is probably Trell's key witness, because she can place Brian at the scene.

Trell asks her where she lives, and establishes that she was Gerry's closest neighbor, though the houses are far apart. "Were you and Mr. Wright friends?" he asks.

"Yes, definitely."

"And do you know the defendant, Brian Atkins?"

"Yes, I do."

"How did you come to know him?"

"I spent time with him at Gerry's house on quite a few occasions. Parties, barbecues . . . that kind of thing. Gerry was a very sociable guy; he threw a lot of parties."

"And Mr. Atkins was often there?"

"Sure. They were partners and best friends."

"Was Denise Atkins often there as well?" Trell asks.

"Almost always. The three of them seemed inseparable."

"Please describe what happened on the day of the murders."

She talks about how she had gone for her three-mile walk, a mile and a half in one direction and then the same distance back. "I saw a car go by me, but I didn't recognize it."

"Is that unusual?"

"Maybe a little. Ours is a very quiet street with only a few houses on it, and it is very lightly traveled."

"What happened as you approached Gerald Wright's house?"

"Well, for one thing, I saw that car sitting in the driveway, down near the street. And I was surprised to see a dog in the backseat."

"Is this the dog?" Trell introduces a picture of Boomer into evidence. It's not a great picture; Boomer is much cuter than that.

"Certainly looks like it," she says, immediately annoying me by referring to Boomer as an "it."

"Then what happened?" he asks.

"Then Brian . . . Mr. Atkins . . . came out the front door. He saw me and stopped, and he looked at me . . . I can't explain it; it's like he looked through me."

"Did you speak to him?"

"I think I just said his name."

"But he didn't answer?" Trell asks.

"No, he just walked by me and got into the car. Then he pulled away. He went down the street, and came back toward me, so that he left the way he came in."

"Did he say anything else to you?"

"Yes. He slowed down almost to a stop, and said, 'Call the police.' Then he drove off."

"And did you call the police?" Trell asks.

"Not right away. Brian had left the door open behind him, so I walked toward it. I was scared, but I just wanted to make sure everything was all right. I didn't even know what Brian wanted me to tell the police."

"So you went in the front door?"

"Yes, I called out and nobody answered. I took a few steps in, and then I saw what was on the floor. I knew it was blood, so I ran out. I probably screamed, but I don't remember. Then I ran home and called the police."

Trell takes her through the horror of it again, and then it's my turn to cross-examine. "Ms. Maurer, you were on the way back from your walk when you saw the car?"

"That's correct."

"How long does the three-mile walk generally take you?"

"Forty-five minutes. Every time."

"And you walk at the same pace all the way?"

"Yes."

Hike hands me a large Styrofoam board that I introduce into evidence. It's an aerial map of the neighborhood. I show it to her and ask her to point to where she was when she saw the car. She does so.

"That is about a tenth of a mile from Mr. Wright's house," I say. "Based on the pace you were going, that would take you about a minute and a half to walk. Does that seem about right?"

"I think so. Yes."

"You testified that you didn't recognize the car, but you didn't mention anything about it speeding. Was it going at a normal pace? The speed limit on that street is thirty miles per hour."

She nods. "That seems about right."

"Ms. Maurer, the prosecution's contention is that Mr. Atkins drove that distance, parked, entered the house, and murdered two people. Based on what we've just talked about, he would have had to accomplish that in the minute and a half it took you to make that walk. Does that seem possible?"

Trell objects that the witness cannot possibly be expected to make such a judgment, and Hatchet sustains. Doesn't matter to me either way; I got my point across, so I move on.

"When you saw Mr. Atkins in front of the house, did you think anything violent had happened?"

"No . . . I mean, I didn't think about it. I just thought he was acting a little strange, like he didn't know me. And I was surprised to see him; I thought he was still in jail."

"There was no blood on him?" I ask.

"Not that I could see."

"No knife or weapon that you could see?"

"No."

"So you weren't afraid of him?" I ask.

"No."

"When he told you to call the police, you thought something was wrong?"

"Yes."

"Did you think he had done something violent?"

"I didn't think about it."

"Had you ever known him to be violent? Ever heard from others that he was?"

"No."

"He would have known you could identify him, is that correct?"

"I'm sure he would have. He would know that I know him. I even called him by name."

"But he made no attempt to hurt you, or worse?"

"No."

"Thank you."

During the lunch break, I meet with Brian in an anteroom. I tell him about the things Sam discovered, without getting into the specifics of it being Westman's computer, etc. I focus more on the capability of the cyber-criminals to essentially hide out in the open without fear of discovery, as well as their being able to inhabit their clients' computers undetected.

"Wow," he says, using a word perfectly suited to the occasion.

"Could Starlight be behind this? Would they have the capability?"

"Well, let's separate this out. The inhabiting of the computers is not that difficult to accomplish. When people accessed the Web site, they were also downloading a program without realizing it. That program starts running on their computer, and allows the people who created it to see everything on it."

"And antivirus systems don't detect it?" I ask.

"No, because it's not a virus; it's a program. The computer doesn't recognize it as an enemy invader; it thinks it belongs there."

"What about the other thing, the Web sites that are just an illusion?"

"That's pretty stunning. I wouldn't know where to begin."

"Would Gerry Wright have been capable of doing it?" I ask.

"With the understanding that I didn't know anyone could do

it, Gerry would be right up there among the possibilities. He was a genius; I was good, but he was head and shoulders above me. Actually, so was Denise. That's why I gravitated toward the business end of things."

"What about Jason Mathers? How good is he?"

"Very good, but more my level."

"Could this have been going on without Mathers realizing it?"

"Absolutely. Andy, you shouldn't be looking at this as a Starlight operation. It doesn't have to have been that at all. This could have just been Gerry; he would have had the money to finance it separate from Starlight."

I nod. "That wouldn't even matter; if Petrone were backing him, financing wouldn't be a problem."

I send Brian back to get lunch, which gives me a little more time to think about the developments. If Petrone is behind this, then he's operating an illegal gambling site and selling drugs and who knows what else online, freezing out the traditional local vendors. That's why he's moving in on everyone's territory. He's doing to them what online retailing has done to the department stores, times ten.

He could control the markets and pay whatever is necessary to get the personnel required to make it run. That might be members of the existing crime organization or newcomers. Their functions would be simple: pickups and deliveries.

The other thing that comes to mind is something that could be even more lucrative, the potential for blackmail. My guess is that Westman was being blackmailed, that Petrone or whoever controlled his computer found out about his predilection for child pornography.

Faced with a ruined business and personal life, and possible jail if his secret got out, he kept paying. Maybe it became obvious that the blackmailer would never stop, and Westman couldn't handle it, taking his own life. He probably never even knew whom he was dealing with, or how they found out his secret.

How many others are possibly being blackmailed? It is almost limitless.

The ability to inhabit these computers may also explain the death of Daniel Bowie. He could well have e-mailed someone about talking to me, and Petrone's people watched him do it. He wound up paying for our conversation with his life.

So I think we're making some progress toward establishing what Petrone is doing in the big picture, how he has dramatically recast his empire from a traditional crime family to one that is capitalizing big-time on technology. It is audacious and remarkable, but probably inevitable that someone would seize the opportunity.

But what is not increasing is our ability to tie it all into our case. Our investigative efforts would be bearing fruit if I were Dominic Petrone's prosecutor. Unfortunately, I'm Brian Atkins's defense attorney, and at this point I'm not close to getting any of what we've learned in front of this jury.

With Trell nearly at the end of his witness list, and the weekend coming up, I only have four or five days before starting the defense case. And since at this point the defense does not actually have a case, that's not much time.

Trell's next witness is Devin Maclin, the warden of the prison that Brian broke out of. It's a throw-in witness, designed to drive another nail in a coffin that Trell already believes is shut.

I objected to the witness; I didn't think he should be allowed to testify, since we've already stipulated that Brian escaped. Hatchet had instructed the jury to accept it as fact. But Trell argued that it was necessary to show that the timing of it allowed Brian to be at the scene when the murder took place. Hatchet agreed with Trell and has allowed Maclin to testify.

"When was it reported that the defendant had escaped?" Trell asked.

"I became aware that he was missing at 3:00 P.M."

"What did you do?"

"I put the facility into lockdown and ordered an immediate

search of the entire complex. I also notified the police, and asked them to put out an alert."

"What did your search uncover?"

"A man named Fred Cummings had been accosted and locked in a small supply room. His clothes had been taken as well."

"Who is Fred Cummings?"

"He is a dog trainer," Maclin says. "Part of a program we were running where dogs were brought in for the prisoners to train."

"And he told you what happened to him."

"Yes, and that convinced me that Mr. Atkins had escaped. From that point on it was up to the police on the outside."

Trell turns him over to me, and my first question to Maclin is, "Yours is a minimum-security prison, is it not?"

"It is."

"Are all prisoners treated the same in terms of the freedoms they are granted within the prison? Or are some watched more carefully than others, and have greater restrictions?"

"The latter, based on our assessment of their history, their actions within the prison population, as well as the underlying reason for them being there."

"And Mr. Atkins was in the group granted the most freedom?" I ask.

"That is correct."

"Had he ever caused any trouble? Ever shown any violent behavior?"

"No."

"Thank you . . . no further questions."

Trell's last witness for the day is Fred Cummings, and he takes him through the frightening experience he had in the prison that day. He doesn't take very long to question him, since Fred obviously can only speak about his experience, and has no knowledge of what happened after being locked in the supply room.

As Fred describes it, Brian led him into a secluded area of the prison on a pretense. Once there, he came up behind him and pushed something into his back, claiming that it was a gun. Cummings was immediately compliant and gave Brian his shirt, pants, and shoes, as asked. He also did not resist being put in the supply room. Brian tied his hands and feet together with electrical cords in the room and put duct tape on his mouth.

"Were you afraid for your life?" Trell asked.

"I wasn't sure," Fred says. "But it was very frightening."

On cross-examination I ask if Fred had, at any point, seen the weapon that Brian claimed to have.

"I didn't," he said. "I felt something in my back, so I took his word for it."

"Did he hurt you in any way?"

He shakes his head. "No. Not at all."

"Did he say anything to you that Mr. Trell didn't ask you about?"

"Yes. At one point he said, 'I'm sorry about this, Fred. But I don't have any choice.' Then when he was leaving me there, he said he was sorry again."

"Did you have a lot of dealings with Mr. Atkins in the months before this happened?"

Fred nods. "I saw him twice a week."

"Did you like him?"

"I did." Then, after a few seconds, "It's weird, but I still do."

"Thank you, Fred," I say. What I don't say is that I couldn't have scripted a better answer.

Hello Andy, haven't heard from you in a while," Cindy Spodek says when I answer the phone.

"I've been busy fighting for truth and justice. How are you, Cindy?"

"Good, thanks."

"Laurie's not home," I say.

"I was calling you."

"You were calling me?" I ask. The way it works is that I call Cindy when I need a favor from the FBI, and she calls me never. That's the way things are; she is upsetting the world order. Chaos is sure to follow.

"I was. It's about Dominic Petrone."

My instincts say that this time she needs me for something. Whereas she always tries to accommodate me if at all possible, I'm not generally inclined to be helpful, unless it benefits my client.

"Dominic Petrone? I have nothing but good things to say about him. He's Tara's godfather."

"Are you going to be a pain in the ass?"

"Do you have to ask? What's up, Cindy?"

"The word is that you are getting somewhere. Maybe we can help."

"Where did you get that word?" I ask.

"Not important. Is it accurate?"

"I'm getting somewhere on Petrone; I know what he's been doing. What I haven't done is link any of it to my case."

"Talk to me about what you've got on Petrone," she says.

An idea has been forming in my brain since I realized I was in a position of some power in this conversation. It's slow developing, because my brain is not used to being in that power position.

"And in return?" I ask, though I know where I'm going.

"Andy, were you absent the day they taught patriotism in grammar school? Your country would be a better place if we put Dominic Petrone away."

"From the mountains, to the prairies . . ."

"What do you want, Andy?"

"Two things. Number one, why are you so anxious to get Petrone? I sensed it last time we talked; you said you wanted him badly."

"He's a criminal," she says.

"That's what you said last time. But he's been a criminal since you were playing with blocks. What's changed?"

"He's expanding his empire, and somehow taking over other territories. He's gotten much bigger, and we want to know how he's doing it."

"Good, because I know how. Number two, I want immunity for a prospective witness."

"Who?"

"Tony Costa." Last time I talked to Cindy, she got me in to see Costa, who was being temporarily held after the shooting death of his boss, Angelo Mazzi.

"What is he going to say?"

"I don't know yet."

"Can you be a little more specific?"

"He's going to confirm what Petrone is doing, and help me tie it into my case. Or he won't say a word, and he'll tell me to get lost."

"When we grant immunity, we try to have a little more to go on than that."

"Okay, I'll get it for you. And then we'll trade."

Tony Costa works out of a bar on Fordham Road in the Bronx. The back room of the place is where Angelo Mazzi used to conduct his business daily, reigning over the dominant crime family in the Bronx.

Now Costa is in charge of that family, but according to Cindy it is a shell of its former self; Petrone has co-opted many of the rank and file and taken over much of Mazzi's former business ventures in the Bronx.

The last time I talked to Costa I got nothing out of him, a rare occasion when the Andy Carpenter charm failed to persuade. But he made it clear that he wants to get Petrone, and suggested I come back when I had something real to make that happen. So here I am.

I'm more than a little nervous about coming here, even with Marcus by my side. Costa doesn't know that I'm coming; I'm not even sure that he'll see me. Part of me is hoping that he won't.

We park in front of a fire hydrant near the bar. It's the only spot available, and while I'm risking a ticket, the good news is that getting one would mean a cop is nearby.

Marcus and I get out and walk into the bar. It's the kind of place that has only "regular" customers, and is not welcoming to others. I would doubt that Fordham University students out on a date are popping in here for a drink. Marcus and I being far from "regular," all eyes turn to us as we walk in.

It's nine o'clock at night, and there are maybe ten people in the place. Behind the bar to the left is a door, and I am guessing that Costa is behind that door. That's because three scary-looking guys are in front of it. Mazzi was taken by surprise the night he was killed; Costa is not planning to let the same thing happen to him.

Marcus and I walk up to the three men. I am petrified; Marcus not so much. "I'd like to talk to Tony Costa."

"Who the hell are you?"

It's not the most welcoming of responses, but I overlook it. "Andy Carpenter. Tell Tony I'm here."

"Tony don't see no little pricks. Get lost."

I've got a feeling he was referring to me, rather than Marcus. I'm tempted to follow his advice and get lost, but I figure I'll take one more shot at it. "No."

The guy moves toward me but never quite gets there. Marcus leans forward and meets him with a right uppercut that just about lifts him off the ground. Gravity wins, however, and he winds up on his back, first hitting his head on the door.

I'm expecting the other two guys to jump into the fray, and then I see that Marcus has brandished a gun in his left hand, causing them to freeze. It's amazing that his right and left hands can work in tandem like that; Marcus would make a great juggler. Of course, if his only skill was juggling, I would be the one lying on the floor.

He indicates with a head nod that I should go into the office. I nudge the fallen guy slightly with my foot so that I can open the door, and I go in, leaving Marcus to watch the three guys, two of whom are conscious.

It's a shaky plan, because for all I know Costa has three other guys with bazookas with him. Mercifully, he doesn't; he's alone, at a desk. He seems to have just stood up, probably because he heard the sound of his guy hitting the ground. There's a look of some alarm on his face, and he actually seems relieved to see me. That's because he no doubt views me as harmless.

"How the hell did you get in here?" he asks. "I told them nobody gets through."

"Sometimes an irresistible force meets a movable object," I say. "I need to talk to you."

"Again?"

"You told me to come back when I had something real. Something to get Petrone."

"Why would I want to get Petrone?" he asks.

"Because he's killed your boss and taken over your operation. Because you're sitting in a room under guard, scared about who might walk through that door. Because you were once a big shot, and now you're nobody."

"I should put a bullet through your head."

"I'd prefer you didn't," I say. "I'd prefer you help me finish off Petrone."

He thinks about this for a few moments, and then says, "Talk to me."

So I do. I tell him about Starlight, and how Petrone had gotten Gerry Wright to sign on with him to create a new business model for criminal activity. "He's taking over from the Angelo Mazzis of the world. Mazzi must have resisted, and you know how that wound up. You are obviously also resisting, which is why you're holed up in this room, with three goons out there protecting you. But believe me, if I could get in, Petrone can get in."

"How much of this can you prove?"

"I can prove all of it, but I can't tie it into Petrone. That's why I need you."

"To do what?"

"Tell what you know. Under oath, to a jury."

"You're out of your mind."

"What's wrong with it? You don't want to squeal on Petrone? You think that violates some ethic you're clinging to? The guy has moved in on you, and will move further. You take him down, or he will eventually take you down."

"I'd rather that than go to prison."

"I can get you immunity," I say, and I can see he's interested.

"How?"

"I have connections to the FBI, and they want Petrone as much as you do."

"I can't get you to Petrone," he says. "The meeting we had was with Joseph Russo."

"That's close enough."

The next two minutes are excruciating. Costa literally walks all around the room, not saying a word, for the entire time. Then, "You get me the immunity, and I'm in."

"Then you're in," I say. "I'll get back to you with the details. But give me your phone number. I'd rather not have to get by your bouncers again."

"How did you do that?"

"Come see for yourself."

We open the door, and see that the two conscious goons are sitting back to back on the legs of the unconscious one, though he seems to be coming to. Marcus just stands there watching them, as is pretty much everyone else in the bar.

"Jesus Christ," Costa says.

"No. Marcus."

I call Cindy and tell her the great news. She's not quite as euphoric as I am. "We want Petrone, not Joseph Russo."

"Let's look at the big picture here, shall we? He's Petrone's number two; you nail him and he'll flip as well. If not, he's a nice catch, considering you're giving up nothing."

"We're giving up immunity."

"Big deal. Costa is nothing; he wasn't even on your radar. You're promising not to prosecute someone you had no intention of prosecuting." Cindy is getting on my nerves; I'm handing her a major victory, and she's acting put upon.

"I'll talk to my people, but the best I'll be able to get is use."

She is talking about use immunity, which is not full. It simply promises that nothing Costa says in his testimony will be used to prosecute him. That's not to say he can't be prosecuted if independent evidence is developed, it just means his testimony can't be used against him.

I would think that should be sufficient, but I don't tell Cindy that. "I'll try to sell it" is what I say.

"You'd better sell hard, because that's all I can get. If I can get that."

"Well, you better get it quick, because it's almost time to present the defense case."

As I'm getting off the phone, Laurie comes into the house. "Where have you been?" I ask.

"Renewing old friendships."

"Boyfriends?" I ask, instantly moving into pathetic mode.

"No. Coworkers," she says, obviously meaning her former colleagues on the force. "I've been asking about blackmail situations that have come up in the last few months, and there are two that fit. Neither was aware of who was blackmailing them, but they paid for a while, and then shut off the tap."

"What happened?"

"The things that they were being blackmailed for were broadcast online. One was stealing money from a company, and the other was having an affair."

"How did they pay?" I ask.

"They wired money. When the cops tried to trace where it went, they wound up in a cybermaze and got nowhere."

"Sounds like our guys."

"There's one other thing. A guy named Lenny Butler was murdered last month; it seemed like a mob hit. He was apparently distributing drugs."

"So?"

"So the drug guys can't figure out where he was getting the goods," she says. "They think he was selling for more than he paid, and turning a profit. But he did not seem to have connections to get the stuff in the first place."

All of these stories seem to fit our scenario, and I would think that at least some certainly do.

"But we still can't tie it to Petrone," she says.

"Maybe we can," I say, and tell her about the situation with Tony Costa and Cindy. "She'll get it done," Laurie says.

"The tough part will be getting Hatchet to buy it."

about a potential attack, he's hiding it well. "Captain Stanton, in addition to Mr. Atkins, who else did you consider a suspect during any point in your investigation?"

"Mr. Atkins was the only suspect," he says.

"So you heard about him from Ms. Maurer at around 6:00 P.M., and at around 9:30 A.M. the next morning you arrested him. Did you sleep that night?"

He nods. "I did."

"How long?"

"I don't remember exactly. Maybe seven hours."

"So if we deduct time for dinner and breakfast, as well as the hour and a half following me, your active investigation prior to arresting Mr. Atkins was about five hours or so, during all of which you were focused on him?"

Pete smiles, as if tolerating this silliness. "I'll go with your math."

"Did your investigation after the arrest include looking for any possible additional suspects?" I ask.

"There was no need for that."

"Because an eyewitness placed Mr. Atkins at the scene?"

"That was a main reason," he says.

"Ms. Maurer was also at the scene. Why wasn't she a suspect?"

"She hadn't escaped from prison."

"So it was the escape that preempted your investigation? Did you ever consider that he might have escaped to prevent the murders?"

"I did not."

"Obviously," I say. Trell objects and Hatchet sustains. "You said when you arrived on the scene, there was a great deal of blood."

"Yes."

"Were there bloody footprints leading from the bodies?"

He nods. "There were some, yes."

"Were the forensics people able to measure the size of the shoes that made those prints?"

"It was very difficult because they were smeared. The estimate was ten and a half."

"Do you know the size the defendant wears?" I ask.

"Nine and a half."

"But that information didn't cause you to question your lack of investigation?"

"No. As I said, forensics had little confidence in the measurement," he says.

"Are you familiar with the earlier testimony that based on the wounds, there would definitely have been blood spurting onto the perpetrators and around the scene?"

"I did not hear that testimony, but I believe that it's likely, though not certain," he says.

"Yet Ms. Maurer did not see blood on Mr. Atkins's clothing, did she?"

"She did not report seeing any, no."

"Seeing blood all over someone is the kind of thing that makes an impression, doesn't it? It's sort of memorable, right?"

Trell objects, and Hatchet sustains and tells Pete not to answer.

I continue. "When you took Mr. Atkins into custody, did you find blood on his clothing?"

"No."

"In his car?"

He shakes his head. "No."

"Not even a trace?" I ask, feigning surprise.

"No."

"What about the motel room where he had spent the night? Any blood there?"

"No."

"Captain Stanton, if you had investigated for an additional ten minutes or so, would you have wondered why there was no blood?"

"He could have changed his clothes and discarded the blood-stained ones."

"Well, the prison officials didn't see him carrying a suitcase with him, so do you think he walked into a store, wearing blood-soaked clothing, and bought a new outfit?"

"I don't know what he did. It was a well-planned escape; he could certainly have arranged for a change of clothes."

"Have any local stores reported that he was a customer?"

"Not to my knowledge."

"Did you canvass local businesses to ask if he'd bought clothes or supplies?"

"No."

"Did you find the murder weapon in Mr. Atkins's possessions?"

"No."

"Any local store come forward to say that they sold him a knife?"

"No."

"So, if I can recap, the only evidence of any kind that you found is the eyewitness testimony of Ms. Maurer?"

"We have him present at the scene, and we have him fleeing the scene."

"Is fleeing the scene the same as leaving?"

"In this case it is."

"Is it possible that he feared you would conduct an incomplete investigation and jump to the conclusion that he was guilty? Could he be smart enough to know exactly what would actually happen?"

Another objection, which is sustained, so Pete doesn't have to answer.

"Last question, Captain. When you and the other police cars arrived on the scene at the Garden State Parkway rest stop, did anything happen with the dog that Mr. Atkins was walking?"

"Yes, it ran in front of the cars as they were pulling up."

"What did Mr. Atkins do?"

"He ran toward it and pulled it away before it could be hit."

"Risking his own safety in the process?"

"Definitely," Pete says, earning him points in my mind, and hopefully earning Brian points in the minds of any dog lovers on the jury.

"Thank you, Captain. No further questions."

t's going to be a long weekend. Just the act of readying the defense case is pressure enough; I need to be completely prepared to elicit exactly what I want from every witness. But this situation is infinitely more difficult, because I have to focus on getting Hatchet to let us present the case we want in the first place.

There is no doubt that Westman's computer, as well as Bowie's, constitutes a strong case of criminality. That is an easy argument to make; the problem is trying to make it to this jury. Because Hatchet's question, posed in judge-speak, is going to be, "What the hell does that have to do with these murders?"

So I have to get by Hatchet and then deal with Trell. The latter presents another series of problems, but those are more traditional, and I face them every time. I have to anticipate the weaknesses he will see, and respond to them in my own head, before I can do so in front of the jury.

There is one thing that has bugged me right from the start. I don't believe in coincidences; I never have. By that I mean I know they can happen, but chalking something up to coincidence is a last resort. Nothing can be classified as a simple coincidence until every other possible explanation is exhausted.

The coincidence in this case is Gerry Wright and Denise Atkins being murdered on the same day that Brian Atkins escaped. The timing worked perfectly to blame him for the crime, even though the killers could not have known he was going to escape, or when he was going to.

Or maybe they could.

I have no idea why I didn't think of this earlier, but I don't have time to beat myself up over it now. I've got to get out to the prison.

I get there in no time, because there is so little traffic on Saturdays. Brian is surprised to see me, since this is an unplanned visit. "Something wrong?" he asks. The question makes sense; the way the trial has gone so far there's more reason to think a new development is negative than positive.

"Just some questions I need answers to," I say. "When you were communicating with Denise in the days leading up to the escape, were you talking on the phone? I assumed you were, because you said cell phones are so prevalent."

"They are, but we were mostly texting."

"So the stuff about Petrone, about the danger, about how worried she was? Those were texts?"

"Mostly. I can't say for sure that it was all of it. We did talk on the phone some."

"What about the escape itself? Did you tell her you were about to do it in a text?"

"Yes, I'm sure I did."

"Why did you text?"

"Because there are listening devices all over jails, Andy. Nobody can hear a text."

"Can't they intercept them somehow?"

He smiles, remembering whom he is dealing with. "No, all texts are encrypted; they can't be intercepted and read."

"Do you still have the phone with the texts on it?" I ask.

"No, they took everything when I was arrested."

I leave the prison and head back home, calling Hike on the way. "Hike, I need you to get some things urgently."

"Hold on," he says. "Let me get a pen."

This is apparently a larger task than one would imagine, because it takes about forty-five seconds. When he comes back, he says, "These things never write. And half of them leak; I got ink stains on three shirts last year. I have to wear a sweater over them."

"Hike, are you familiar with the concept of 'urgently'?"

"I'm ready," he says. "Go ahead."

"I need Brian's cell phone, the one they took from him when he was arrested. I also need Denise Atkins's cell phone and personal computer."

"Okay, I'll go right to Trell on this," he says, uncharacteristically springing into action. "If he gives me any trouble, we'll get a judge to authorize it."

"Perfect. Get back to me as soon as you can." Hike is actually an outstanding attorney, for a pain in the ass.

When I get home I brief Laurie on what is happening, and she has some more good news to give me. Cindy called, and her bosses are willing to give Tony Costa the use immunity we talked about.

I call Costa on the number he gave me and tell him what the government is going to do. I expect some resistance, some hesitancy to follow through on our deal, but I get none. The chance to help nail Petrone is very appealing to him.

Almost as appealing as it is to me.

Besides being really smart, the upside to Hike is that he's an equal opportunity pain in the ass. When he wants something from people, he doesn't just ask for it. He chews on their ankle and tortures them until they beg him to take it, just to get rid of him. It's a somewhat-less-than-endearing quality, but I'm okay with it when I'm the one sending him on the mission.

In this case, Norman Trell was the unfortunate victim of Hike's personality, and it took him little more than a day to cave. To get the bureaucracy to move on a weekend is no small task, but under pressure from Hike, Trell managed to secure and turn over Brian's cell phone, as well as Denise's computer and cell phone.

"What do you want me to do with them?" Hike asks when he calls to tell me the good news.

"Take them to Sam's office. He'll be waiting for you."

I had called Sam to tell him what was going on, and of the need to go over the devices as quickly and thoroughly as possible. He promised that he would, and we arrange to meet before court in the morning.

My preparations for tomorrow's court session are finished, and Sam is off doing his work, so I have some rare downtime. "You want to go out for dinner?" I ask Laurie.

"I thought you'd never ask."

"Where do you want to go? Fancy as you like; money's no object. You can even order an appetizer if you want."

"Thanks, Diamond Jim," she says. "Let's go to Charlie's."

This is my kind of woman.

On the way there, Laurie says, "We need to talk."

Uh-oh. I can't remember ever enjoying a talk that I needed to have. "Hurry up and tell me," I say. "It's not safe for me to cringe and drive."

"Nothing to cringe about," she says. "I just think I should go to be with Ricky. The investigating phase is about over, and I can tell from our conversations on the phone that he's missing us. And I'm sure as hell missing him."

I nod. "So am I. It turns out that having a child is different than having a turtle."

She smiles. "That it is. And as great as Celia is, and as much as Ricky likes her, I just don't want him to feel like we dumped him there."

"You think we should bring him home?" I ask.

"Not yet, not when we've gone this far. There's too much downside risk. Soon."

"Okay, I think you're doing the right thing."

She smiles. "Good."

When we get to Charlie's, Pete is sitting at our regular table. I'm not happy about that, but it could be worse. Vince could have been here also.

I'd prefer to sit alone with Laurie at a different table, but she lights up when she sees Pete and drags me over there. "Can we join you?" Laurie asks.

Pete looks at me, then says to her, "Just you? Or F. Lee Shithead as well?"

She laughs. "Both of us." And she sits down, not waiting for an answer. I sit down as well.

"Pete's upset because I made him look like a blithering idiot on the stand. Actually, that's not accurate. I merely brought out the fact that he's a blithering idiot."

"I wiped the floor with you," he says.

Neither of us are telling the truth, so we move past it quickly enough. The presence of Laurie and beer are more than enough to take us both out of our bad moods. Before long we're actually having a good time.

As we're getting the check, or more accurately, as I'm getting the check, Pete says, "So, you going to throw yourself on the mercy of the court tomorrow?"

"Actually, I'm going to do something you've been trying to do for years, without any success. And I don't mean look presentable and not sound like an idiot."

"What might that be?" he asks, ignoring the insults.

"I'm going to get Dominic Petrone."

"You got life insurance?" he says, as I see Laurie wince slightly.

"Of course. Marcus."

He nods. "Good enough."

As we're getting up, he says, "Andy, wait a minute."

"What now?"

"If you need help, I'm the first call you make. You got that?"

"Got it."

"You're an asshole, but you're my friend," he says.

"This is a moment I'll cherish," I say.

"Thank you, Pete, sincerely," Laurie says. "He's an asshole, but he's my husband."

"I promised myself I wouldn't cry," I say, and head for the exit.

meet Sam in the office at 7:00 A.M. to hear what he found on the devices. He doesn't look tired, which leads me to observe, "Doesn't look like you stayed here all night."

"I didn't. I just got here. It took much less time than I thought last night."

"Why is that?" I ask.

"Because Denise Atkins's computer was wiped clean."

This is horrible news. "What exactly does 'wiped clean' mean?"

"Actually, I used the wrong term," Sam says. "The applications and programs are still on it, but anything you would care about is gone. E-mails, surfing history, that kind of stuff . . . all gone."

"Obviously someone did that deliberately?"

"No doubt about it," he says. "I can't tell when it was done, but maybe the cops did it?"

I shake my head. "No chance; that would be destroying evidence. They would know I could nail them on it. Can it be retrieved?" I ask.

"No doubt about that either. But I don't have the material to do it. Send it off to the FBI lab, and they can get just about everything back. Also, her e-mails can be retrieved from her provider, but it would take time."

"So you learned nothing from it?" I ask, although just the fact that it was wiped is significant and enlightening in and of itself.

"I learned a couple of things. The same program that was in Westman's computer was in this one. They were inside her computer, watching every cybermove she made."

"Could they have erased all the material from where they were, without physically having it?"

He nods. "Absolutely."

"What about the cell phones?" I ask.

"Hers gave me nothing, everything was wiped in the same manner."

This surprises me. "So they were in her phone?"

He shakes his head. "No, not likely at all. These were all Apple devices, so they were synched together. If you erase these things on the computer, especially e-mails and texts, you erase them from the phone as well."

This is not going well; the bad guys seem to stay one step ahead of me. "You said you learned a couple of things from her computer. What's the other one?"

He smiles. "I thought you'd never ask. Have you ever googled anything?"

It's an annoying question; I'm not a complete loser. "Of course I've googled," I say. "I was captain of my high school googling team. Get to the point, please."

He nods. "Okay. You know when you're typing in your search request, how Google automatically fills in the rest, anticipating what you're looking for? Like if you typed in B-A-R, it would guess 'Barack Obama.'"

"Yes."

"Well, it knows what you've searched for in the past, so if you had recently searched for 'bar stools,' that might come up with your B-A-R instead of Obama."

"Right."

"Well, I tried some on her computer, just to see what would

happen. "D-O-M brought up Dominic Petrone. When I tried the same thing on my computer, I got Domino's Pizza. She obviously searched Petrone."

"I'm not surprised, but I doubt I can use it in court. Anything else?"

"Yes. When I typed in S-T-E-V on my computer I got Steve Jobs. On hers I got Steven Thurmond."

"Wow," I say, because what I'm thinking is, "Wow." Steven Thurmond is the ex-con hacker who's living like a king on other people's money, and Denise was searching for information about him. Gerry Wright had called him the day before he was killed.

Sam tells me that's all he got from Denise's computer and phone, so I ask, "What about Brian's phone?"

Another smile; the man loves doling out good news. "Pay dirt," he says. "The text messages between Brian and Denise are all there. I printed them out for you."

He takes a piece of paper off the desk and hands it to me. "I think you'll like it," he says.

I take a quick glance at the paper and see enough to confirm that Sam is right; I'm going to like it just fine.

"Sam, you do nice work."

"I'm here to serve," he says.

"Good, because I need you to go see Jason Mathers. Show him everything you've learned . . . the fact that the sites are essentially invisible, how Westman's computer and Denise's computer were compromised, and show him what you found on Denise's computer. I'm going to need him to testify to all of it. I'll call and tell him you're coming."

"Will do," Sam says. I'm glad I took him to meet with Mathers the first time.

I thank Sam and head for court, holding copies of the text transcripts. If I'm lucky, in a couple of hours they're going to let me present my case.

would suggest we do this in chambers, Your Honor." Trell has complained to Hatchet that the defense has turned over nothing in the way of discovery, and has not previewed its case at all. His fear is that we will go off on a tangent and present specious and irrelevant testimony.

The man has a point.

"Very well," says Hatchet, granting my request. "With a court reporter present."

Trell, Hatchet, and I go into his chambers, and Hatchet sits behind his desk, sighing at the annoyance that we attorneys represent. I think at some time in the future someone is going to dig up his backyard and find the bones of enough lawyers to fill an ABA convention.

"Mr. Trell" is how he opens the discussion.

"I'm sure Your Honor remembers that Mr. Carpenter did a newspaper interview a while back and announced he was going to prove an organized crime connection to these murders. He has to my knowledge never recanted that, nor has he provided the state or this court with any evidence to support that contention."

He takes a breath and continues. "If that is still Mr. Carpenter's intention, I would ask that he give the court an offer of proof before he goes off on some wild tangent."

"Mr. Carpenter?"

"I have no intention of going off on a wild tangent, Your Honor."

"How comforting," Hatchet says. "Now that that's out of the way, perhaps you can reply to Mr. Trell's main point."

"With pleasure. When I gave that interview, I believed that what I was saying was accurate. Our investigation has continued, and I am now positive of it. And I am prepared to prove it."

"Then let's have an offer of proof," Trell says.

I shake my head. "Your Honor, I need to develop the case as I see fit. The initial witnesses will be significant, but their absolute relevance will only be established as further witnesses testify. I would ask that you allow me to proceed subject to connection."

My "subject to connection" request means that Hatchet would allow it essentially on my promise that it will all connect. If it ultimately doesn't, he can tell the jury to disregard all of it, and admonish me in their presence.

That would be devastating to the case, but for me it wouldn't change anything, since if I can't prove my case, we're going to lose anyway.

"Your Honor," I continue, "if I don't fulfill my promise, you're going to crucify me in front of the jury, and I'll deserve it."

Trell seems concerned, fearful that he might be losing this. "Your Honor, we have seen not a single page of discovery from the defense."

"We've withheld nothing subject to discovery, Your Honor. No reports, no transcribed interviews, no science, nothing. And much has developed in the last thirty-six hours. But Mr. Trell is the last one who should be complaining about discovery failings."

"What does that mean?" Trell asks, as indignantly as he can.

I take two sheets of paper from my briefcase and hand one to Hatchet and one to Trell. "Your Honor, these are transcribed texts taken from Mr. Atkins's cell phone. On page two, you can see a text from Denise Atkins to her husband, expressing fear that Mr. Petrone was involved with Starlight, and that she was fearful of him."

"This is discoverable," Hatchet says, meaning I should have turned it over to Trell.

"Yes, it is, Your Honor. Except the phone was in the prosecution's possession until yesterday, when we made a special request for it."

Trell looks stricken. "I knew nothing about this information, Your Honor."

"If you didn't, you should have," I say. "There would be no reason to impound the phone if your investigators were not going to look at it. You were in possession of Brady material, and we were entitled to it." Brady material refers to exculpatory evidence that the prosecution must turn over according to the Supreme Court case, *Brady v. Maryland.*

"Mr. Trell?" Hatchet says, in a prompting tone.

"This doesn't change our position at all."

"Well, it should," Hachet says. "You came in here saying that the defense had made no connection at all between this case and organized crime, and you had that very connection in your possession all along."

"We were not aware of it," Trell says, sounding increasingly lame.

"Well, you are now. Consider it an offer of proof. Mr. Carpenter, I will allow the witnesses subject to connection. But it is not a blank check. If I do not see progress and relevance, I will cut you off."

"As you should, Your Honor. But I must request a one-day continuance. I literally received these documents an hour ago, and need a little time to work them into my case. It is not the defense's fault that we are in this disadvantageous position, and we need at least a day to adjust."

Hatchet would rather eat nails than grant continuances, but I think he wants to stick it to Trell, so he agrees.

Trell doesn't bother to object to Hatchet's decision. He probably knows it's final, and I think he just wants to get out of here as soon as possible. I truly don't think he had any idea what these texts said, and I certainly don't think he deliberately withheld them. I feel bad about nailing him like this, but I'll get over it.

We leave the chambers. Starting tomorrow, I'm going to present my case as I wish, based on my promise that I will conclusively demonstrate the relevance and firmly establish that connection.

I wish I knew how the hell I am going to do that.

Things have worked out well, at least geographically. I'm dropping Laurie off at Newark Airport for her flight to Wisconsin, and then heading over to the FBI offices in Newark for a meeting.

I'm old enough to remember when you could take someone to the airport for a flight and actually go with them to the gate. Now you have to say goodbye at security; if they were remaking *Casablanca* today, they'd have some trouble shooting the final scene.

Saying goodbye to Laurie is one of my least favorite things to do, but I understand and agree with her decision to go. "Give Ricky a hug and kiss for me," I say.

She nods. "I will. We'll be back as soon as this is over. Take care of yourself, Andy."

Way back in the day I would have stayed at the gate, watched the plane taxi out to the runway, and followed it as it soared into the sky. Now the best I can do is watch Laurie step into what looks like some kind of time machine and raise her arms over her head, so that some people in another room somewhere can see a picture of her through her clothing.

I leave and go straight to the FBI offices, where I discover that I'm the last to arrive for the meeting. Present are Assistant Director Stanley Brasso, two other agents whose names I don't catch and whose main functions are to stand and look ominous, Tony Costa, and his lawyer, Wilbur Stetson.

Also, much to my surprise, Cindy Spodek has flown down to be at the meeting, no doubt to try and keep me in check. It's unnecessary, since I have no intention of causing any problems. I want this to go smoothly.

Assistant Director Brasso starts by thanking Costa for coming in and explaining the ground rules, including the meaning of use immunity. It's no doubt unnecessary, since I know his lawyer, and I'm sure he's adequately gone over it all with his client.

Costa receives the written immunity grant from Brasso, and he hands it to Stetson to read. Once the attorney nods his agreement, Costa signs it, and we're off and running.

He takes them through the story as he understands it, including Joseph Russo's meeting with Mazzi, which started Petrone's moving in on his territory. Costa also relates how he knows that the same thing has happened in other cities.

Costa does not go near the murder of Mazzi, or the attempted murder of Petrone. Brasso tries to get it out of him, but he disclaims knowledge of it. The truth is that he knows it was Petrone's people that killed Mazzi, and he knows that someone alerted Petrone to the impending attack on his own life.

So he's lying, and I must admit that I don't care, because it really has nothing to do with my case. I'm not even sure the FBI cares; it's enough to get Petrone on massive drug dealing. The Al Capone tax evasion case comes to mind.

By the time we're finished, everybody seems happy, and I've been a good little boy, barely saying a word. Cindy is beaming at me; I've got a feeling she's going to give me a lollipop.

Costa leaves, and per our agreement, I take the FBI people through what I know about the cyberoperation behind all of this. They bring some technology people in to hear it, and my sense is that they're skeptical it could all be real.

I offer to have Sam take them through the same information.

He'll speak their language, and they'll understand it better. Then they'll believe.

Before I leave, I ask if any of them are familiar with Steven Thurmond. Brasso and Cindy are not, but the tech guys definitely are. "Thurmond is involved in this?" one of them says.

"His name has come up," I say. "I'm not sure exactly how he fits in."

"That's something we would be very interested in."

I promise to keep them informed on what I learn and then head home, where I'm greeted at the door by Tara and Sebastian. So I grab the leashes and take them for a long walk through the park. We come back down to Park Avenue and I stop to buy us all bagels. If Marcus would make an appearance, I'd buy him one as well, but that's not his style.

Tara chews her bagels slowly, savoring each bite, while Sebastian sort of vacuums his up. The net result is that he finishes way before her, and stares at her while she eats, hoping that she'll share it with him. Good luck with that, pal.

All in all, the walk takes an hour and a half, and all three of us enjoy every second of it. I don't want to get home for a number of reasons. I hate to curtail their enjoyment, plus getting home means having to prepare for court by again digging into case documents. But most of all I hate getting home because Laurie and Ricky won't be there.

I used to love an empty house. I could watch television in my underwear, leave clothes and dirty plates strewn around the house, and belch if the urge hit me. I'll still do that stuff on nights like tonight, but I'll somehow feel guilty about it.

But the bottom line is that I used to cherish "alone time," and now I don't. Now I want Laurie and Ricky with me.

Love is a pain in the ass.

My focus tonight is on Denise Atkins and Steven Thurmond. He clearly is an important player in whatever scenario I come up with.

Denise was worried about what was happening with Gerry Wright; she had learned something wrong was going on, and that it included Dominic Petrone. She also knew that Thurmond was somehow involved; that's why she was googling his name and searching for information on him. That Thurmond was mixed up in this does not come as a surprise, but this new information causes me to wonder just where Denise Atkins fit in.

If she was trying to uncover and maybe stop the wrongdoing, is it possible that she was the target, and not Gerry Wright? Was Gerry actually trying to protect her, and that's why he died also?

Denise's death has always left me wondering who was running the tech side of the Petrone operation with Gerry gone. Thurmond fits that bill perfectly.

It's midnight when I finally put down the case documents and get into bed. Tara never used to sleep in bed with me, but she began doing so when Laurie came into the picture. Now, when Laurie is away, Tara plants herself back on the floor.

"You like Laurie better than me?" I ask Tara, then think better of it. "Don't answer that."

Jason Mathers has put on a suit and tie to come to court. It doesn't quite fit; it looks a little snug and the sleeves are a bit short. My guess is that it's been a while since he dressed up.

Sam has assured me that he's told Mathers everything, and that he fully understands all that has gone on. Sam says it as if getting Mathers to understand was a personal triumph, as if Mathers is his young protégé. Of course, Mathers was head of technology for Starlight, so he had some insights going in.

I take Mathers through his résumé. He dropped out of MIT, though he subsequently finished his degree at Cal Tech. He had two jobs in Silicon Valley before coming back east to work at Starlight.

About three years ago, he assumed the job as head of technology, and he only left the company when CFO Ted Yates was temporarily named to replace the deceased Gerry Wright as CEO. It was obvious that Yates was going to get the position permanently, so Mathers took his ball, or his data, and went home. He could afford to: he made a huge amount of money there, and had a lucrative buyout as well.

The best thing that Mathers has going for him, other than his tech ability and knowledge, is his ability to explain it in simple terms. Like most average citizens, this jury doesn't strike me as being particularly computer savvy, so Mathers is the perfect guy to talk to them.

Mathers basically gives them a tutorial on how the Internet works; it's painstaking and slow, but the jury seems interested and alert. I'm watching them carefully, and if at any time I see their interest starting to wane, I'll speed things up.

Eventually I lead Mathers to the key points, and I use an overhead screen to show the gambling and drug sites, briefly mentioning Daniel Bowie and Joseph Westman. I ask him if there is anything technical that distinguishes them from other sites, other than the content.

"Absolutely," he says. "They can't be traced to a source."

"What does that mean?"

"They're masked. It's as if they reside in an area of the Internet that can't be reached, by law enforcement or anyone else."

"How is that done?"

He smiles. "The truth is, until yesterday I wouldn't have thought it possible. But it's very real. The how is something I don't quite understand."

"So the people that created this would have to be very good?"

"They'd have to be better than good, and better than me," he says.

"Was Gerry Wright better than you?" I ask.

"Gerry was the best I've ever seen. He had a gift, an instinctive understanding of the way the cyberworld operates."

"So he could have set this up?"

"I can't answer that. But if anyone could, he'd be at the top of the list."

I then switch topics and ask him if I gave him computers to examine, and he says that I have.

"Did one of those computers belong to Denise Atkins?"

"Yes."

With very little prompting from me, he talks about how an outside force had occupied her computer, as a result of her downloading a program that she no doubt did not realize was there for that purpose.

"So whoever was responsible for that program could see everything she was doing on her computer?

"Yes."

"Was that the only computer that this was done on, to your knowledge?"

"No. The same was true of the personal computers of Mr. Bowie and Mr. Westman."

Something about his answer triggers something in my mind, but I can't identify it, which means I can't use it to my advantage, so I move on.

I've taken Mathers as far as I can in the tech area; the jury is either going to get it or they're not. I wrap up with some questions about Brian Atkins; Mathers testified on Brian's behalf in the first trial.

"How long have you known Brian Atkins?" I ask.

"Almost six years."

"Have you ever known him to show a temper?"

He shakes his head. "No."

"Ever known him to be violent?"

"No."

"Do you consider him a friend?" I ask.

"A mentor and a friend, yes."

"You've never felt threatened by him?"

"I would trust Brian Atkins with my life," he says.

I couldn't have written a better closing line than that, so I turn him over to Trell.

"Mr. Mathers, that was a fascinating presentation; I learned a lot," he says. "Thank you for sharing your knowledge."

"You're welcome."

"You said that you learned about these illegal sites yesterday, is that right?"

Mathers nods. "Yes."

"Yet you worked at Starlight for years?"

"Yes."

"With Gerald Wright?"

"Yes."

"You worked closely with him?"

"I did."

"Yet you saw no evidence of any wrongdoing in all that time?" Trell asks, feigning surprise.

"That's correct."

"Never suspected anything?"

"That's correct," Mathers repeats.

"Did it bother you that your close friend and mentor, Mr. Atkins, stole a fortune from the company where you worked?"

"I don't believe he did."

"So the jury that convicted him beyond a reasonable doubt was wrong?" Trell asks.

"I believe they were. Maybe they weren't presented with all the facts."

"You testified in that trial, did you not?"

"I did."

"Did you have facts pointing to Mr. Atkins's innocence that you forgot to tell that jury?"

"No."

"Is it fair to say that you do not believe Mr. Atkins would commit a serious felony?"

"It's fair to say that, yes," Mathers says.

"Are you aware that it's already been stipulated by the defense that he committed a serious felony by escaping from jail?"

"He must have had a reason."

"Mr. Mathers, let's end this examination on that note of agreement. I also believe that Mr. Atkins had a reason for escaping from jail."

Trell has done a very effective job on cross, and my redirect is of limited value. Mathers has been on the stand for most of the day, and rather than start with a new witness at this late hour, Hatchet adjourns.

"Please thank Jason for me," Brian says, before the bailiff takes him away.

"I will," I say. Once Brian is gone, I take a photograph of Denise Atkins out of the file. I've got an important stop to make before I go home.

It takes me twenty minutes to get to Harbor Towers in Fort Lee. I didn't want to call ahead and alert Steven Thurmond to the fact that I was coming, so I just have to hope that he's home.

I catch a major break when the same doorman I met last time I was here is again on duty. When I was here before, he could not conceal his disdain for Thurmond and delighted in letting me up unannounced.

"Well, you're back," he says. Doormen have to be good at remembering faces, and this guy clearly is. "Thurmond again?"

I nod. "Thurmond again. But first I have a question."

"Shoot," he says.

"Last time I was here, you said something about sending up someone else that Thurmond didn't want to see."

"Right . . . a woman."

I take out the picture of Denise Atkins and show it to him. "Was it her?"

He looks at it for about fifteen seconds, then puts on his glasses and looks again. "Definitely," he says. "No doubt about it. I remember she might have been pissed off about something; she was just really intense."

"She was here to see Thurmond?"

"Yup."

"How many times was she here?"

"Just the one time that I know of. But I'm not on all the time, so I can't say for sure."

"That one time, how long did she stay for?"

"I . . . maybe twenty minutes?"

"Do you know when she was here?"

"Not off the top of my head, but I can check through my lists. I mark down every person who comes in. What's her name?"

"Denise Atkins."

"I'll check it out and let you know," he says.

The doorman says that he thinks Thurmond is home, so I thank him and head upstairs. I ring the bell on his apartment door, and after a few seconds I can sense someone is on the other side. He must be looking at me through the eyehole.

"What the hell do you want?" he asks.

"We need to talk, Steven. I'm here to help you."

"Get out of here."

"Steven, just talk to me. Believe me, it'll go much better for you if you do."

A good thirty seconds go by, and finally the door opens. "God-damn doorman," he says, as he lets me in. "What do you want?" he asks, after he closes the door.

I decide to hit him with both barrels. "Steven, here's what I know. I know you were working with Gerry Wright to create Web sites for Dominic Petrone, Web sites that have allowed him to conduct illegal activities. I know that Denise Atkins learned of your involvement, and came to see you. I know that Petrone had Wright and Denise killed."

"You're crazy," he says. "Get out of here."

He looks and sounds scared, and I want to scare him some more. "Steven, you think you can handle this yourself, but you can't. You're in way too deep. I can help you; I'm the only one that can help you. But you have to help yourself. You have to tell your story."

"I said get out!" he says, yelling now, his panic evident.

I nod and put my card on a table. "Okay, it's your call, Steven. But here's my number if you change your mind. You can call me twenty-four seven."

With that I leave, at least for the moment having accomplished nothing.

As I exit the building, I thank the doorman again. He smiles. "Come anytime."

The phone rings at two thirty in the morning. It is not something I will ever get used to, but I'm relieved when I see a local number that I don't recognize. It's not Laurie calling from Wisconsin.

Tara and Sebastian have no reaction; they don't even bother opening their eyes or lifting their heads. They are obviously better able to handle a crisis than I am.

"Hello," I say, demonstrating that my conversational eloquence is with me around the clock.

"Carpenter, it's Steven Thurmond."

"Steven, I'm glad you called."

"What kind of deal can you get me?" he asks. I can hear the panic in his voice.

"It depends on what you have to say. Are you ready to tell what you know?"

"Yeah. I've got no choice."

"Are you at home now?" I ask.

"No."

"Where are you?"

"I don't want to say."

This is getting frustrating. "How do you want to play this, Steven? You need to trust me."

"I'll meet you in the morning," he says. "You tell me where."

"My office," I say, and I give him the Van Houten Street address. "I have to be in court at nine, so I'll meet you there at seven."

He hesitates. "Okay."

"Steven, you're doing the right thing."

"Yeah," he says, without sounding close to convinced. Which in turn means that I'm not convinced he's going to be there.

I go back to sleep, no easy task after that phone call. Steven Thurmond sounds like he's standing on the edge, and can fall either way. I need him to fall our way at seven o'clock.

I'm up at five thirty, have some coffee, and take Tara and Sebastian for a quick walk. Once I bring them back, I head down to the office, because I want to be there when Thurmond arrives.

If he arrives.

My office is a second-floor walk-up above Sofia Hernandez's fruit stand. She and her daughter are setting up for the day, preparing to open at 7:00 A.M., in twenty minutes.

I open the ground-floor door, and that's when I hear the noise. It sounds like a firecracker, but I've heard that sound enough times to know that it's a gunshot.

My first thought is that Thurmond is up there, and he's killed himself. But I still pull back; it's not exactly a natural instinct of mine to head toward the sound of a gunshot.

I almost get run over by what seems like a speeding bus, but it's actually Marcus Clark, running by me and through the door. It closes behind him, leaving me standing there like a jerk.

After a few seconds of paralysis that seems like an hour, I grab for my phone and call 911. "I want to report a shooting," I say, and give my address.

Just then two more shots are fired, even louder than the earlier one. "Is the shooting continuing?" the operator asks.

"Yes. Hurry."

As I hang up, the door opens. If it's Marcus, I'm alive; if it's not, he and I are dead.

It's Marcus.

Three patrol cars arrive on the scene within minutes. They enter the office, guns drawn, though Marcus and I assure them that no one up there remains alive. There are two bodies lying in the hallway, Steven Thurmond and his killer.

Pete Stanton shows up a short time later, consults with the patrolmen, and then comes over to me. "Let's hear it," he says.

"There's a guy up there named Steven Thurmond. He was shot and killed by the other guy, whose name I don't know. Marcus killed him, before he could shoot me as well."

Pete turns to Marcus. "You have anything to add to that?"

"Nunh," or something to that effect, says Marcus.

"Why are they outside your office?" Pete asks.

"Thurmond was integral to my case, and was going to help me put Petrone away. My guess is that the other guy works for Petrone. Or maybe you think that Brian Atkins broke out of jail again and killed them both."

He doesn't seem to find that worthy of a response, and instead heads back into the office, telling us to stay where we are.

I make two phone calls. The first is to Rita Gordon, the court clerk, to describe to her what has happened and to explain that my obligations to file police reports will prevent my being in court this morning.

Rita is a good friend, and we actually had a forty-five-minute affair during the awful five-month period when Laurie had gone back home to Wisconsin and was out of my life. Rita hasn't mentioned our fling since, and I'm afraid she might not even remember it.

Rita and I have a bantering relationship, but there's no bantering now. "Damn, Andy, that's awful. Are you all right?"

"Yes, thanks to Marcus. Tell Hatchet I'll be there as soon as I can."

"He's going to be pissed," she said.

"He's going to be pissed at me for almost getting killed?" I ask.

"You're messing with his trial schedule," she says. "He'd even be pissed at you if you were killed."

The second call I need to make is to Laurie in Wisconsin. It's early there and I know the call will both wake her and scare her, but I do it anyway. I don't want her to turn on the news and possibly see that two people were shot to death in my office; she might think that one of them is me.

"Andy, are you all right?" she says instead of "hello."

"I'm fine, but there was an incident, and I want you to hear it from me." I then proceed to tell her what happened. She's both upset and relieved, and I'm glad I called her.

We talk a little bit about the case, and how Thurmond's death will affect it. "Petrone is obviously cleaning up the loose ends," she says.

"What I don't understand is how Petrone found out that Thurmond was talking to me."

"He must have told them, either directly or through someone. He would have been too savvy to be monitored online like the others. He wrote the book on that."

The devastating effect of his death on my case is becoming clear. "I don't know exactly what he was going to say, but I'm sure he could have been the link from the computer stuff to Petrone. It's an easy jump from there to the murders."

As we're getting off the phone, I tell her that I love her.

"And I love Marcus," she says.

I find Pete and tell him that I can't stay long, that I have to get to court.

He smiles. "Hatchet will set fire to you. I wish I could be there to see it." But he promises to take my statement and get me out of here within the hour.

"Do you know who the other dead guy is?"

He nods. "Name is Richie Phalen. You were right: he's one of Petrone's guys. He works under Joseph Russo."

"What a surprise," I say, as drily as I can.

"Marcus put two bullets in his forehead, about a quarter of an inch apart." He holds two fingers together to demonstrate how close they were, and shakes his head in amazement. "Remind me never to annoy Marcus."

D id you send Phalen to kill Steven Thurmond?" Joseph Russo asked. He had come to Dominic Petrone's home uninvited, something he rarely did. But Russo did not want to wait until Petrone got to the office; this was too important.

His tone was accusatory, but if Petrone was concerned, he did not show it. "Yes, I did."

"Why did you go around me?" Russo asked. "Phelan works for me."

"And you work for me, Joseph. You seem to be forgetting that lately."

"Why did you go around me?" he repeated.

"Because I told you to get rid of Carpenter. You didn't follow those orders, so I lost some faith in your ability to follow others. Now Thurmond, I assume, is dead?"

"He is, and so is Phelan."

"That's unfortunate," Petrone said.

"Why did you want Thurmond dead?"

"I was informed that he was about to testify."

"Who told you that?" Russo asked, pressing him.

"That is not your concern. Joseph, I don't know where you got the idea you can cross-examine me in this manner. The fact is that had you killed Carpenter, we would not be in this position."

"The position is worse than you think," Russo said. "Tony Costa has turned state's evidence. He got immunity, and he's talking to Carpenter and the Feds."

A brief flash of worry crossed Petrone's face, but he covered it quickly. "You know this?"

Russo nodded. "I know it. I also know that I'm the one who is exposed here. I'm the one who met with Mazzi and Costa, and Phelan worked for me."

"And I must repeat that you work for me, Joseph. Everyone knows that."

"So what now?"

"The source of our difficulties remains Carpenter. Kill him."

"You think that will make all of this go away?"

"Perhaps, perhaps not. But it will certainly make him go away."

Russo started to respond, but Petrone cut him off. "Joseph, this time do what I say. Kill him."

Hatchet is less angry than I thought. Apparently, two murders is a big enough event to justify missing one morning of court time. But he's not pleased, and when I show up for the afternoon session, he gives me a dry, "Glad you could join us, Mr. Carpenter."

"Always a treat, Your Honor."

"Call your next witness."

"Anthony Costa."

I'm a little anxious about this testimony. I didn't have time to prep him personally; I had Hike do it. The fact that Costa didn't kill Hike is evidence that maybe he's giving up his life of crime, but that's another story.

Hike isn't even here now; I sent him off to get the doorman at Harbor Towers to testify in the trial. I'm hoping the guy will cooperate, but if not then I told Hike to get a subpoena to compel it.

Costa takes the stand; if he's nervous, he's a great actor. He smiles and seems perfectly at ease. As I get up to question him, I notice that two of the FBI agents are in the courtroom to take in his testimony.

"Mr. Costa, have you entered into any agreement with the government as it relates to your testimony?" I'm starting with this to get it out in the open, since Trell will no doubt use the existence of the deal to try to impeach Costa's testimony.

"Yes, I've given up my Fifth Amendment rights, and in return I've been granted immunity. They won't prosecute me as a result of anything I say here today."

"So there is no downside to you for being truthful?"

He smiles. "I certainly hope not."

Unlike with most witnesses, I don't spend much time on Costa's résumé, as it doesn't exactly include time spent as a Boy Scout leader.

I move quickly to the case at hand. "Are you familiar with Gerald Wright, one of the murder victims in this case?"

"I am."

"Did you meet him personally?"

He nods. "Once. He attended a meeting with myself, Angelo Mazzi, and Joseph Russo. Russo and Mr. Wright came to see Mr. Mazzi; I sat in on it."

"Who is Joseph Russo?"

"He works for Dominic Petrone."

"Why were Gerald Wright and Joseph Russo there?"

"To demonstrate a computer thing they set up. People could order stuff . . . drugs . . . they could bet on sports . . . whatever. Wright showed us how it worked, and said it could never be traced. Russo said it was the way business was going to be conducted in the future."

"And why were they talking to Mr. Mazzi?"

"Because they were planning to take over his territory, and they wanted to use Mazzi's people. They said customers would rather deal with them this way, than the old way. They'd pay us . . . Mr. Mazzi . . . forty percent."

"What did Mr. Mazzi say?" I ask

"He told them to 'f' themselves."

"What did they say to that?"

"That they were taking over other markets as well, and that the money they would make would let them buy off our people anyway. So either Mazzi would take forty percent, or he'd get nothing."

"So did he take the deal?" I ask.

"No, he threw them out."

"Where is Mr. Mazzi today?"

"Six feet under," he says. "They came into his restaurant and killed him."

"Who did?"

"People that worked for Russo and Petrone."

"What is the status today, as we speak, of Mr. Mazzi's business?"

"Russo and Petrone control the territory."

I sit down thinking the testimony has been powerful and convincing, and I hope the jury feels the same. I also hope Trell doesn't get anywhere on cross.

"Mr. Costa, this meeting you said you attended, Joseph Russo and Gerald Wright were there as partners?" Trell starts.

"Yes."

"And Mr. Wright was presented as the brains behind the computer operation?"

Costa nods. "Yeah, Russo said he didn't even know how to send an e-mail."

"So Mr. Wright's death would have been a blow to their business?"

"Seemed like it."

"But the operation continues today, is that your testimony?"

"Yes."

"You worked for Mr. Mazzi?"

Costa nods. "Yes."

"And he was a criminal? The head of a mob family?"

"You could say that."

"I did say that," Trell says. "Would you?"

"Yes."

"Does that make you a criminal as well?"

Costa hesitates. "I've done some things I'm not proud of."

"Like murder? Extortion? Those kind of things?"

"My agreement was that I would testify only to matters related to this case."

"Have you ever had dealings with the police in the past? Ever been questioned by them?"

"Of course."

"Did you provide truthful answers on those occasions?" Trell asks.

"Sometimes."

"And sometimes you lied?"

"Sometimes I left stuff out," Costa says.

"In order to protect and benefit yourself," Trell says, more a statement than a question.

"Yeah."

"So you'll lie if it's to your benefit. Does the immunity deal you've made provide you any benefit?"

"I'm telling the truth."

"The jury will make that decision," Trell says.

The doorman's name is Paul Tarpley," Hike says. It's nine o'clock at night, and he's calling me at home.

"You sure you got the right one?" I ask. I didn't know the man's name, and since he can't work twenty-four hours a day, I want to make sure we don't call someone to the stand who doesn't have the slightest idea what I'm talking about.

"Positive," Hike says. "He remembers you well, and didn't seem too broken up that Thurmond isn't going to be a tenant anymore."

"Will he testify willingly?"

Hike laughs. "Are you kidding? I couldn't fight him off with a stick. He's probably in 'hair and makeup' right now."

"Good. I'm going to call him first tomorrow."

"Without prepping him?" he asks.

"It'll be okay. He'll be on and off in fifteen minutes, and I know what he'll say."

"Famous last words," Hike says, upbeat as always.

I hang up feeling a bit better about our case. In order to get an acquittal, I don't have to prove that Petrone is guilty of the murders. What I have to do is throw enough "Petrone mud" against the wall so that that the jury will think it's reasonable that he could have ordered them. As far as that goes, I'm getting there.

My other problem is personal. I'm not going to feel safe, more importantly I'm not going to feel that Ricky is safe, unless Petrone gets put away. He's not really a turn-the-other-cheek kind of guy, and I don't want my family under a cloud of danger from here on.

I really need to nail him.

But first things first, and I'm a long way from winning the case. I'd love to watch the Knicks game from the West Coast tonight, but I need to study and prepare.

I take Tara and Sebastian out for their nighttime walk at nine thirty. I think I like it more than they do; it relaxes me and focuses me at the same time. We walk for about an hour, not nearly long enough to prepare me for who I see in my den when we get back.

Joseph Russo. And Marcus Clark.

The weird thing, beyond the fact that they are there, is that there doesn't seem to have been any kind of a fight. Russo is not battered or bloody, as he would be if he tangled with Marcus. He's just sitting casually on the couch, while Marcus is in a chair across the way. Marcus is not holding a gun, or in any way restraining Russo.

Russo speaks first, which is just as well, because I am so stunned that my throat is paralyzed. He points to Marcus. "Whatever you're paying this guy, it's not enough."

"Tell me about it," I say. "Did you come here to kill me?" I ask.

"If I came here to kill you, you'd be dead. I'd have brought so many guys even Superman here couldn't have stopped us."

"That's comforting. So why are you here?"

"I want to make a deal," he says.

"To testify about the case?"

"To talk about the entire Petrone operation. He's been setting me up, and he's going to regret it."

"What do you know about the computer operation?" I ask. "The way Petrone is moving in on other territories?"

"I know everything. But I'm not going to talk unless I get immunity."

"Costa got use immunity. That means—"

"I know what it means, and it's not good enough. I want full immunity."

"I'll see what I can do," I say. The truth is that I have no idea what the Feds will do in this case. They want to get Petrone badly, and are close. There is no doubt that Russo can hand him over on a silver platter. But Russo's hands are about as dirty as they can be, and letting him completely walk may not work for them.

"You do that," Russo says. "Make sure they realize I know everything."

"Why were Denise Atkins and Gerald Wright killed?"

"Except that."

"What do you mean? You didn't have them killed?"

"No. If Dominic did, he did it behind my back. Until recently, I wouldn't have thought that was possible."

Those are Russo's last words on the subject. In fact, they are the last words of his life. The window shatters, and a nanosecond later, Russo's head follows suit.

I see the bloody mask that was once Russo's face, and before I can react, a huge mass lands on me and pushes me to the ground. It's Marcus, reacting with unbelievable quickness to the danger.

Once I'm safely behind the couch, Marcus goes to the window and peers outside into the darkness. There's no way he can see anything, and no way he can determine if the danger has passed.

Marcus heads for the back of the house, and I can hear the door opening and then closing. My assumption is that he's going to circle around to the front, in order to determine if Russo's killer has fled.

The net result is that I am alone in a room, hiding behind a couch, next to a dead, bloody, fat mobster. I've had more pleasant interludes in my life, and it's a long ten minutes until Marcus comes back in and signals that things are safe.

I call 911 and report what has happened, and Pete shows up with a bunch of cops, just like last time. "I think we got a déjà vu thing going on," he says. "Marcus again?"

I shake my head. "Not this time. The shooter got away; I didn't see him."

Pete walks over and looks at the body, which is hard to identify without very little face remaining. "Russo?"

"Yes."

Pete nods. "Mmm . . . stepping up in the world."

Once again I head for the phone. I call Willie to tell him of Russo's death. I can tell he's upset about it, and he says, "Andy, I know he was a bad guy, but he was my friend."

"I know that, Willie. And I'm sorry."

Next I again call Laurie, to head off her learning about the shooting from anyone else. I'm tired of making this call, and I'm tired of people getting killed.

And I'm very tired of losing witnesses.

If Paul Tarpley had his way, he'd be on the witness stand for a week. He's clearly loving being in the spotlight, and my guess is he's also loving a day off from screening visitors and signing for FedEx deliveries. But he's about to be disappointed; he's going to be on and off in a hurry.

"Mr. Tarpley, how are you employed?"

"I'm a doorman at Harbor Towers in Fort Lee," he says.

"Was Steven Thurmond a tenant there?"

"He was. Until he got himself killed."

Trell objects, and even though it's sustained, I have to fight off the urge to smile; Tarpley is putting in my case for me.

I introduce as evidence a police report and newspaper article, both confirming Tarpley's comment that Thurmond was killed.

"Mr. Tarpley, did I ask you if Denise Atkins had been to see Mr. Thurmond?"

"Yes, and I told you she had. I checked, and it was on October twenty-eighth."

"Two days before she died," I say, only to remind the jury. "Thank you, no further questions."

Trell has no questions for him on cross, and Tarpley has to leave the spotlight. For a second, I think he's going to take a bow, but he just walks off.

Next I call Pete Stanton back to the stand. He wasn't happy

when I told him I was going to do it, but he knew I could force him, so he agreed.

"Captain Stanton, were you called to my office by a 911 call that I made two days ago?"

"Yes," he says.

"What did you discover when you arrived there?"

"Two people deceased; cause of death, gunshot wounds."

"Did you identify the people, and can you tell us who they were?"

"Yes. One was Steven Thurmond. The other was Richard Phalen."

"Were you familiar with Mr. Phalen prior to that day?" I ask.

"Yes."

"In what context?"

"He was a known associate of Dominic Petrone and Joseph Russo. He reported directly to Russo."

"Thank you. Did you also answer a 911 call at my house last night?"

"Yes, because there was another shooting death."

"Who was it this time?"

"Joseph Russo."

There is chattering in the court gallery; the Russo killing was on the news this morning, but apparently not everyone had seen it. Hatchet gavels for quiet.

"Was the killer arrested?" I ask.

"No, he is at large."

"And Mr. Russo was an associate of Dominic Petrone?"

Pete nods. "For many years."

"Just to recap," I say, "all of these murders happened within the last few days?"

"That's correct."

"Is Brian Atkins a suspect in any of them?"

"No."

"Because he has been in jail throughout this trial, is that correct?"

"Yes."

Next I tell Hatchet that I have an FBI-prepared document that I want to introduce as evidence. I need a witness to read it for the jury, and I ask that Pete be allowed to do so. Failing that, I say that I could have an FBI agent in to read it, but I'm suggesting Pete in the interest of saving time.

Trell doesn't object; I'm sure he'd just as soon the jury not see the FBI weighing in on our side.

I tell the jury that the document is a transcript of the text messages between Brian and Denise, in the days leading up to her death. Pete reads it, and when he is done, I throw in a couple of questions, just so I can be sure that the jury hasn't missed the key facts.

"So, Captain, based on what you have just read, is it fair to say that Denise Atkins was concerned about what was happening at Starlight, and afraid of Dominic Petrone?"

He nods. "That's what it says."

"And she was aware that Brian was planning to escape on that day?"

"Yes."

"And is it fair to assume that Mr. Atkins at least expressed guilt about his wife being in this position, and that he said he was coming to help?"

"That's what it says."

Trell finally objects that Pete only knows what he's read, and shouldn't be giving an opinion on it. Hatchet sustains, but the objection has come three questions too late.

I continue. "Are you aware that there was previous testimony from Mr. Mathers that Denise Atkins's computer was compromised, and that whoever was behind it could have seen these messages?"

"I am now."

"Thank you."

Trell has only perfunctory questions for Pete; he hasn't said anything controversial enough to challenge. He simply recited facts.

The next words out of my mouth are always very difficult for me to say, because they are momentous, and can't be taken back.

"Your Honor, the defense rests."

Ladies and gentlemen, you've gotten to hear quite a story," says Trell. "I won't even say it's all fiction, because it isn't. Some of what the defense told you is true. Some other things they told you might be true; at this point there's no way to know. And some of what they told you is nonsense, pulled out of thin air.

"But there's one thing that I can say for sure about all of it. It is not relevant.

"Starlight Systems was a hot company; they were right near the front of the tech industry almost from the day they were founded. They made products that were unique, and that companies needed.

"But Starlight was not a company where you'd want your son or daughter to intern. Because there was a pervasive corruption and lawlessness there, and it started at the top.

"Brian Atkins was convicted of embezzling a fortune from his own company. His huge salary and equity interest were not enough for him; he had to have more.

"And as you've heard, as Mr. Carpenter himself said, Gerald Wright continued that illegality. He went into a partnership of sorts with criminals, using his technical capabilities to spread drugs, and to commit blackmail, and who knows what else.

"Yes, you've heard it all, and I haven't even gotten into the child pornography, or gambling, or affairs among the company executives.

"Well, Brian Atkins heard that all this was happening. He heard it from his wife, who was betraying him. He discovered that his ex-partner, who testified against him and helped to put him behind bars, was growing rich beyond imagination. He knew what was going on—for all we know he may have instigated it before he went to jail—and he snapped.

"He told his wife he was coming to help, probably so she wouldn't suspect what he had in mind, so she wouldn't be on the alert. And then he killed them, the wife and partner who betrayed him.

"There are a lot of bad actors in the stories you've heard; in a murder trial there always are. Gerald Wright may have been a bad guy, and Denise Atkins not much better. But they did not deserve to die, and Brian Atkins did not have the right to kill them.

"So beyond the stories, beyond the guesswork and supposing and theorizing, let's look at the facts. Brian Atkins had a motive for murder. He escaped from jail, stole a car, and went directly to the house where he found the two people he was looking for. A neighbor saw him leaving the house shortly after they died. And he ran.

"Those are the facts.

"These two people were brutally murdered, slashed multiple times by someone obviously in a rage. That is not how organized crime operates. To hired killers, murder is a business, and their preferred method is a bullet in the back of the head. That is not what happened here.

"What happened here is that Brian Atkins took two lives, and for that he should be punished. It's a large responsibility, but you are the only ones who can do it. Thank you."

My turn.

"Brian Atkins should not have escaped from jail," I say. "He knows that now, but it's too late. What's done is done. But he did it because he thought his wife was in danger, and he felt partly responsible for putting her in that danger. So we know why he escaped; we read it in the texts.

"Mr. Trell is correct that there were bad things going on among certain employees in Starlight. Huge money was at stake, and they were teaming up with people who were dangerous and lawless. Something had to explode, and it did.

"Repeatedly.

"Think of the things you heard about here, and Mr. Trell talked about many of them. Drugs, gambling, blackmail, child pornography, and murders. Five murders . . . Denise Atkins, Gerald Wright, Joseph Russo, Steven Thurmond, and Richard Phalen.

"Except for the deaths of Denise Atkins and Gerald Wright, all of it happened while Brian Atkins was behind bars. Think about that. The drugs, and gambling, and murders, and all the rest . . . Brian Atkins could not have done any of it.

"With all of that, how could anyone possibly conclude, beyond a reasonable doubt, that someone else did not commit these murders? How can anyone say with certainty that Brian Atkins committed these horrible acts, without getting blood on himself in the process? It just doesn't make sense.

"Mr. Atkins escaped from jail, so he pleaded guilty. He did not kill these people, so he pleaded not guilty. I hope and believe you'll agree with him on both counts."

I head back to the defense table, and Brian greets me with his hand outstretched. "Thank you, Andy. No matter how it turns out, thank you for all you've done, and for convincing me to fight."

"I'm glad you did," I say.

Hatchet announces that the jury will be sequestered during their deliberations. He says that he's doing it because of the unusual amount of publicity that the proceedings are getting. I suspect he also thinks that the verdict will come quickly, but I have no idea which way he thinks it will go.

The bailiff is walking toward us to take Brian away, but Brian has enough to time to ask one question. "Andy, who killed Denise?"

I have time to give him an answer. "I don't know."

I am pretty much impossible to live with while I'm waiting for a verdict. I get irritable, and obnoxious, and disagreeable. I know that I'm doing it, and I don't want to be like that, but I just can't seem to help myself.

Of course, none of that matters right now, since there is no one here living with me. Laurie and Ricky are a thousand miles away, stuck there because some assholes are threatening him.

That fact makes me even more irritable, obnoxious, disagreeable, and impossible to live with. Which still doesn't matter, since there is no one here to live with me.

Waiting for a verdict turns me into a circular nutcase.

I try not to anticipate what the jury is going to do, but most of the time I can't help myself. And when I do, I become a complete contradiction. For one thing, my logical mind can't imagine how rational human beings might not understand and appreciate the arguments I've presented. They have to agree with my point of view, because that point of view is obviously correct.

On the other hand, my pessimistic nature is positive that those idiots will vote guilty.

One of me is going to be wrong.

So basically I'm sitting at home and waiting by the phone. I wish the damn thing would ring, because I want to get this over with. I also wish it wouldn't ring, not for a long while, because I instinctively feel that a quick verdict would not be good news.

So far it hasn't rung, which pleases and displeases me.

I may have mentioned this, but waiting for a verdict turns me into a nutcase.

It's bugging me that Joseph Russo didn't know who killed Denise Atkins and Gerry Wright. He had nothing to gain by lying when he said it, which makes me believe him.

It's possible that Petrone had gone around Russo to order the killings; certainly recent events demonstrated that their relationship was deteriorating. But I believe that the murders preceded that deterioration, and I would have thought Russo would at least have known, and would likely have been involved.

When I'm stuck in a situation like this, a technique I use is to break things down to winners and losers. A lot of bad things have happened in the development of this case. People have died, and money has been lost.

Denise Atkins, Gerry Wright, Daniel Bowie, Steven Thurmond, Joseph Russo, Joseph Westman, and others have lost their lives. Jason Mathers has lost his job. Brian Atkins has lost his wife, his chance at parole, and maybe much more. So who won?

Ted Yates.

Ted Yates has seen the two men above him at Starlight, Brian Atkins and Gerry Wright, get pushed well out of the picture. He's been appointed by the company's board to move into the CEO spot, and his main rival, Mathers, has left the company. He's even packed up his things and moved upstairs, to Brian's old office.

Things have worked out for Ted Yates.

Of course, none of this makes him a criminal. He could just have been really lucky, in the right place at the right time, with the competence and savvy to capitalize on it.

I'm not going to find out the source of that luck by sitting and waiting for the phone to ring, so I call Yates. His assistant tells me that he's really busy, and my response is to say that it's really important. That gets him to the phone.

"I'd like to come down and talk to you," I say.

"Join the club."

"What do you mean?"

"Every federal agent in America is here."

"Why?"

"They're not saying, but they're going over our entire operation. And none of them are smiling."

"So talking to me will be a pleasant change."

"Or not," he says. "Come on over; I'll try and give you a few minutes."

I thank him, take Tara and Sebastian for a quick walk, and then get ready to head down to Starlight. But I don't make it out the door, because something happens.

The phone rings.

It takes me twenty minutes to get to the court-house. I would have made it in eighteen min-utes, but on two occasions I waved in drivers who wanted to get in front of me. Just in case there is a Verdict God, I want him or her to see that I'm a good guy.

Hike is already at the defense table when I get there. He's got a downbeat expression on his face, which doesn't exactly qualify as breaking news. "Way too quick," he says, shaking his head and referring to the jury's verdict. "Way too quick."

"We'll see," I say.

"You did the best you could," Hike says, making a compliment sound like a postmortem.

Norman Trell comes into the courtroom, sees me, and walks over to shake my hand. "We fought the good fight," he says.

I nod and ask, "Who do you think is going to win that good fight?"

"I think you are," he says, and then nods toward Brian, being led toward us by the bailiff. "But I think he killed them."

Trell heads back to the prosecution table, and I shake hands with Brian. I can see the tension in his face; I feel like my head is going to explode from the pressure, and I'm just the lawyer. I'm going home after this no matter what. I cannot even imagine what he feels.

I will never get used to this.

The courtroom is packed as Hatchet enters and takes his seat behind the bench. He asks that the jury be brought in, and the bailiff goes to get them. They must be in Connecticut, because it feels like forever until they finally enter and take their seats.

Hatchet gavels to quiet down the noisy gallery, admonishes everyone about the need for decorum after the verdict is read, and then asks the foreman if they have reached that verdict.

"We have, Your Honor."

"Bailiff, please retrieve the verdict and give it to the court clerk to be read."

I'm not sure why the bailiff chooses to do all of that in slow motion, but it finally arrives on the clerk's desk. She looks at it, and then starts to read.

"In the matter of the state of New Jersey versus Brian Atkins, count one, the first-degree murder of Denise Atkins, the jury hereby finds the defendant, Brian Atkins, not guilty."

She reads the second count, but it's hard to hear, since the gallery has erupted in noise, and Brian is hugging me. It doesn't matter, since I know what she must be saying. There is no way to find Brian not guilty of one murder and guilty of the other.

"I can't believe you pulled it off," Brian says.

I smile. "Piece of cake."

"It's weird, we won, but I've got to go back to prison. How long do you think it will be before I get out?"

"I don't know, but I'll do my best."

Hatchet adjourns, and they take Brian away. I leave the court, stopping in front of the assembled press to give my obligatory "Justice has been served" speech.

As soon as I get in my car and pull away, my phone rings, and I see on the caller ID that it's Cindy Spodek. "Congratulations," she says.

"You heard already?" I ask.

"Heard what?"

"That we got an acquittal."

"No, but congratulations for that, too."

"Then what were you talking about?" I ask.

"You haven't heard?"

"Cindy, we've now been talking for twenty minutes, and I still don't know what the hell we're talking about."

"We executed a raid on Petrone and his operations about an hour ago. He's been arrested; it's all over the news."

"Can you make it stick?"

"He couldn't get out of this even if you were his lawyer. Costa testifying opened the floodgates, and now others are coming out of the woodwork to nail the bastard. We've shut down his computer operation; he's history, Andy."

This is spectacular news, and I want to hear more about it, but I get off the call, because I have to make one of my own.

As soon as Laurie answers, I say, "Time for you and Ricky to come home."

Ted Yates hasn't even unpacked the boxes in his new office. When I comment on that, he says, "Thanks to you I doubt that I will."

"What do you mean?"

"I would hope and assume that Brian will be back. Although that will be up to the board; he's still got the felony embezzlement issue to deal with."

"That was a bullshit charge," I say.

He smiles. "Is that the legal name for it?"

I'm not sure what I'm doing here. I have no evidence that Yates is guilty of anything, just a suspicion based on how well it all worked out for him. So I guess I'm just here to talk and learn, hoping something will lead me to understand who killed Denise Atkins and Gerry Wright.

"How big a hit is Starlight going to take in this?" I ask.

"No way to tell, but it's not pretty. The publicity has been horrible, but we have three things going for us."

"What might that be?"

"We're good at what we do, our legit customers need our products, and the investigation will show that we're clean."

"You're sure of that?"

He nods. "I'm sure. I had our people go over everything. But things are going to change around here."

"How so?"

"There will be much more scrutiny, both by the board and by regulators. But that's okay, that's how it should be. And I can use all the help I can get; I've got a lot on my plate. Just the personnel alone . . ."

"You'll make a lot of changes?"

He shrugs. "I've got no choice. Gerry Wright and Jason Mathers were a huge piece of this company. They had amazing talent, and in this business talent follows talent. We've got to avoid losing our people to other tech companies; these kind of people want to be part of the new, bright, shiny object. We're a bit tarnished right now."

"You replaced Mathers from inside the company, right?"

He nods. "Yes, Stacy Mullins. Good, solid, smart guy, but I'm afraid he's not in Jason's league when it comes to talent."

"What about Denise Atkins?" I ask. "Have you replaced her?"

"Not yet, but that will be up to Stacy. Denise's position reports to him."

I'm getting nowhere; Yates seems at ease and not on his guard. "Did you follow the trial?"

"I did, especially the technology stuff. I'm not an expert, the people who work for me are the experts, but in the wrong hands it can be very dangerous. It's a lesson we all need to learn."

"I've given up on trying to keep up," I say.

Yates laughs. "I'll tell you, when I heard about how many people had lost all their privacy, even in their own computers, I got worried and had mine checked out. That could be embarrassing."

I don't say anything; Yates's comment has shaken me and I'm wracking my brain trying to makes sense of it.

He takes advantage of the silence to say, "Well, I've really got to get back to work."

I stand up and nod. "So do I."

I get into the car and call Norman Trell. The first thing he says is, "I was hoping not to have to hear your voice for a while."

"You sound like Laurie," I say. "I just have one question."

"Shoot."

"During the trial you alluded to the fact that Denise Atkins and Gerald Wright were having an affair. Her friend said on the stand that she was sleeping with her boss."

"Right."

"It fit right in with a revenge motive for Brian, but you didn't push it. Why not?"

"Because we couldn't pin it down," he says. "We believed it to be true, but there was no hard evidence. If we went for it, and you were able to shoot it down, we would have lost credibility with the jury."

"Okay, thanks."

"Why are you raising this now?" he asks.

"Because I was too dumb to see it before," I say.

W hat are you doing here?" Jason Mathers asks when he opens the door. "You won. Isn't your job over?"

I walk past him into the apartment, then point to the amazing view of New York through the glass wall. "I just wanted to see that view again."

He laughs. "Actually, you can sublet the place if you want. I'm leaving."

"Where are you going?"

"California. Time for me to get back into the workforce . . . maybe a start-up. The money guys don't think you're smart enough unless you're in Silicon Valley."

"I also wanted to thank you for testifying. It was a big help."

"Glad to do it. Brian's a good guy."

"That he is," I say. "But he's going to be pissed when he finds out you murdered his wife."

I expect at least a double take from Mathers, but none is forthcoming. "Is that a joke?" he asks.

"If it is, it's the worst one of all time," I say. "Killing two people in cold blood, helping a gangster peddle drugs, blackmail . . . that's not really stand-up comedy material."

"You're dreaming."

"If I am, it's one of those really detailed dreams where everything seems real."

"Let's hear what you've got," he says, almost sounding amused.

"Okay; I'm actually pretty proud of it. For one thing, Denise Atkins said she was having an affair with her boss. Everybody assumed that was Gerald Wright, because he was head of the company and they were so close, but you were actually her boss within the company. Her affair was with you."

"Bullshit," he says.

"You want to hear this, or not? She found out that Wright was doing bad business with Petrone, and she was going to confront him. She told you what was happening; you were her boyfriend, she didn't know you were part of it, and she thought you'd help. But you killed her instead."

"This is all guesswork."

I nod. "Some of it. But when Steven Thurmond was killed, I couldn't figure out how Petrone found out he was talking to me. But then I realized that I had sent Sam to update you on all the computer stuff the day before. He told you about Thurmond."

He doesn't respond, so I continue. "When you were on the stand, you mentioned that Bowie's, Westman's, and Denise's computers were all invaded by the program that let others see what they were doing. But you couldn't have known about Bowie's computer. You never saw it."

"Sam told me about it."

I shake my head. "Sam never saw it either. None of us did. I just copied the address of the gambling site from it. But you knew it was taken over, because you did it. And that's how you found out he was talking to me, and that's why you had Petrone kill him."

"You're pretty good at this," he says.

"Why did you have to kill Denise?"

"She was in the way. She went to Thurmond first, and scared the shit out of that little weasel. Then she scared Wright; he was going to put the brakes on the whole thing because he was afraid of what she might do. So I had to take him out as well. We didn't need him anymore anyway."

"You should have stopped when you had the chance," I say.

"And you should have stayed out of it. There is no way I can be caught."

"How do you figure?" I ask.

"You know how many identities I have set up? You know how easy that is for me? I walk out of here, and I can be a different person every year for the rest of my life if I want. You exist if computers say you exist."

"Wow, that's pretty cool. You can teach computer class in prison."

He laughs. "What made you think you could come here and get out alive?"

"I'll show you," I say, as I reach into my shirt pocket. "See this? It's a wireless microphone; it's pretty high tech, so I'm not sure you can understand it. But it has relayed everything you've said to the police. They're right outside, so you might want to hurry up and assume one of your secret identities. Because this conversation will give them probable cause to arrest you, and to search your computers. They might even find specks of blood in here or in your car; it's really hard to get all of it up."

The good news is that I can see in his face I've finally gotten to him. The bad news is that his face is not my problem. My problem is his hand, which is holding a knife.

He picks up the microphone and throws it through a door into another room. "If you're telling the truth, and they're out there, it's over for me. If you're lying, then I'll go on. Either way, you're a dead man."

He slashes at my face with the knife, but I'm out of range. I back up and out of the way, as he lunges again.

"Pete, get the hell in here!" I scream. I have no idea if he can hear me, either through the microphone or the door, both of which are in the other room.

Mathers's stalking me around the room now, taking his time.

I grab a small vase from a table as I back up. As scared as I am, a ridiculous variation on the old line comes into my mind: "never bring a vase to a knife fight."

I hear loud noises, but can't tell what it is. It could just be my heart pounding. Mathers is getting closer; if I don't throw the vase now, I'm going to die holding it.

It's not easy to throw a vase; it's too big to throw like a baseball, and two weirdly shaped to throw like a shot put. But I throw it, as hard as I can, right at his face.

He raises his left arm to block it; the knife is in his right hand. I think I hurt him; he yells in pain. But he keeps coming, and I'm out of vases.

A voice yells, "Freeze!" but I don't really think Mathers has the time to decide whether that is a good idea before the bullets slam into him. He's thrown back into the glass wall, but bounces off it. The bullets smash into the glass in two places, but it's unbreakable, and simply spreads into that cracked mosaic that often happens to car windshields.

Pete is one of the cops who did the shooting. "Glad you could make it," I say.

He nods. "Happy to do it. You owe me two tickets to the Giants game this Sunday."

W e've waited four months to have this victory party. It would have been longer, but I managed to convince the parole board that the one-year additional sentence for Brian's escape could be disregarded in light of subsequent events. Especially since we were able to provide evidence linking Mathers to the evidence that convicted Brian of embezzlement.

It's at Charlie's, of course, and everyone from our team is here except Willie, who promised to stop by later. Even Edna is here; we couldn't have won the case without her, except for the fact that we won the case without her.

Ted Yates, the recently named permanent CEO of Starlight, has dropped in to pay his respects to Brian. The board determined that Brian was worthy of reinstatement to his previous position, but he declined. He's going to take some time off, relax, and adjust to life on the outside.

Vince is in attendance because there is free food and beer; he would go to a party honoring the Ayatollah if they were serving free food and beer. Pete is here as well, and displays uncharacteristic classiness by shaking Brian's hand and wishing him well.

Laurie is here, while Ricky is at home with a sitter. It has been great having them back, and I hope we never have to go through that again. With Petrone certain to live out the rest of his unnatural life in prison, we shouldn't have to.

We're going to Disney World next week, and I'm actually looking forward to it.

Willie finally shows up, a half hour into the party. With him is Sondra and another guest, who stands at the end of a leash that she holds.

Boomer.

I walk over to them. "The family that adopted him was you?"

Willie smiles. "Just like I said. Nice couple, no kids, and another dog that Boomer got along with great. A perfect match."

"And why is he here?"

"Because there's an even better match over there," Sondra says, and she takes the leash from the woman and walks Boomer over to Brian.

I try out my stern voice on Willie. "You violated a direct order."

"Ask me if I give a shit," he says.

I decide not to ask him, and instead watch the look on Brian's face when he sees Boomer. He gets down on one knee and hugs Boomer, whose tail is wagging a mile a minute. I can't tell if Brian is crying, because Boomer is licking his face, so it's wet anyway.

I look over at Laurie, who is laughing and crying at the same time.

I have absolutely no idea how women do that.